W9-BYL-088

THE
GOD
COMPLEX

A Novel by

Chris Titus

GuruKnee Press

THE GOD COMPLEX. Copyright © 2011 by Chris Titus. All rights reserved. Printed in the United States of America. No part of this book may be used or reproduced in any manner whatsoever without written permission from the author except in the case of brief quotations embodied in critical articles and reviews. For additional information please write to info@godcomplexnovel.com.

This book is a work of fiction. Names, characters, places, and incidents are products of the author's imagination or are used fictitiously. Any resemblance to actual events or locales or persons, living or dead, is entirely coincidental.

Kata design and artwork by Sensei Troy Price

Second Edition

Designed by Chris Titus

Library of Congress Cataloging-in-Publication Data

Titus, Chris, 1974—

   The God Complex : an adventure through Eastern medicine that draws upon a real life health care crisis spanning fifteen years and confounding over 140 health care professionals / by Chris Titus.—1st ed.

LCCN: 2010911096
ISBN-13: 978-1453717028
ISBN-10: 1453717021

1. Traditional Chinese Medicine—Five Element Theory—Fiction.
2. Prague, Czech Republic—History—Culture—Travel—Fiction.
3. Boston, Massachusetts, United States—Western Medicine—Fiction.

To anyone desperately seeking a cure ...

ACKNOWLEDGMENTS

The past fifteen years have led me to the doorsteps of many gifted teachers whose care and guidance proved invaluable in my search for a cure. Without your support, I might never have overcome my ailments. I would like to thank a few people in particular who influenced my journey—Sensei Dave Castoldi, Ines Hudson, Dr. BJ Wang, Dr. Kwok Lap Wong, Dr. Song Li, Dr. Ariana Fucini, Sensei Darryl Rambo, and Dr. Tom Tam.

I would also like to extend additional thanks to Sensei Troy Price for the use of his Kyusho-Jitsu kata and artwork.

AUTHOR'S NOTE

Let me start by saying that this is a fictional work and is not intended to provide any medical advice. The *kata* described in this book is potentially dangerous and should not be attempted—period.

The God Complex takes readers on an adventure through Eastern medicine that draws upon a real life health care crisis spanning fifteen years and confounding over 140 health care professionals. Passages from my own personal journal have been woven into the story, detailing symptoms and situations I faced along the way. By constructing a story around the emotions, pain, drama, intrigue, and enlightenment that come through such a journey, my goal is to provide you with an entertaining and effortless way to learn about traditional Chinese medicine.

I have written this book to address many audiences—family, friends, patients, health care professionals, and martial artists. In my opinion, we all need to take greater responsibility for our own health care. An important first step is to better understand the options available—namely complimentary medicine. I believe the solution to the world's health care problems can be found in a combination of Eastern and Western medicine.

It should be noted that I am not a health care practitioner and make no claims to be. The views of traditional Chinese medicine I have presented are admittedly limited and rudimentary. The leaps I have made to bridge Eastern and Western medicine were done so to fit within the context of the story and may not be entirely accurate. It is my intention to use the proceeds of this book, if sufficient, to return to school and study traditional Chinese medicine.

In some sections, dates have been changed to fit within the context of certain historical events.

Chapter 1

Prague, Czech Republic

The scent of burnt flesh canvassed the quaint Czech neighborhood of Nusle Valley, lying low in the shadow of the Nusle Bridge. It was another reminder of this neighborhood's unwanted infamy.

Shortly after dawn, the local police station had received multiple calls complaining of a nauseating stench conflicting with breakfast. When the call came from his station's dispatcher, Lieutenant Marek was long awake, engaging in his strict early morning routine of stretching and martial arts practice. Once a labor of love, his efforts had become a tedious burden for this middle-aged lieutenant to keep pace with younger subordinates whose structured buzz-cuts and chiseled physiques outshined the glistening sweat now rolling over his slightly protruding belly. Before the phone made its way to the cradle, Marek's mind had already concluded the obvious.

The Nusle Bridge, known as Suicide Bridge, had been the site of approximately three hundred suicides since opening in 1973. Anytime he was called to this part of town, it had been to investigate a jumper. In the past year alone, there had been sixty-three attempts, averaging more than one per week.

Something was peculiar about this jump. *Burnt flesh.* It was obviously a jumper. It's always a jumper. *But burnt flesh?*

Traffic on the E50 was beginning to pick up speed at the same rate thoughts accelerated around Marek's brain. Uncomfortable with the details, his mind darted down every path that rose from the chaotic amalgam of thoughts stewing in his head. *Was he burning on the way down or after? Did this poor soul get tangled up in a part of the local electrical grid? Was it a mafia hit made to look like a jump? After all, the Russian mafia's strength in Prague had been growing in recent years.*

"We've never had a fireball," he muttered aloud in Czech.

He arrived to the valley where he was greeted by his band of subordinates at the bottom of Kresomyslova Street. From there, they followed the pungent odor down a grassy path leading from the roadside. Noses angled toward the sky and sniffing like bloodhounds, their pace quickened with each new waft of singed flesh. The group encircled a small construction site storage area at the bottom of the valley. A chain-link fence covered by dark army green tarps kept Marek and his hounds at bay. After circling the boxed-in area a few times, it was clear that the smell was originating from inside.

Marek barked out an order. A junior officer jumped forward to cut the lock on the fence door and tried opening it to no avail. Marek shoved the officer aside and buried his shoulder into the metal mesh. It refused to budge, dragging something with it in the dirt. With the help of another officer, Marek finally forced the door open a crack and squeezed through.

Two-by-fours were strewn about the yard. In the middle lay a disfigured body, charred and smoldering. The sight of the encrusted body revolted Marek, making the stench emanating from it much more unbearable. Marek started choking and reached for a handkerchief to cover his face. The body slumped over a shortened stack of lumber where its initial impact had sent wood scattering in all directions.

"We've got another jumper—a male who went down in a ball of fire. Send over a clean-up crew. We're in a construction storage area at the bottom of Kresomyslova under the Nusle." Marek turned off his radio and began clearing the pile of wood blocking the door. He felt clever for deducing what he deemed to be an obvious conclusion.

Neighbors gathered at the U Skokana (Czech for *At the Jumper*), a local bar within shouting distance of the bridge. Business always picked up on these days, with locals streaming in and out, mimicking an informal wake for a victim they never knew. Many would sit chatting about the possible problems that could drive someone to take such actions. Others would complain about how such events have cast a pall over their neighborhood, wishing these people would solve their problems elsewhere. On rare occasions, a family member of the deceased would venture into the bar.

Marek had become a regular at the Skokana, greeted each time with a cheerful smile by its owner.

"Don't get me wrong, Jaroslav, but I'd rather not see so much of you," Marek said with a short-lived grin. "What can you tell me?" His tone turned matter-of-fact.

Jaroslav had become one of Marek's best pulses on the neighborhood. "Nothing. Nobody saw anything. I smelled the body as I was cleaning up from last night, probably around four thirty this morning. I didn't even bother going home. I can tell you this—if this keeps up, I may be the next one up there. The only thing keeping me from doing it is that there would be nobody here to open the bar for you in the morning." Jumpers turned Jaroslav's twelve-hour workday into thirty-six. More than one jumper a week had taken a toll on this forty-eight-year-old, painting his hair prematurely gray.

"Well, you better hurry before they build the barrier up there," Marek responded with a smile. He was referring to a city-commissioned metal overhang to be built atop the existing fence that would make it impossible for people scale it and jump.

"If they'd hurry up and agree on a design, I might start getting some sleep and wouldn't have to think of such things."

Marek heard the clean-up crew arrive. A forensics team wearing white lab coats and carrying expensive-looking equipment exited a procession of boxy Mercedes vans. Photographers and forensic analysts scoured the grounds looking for clues. Samples of hair, clothing, and possible accelerants were bagged for evidence.

A junior detective called out Marek's name. He found the detective bent over behind a pile of lumber. As Marek approached with the lead forensic specialist in tow, their gaze landed upon a partially burnt wallet three meters away from the victim. The forensic team began measuring its distance from the body and the possible trajectory it traveled after falling forty-two meters from the bridge above. Holding the bagged wallet, the lead specialist carefully removed a blue plastic identification card.

"Steve Benson." The library card identified him as an employee of one of the many language schools dotting the city.

Each year, thousands of Americans, Brits, and Aussies flocked to Prague to live a twenty-two-year-old's dream of drinking $.50 pints of the world's best beer, dating Czech supermodels, and wandering streets paved with extravagant architectural wonders.

In exchange, teachers worked a grueling schedule with the majority of class hours beginning early in the morning and ending late at night. The middle of the day provided just enough of a break to scarf down lunch, plan afternoon lessons, and travel to class. Shortly after arriving home, lesson planning resumed for the following morning. When a teacher's pay was averaged across the total hours spent planning, traveling, and teaching, the true hourly wage fell to less than $5 per hour, far from the vacation they envisioned. As a result, many teachers turned into *runners*.

"British?" Marek asked.

"American," the specialist replied.

"Age?"

"Thirty-nine years."

"That's a bit unusual." Marek cocked an eyebrow. "Most teachers are typically recent college graduates or retirees. How long has he been here?"

"Eight months."

The lieutenant's voice showed signs of apprehension as he called the victim's name into the station. With thousands of teachers flowing through Prague each year, this was the first jumper who was a teacher. His thoughts turned to the international stir this might create—crisis management, media, public relations, and all in English. Like most officers in his department, Marek's English skills were poor enough to make him fret over the media circus that might follow if not properly managed.

"Who here speaks English?" Marek's voice carried across the storage area.

A nearby forensic analyst stood up. "I do."

Marek told her that she would help by contacting the family and school and that under no circumstances was the press to be informed. She gave a halfhearted smile and nodded before resuming her work on the wallet's trajectory.

Chapter 2

Boston, Massachusetts

A woman's voice crackled over the loud speaker. "We will begin boarding sections one through three." Paul Benson remained seated by Terminal E's Gate 32 at Boston's Logan International Airport. He dug his ticket out from the inside pocket of his leather coat. *Section 5 Row 18 Seat B. The middle seat.* Unlike most travelers, Paul preferred the middle seat. Aware that most people are overly conscious of the middle person, overcompensating in the amount of room they leave, he was often afforded extra room on most flights. It was a gamble he was willing to take.

Gripping his newspaper firmly, his eyes were unable to focus on the words in front of him. He repeatedly turned to his carry-on bag, rummaging through it as if he was looking for something, but he didn't know what he was looking for. The news of his brother's death was overwhelming. Unable to focus, he decided to stand up and walk around. Realizing his section would be called any minute, he sat back down.

"Sections four through six may begin boarding at this time."

The sound system electrified Paul. He shot out of his seat like a wound spring and queued up in line.

Upon finding his seat, he promptly popped one of the Valium pills his doctor had prescribed for the trip. Paul had never been good at relaxing. Unable to easily let go of things, his stress was constantly spilling over into his sleep. When they had lived together years earlier in Boston, his brother Steve would routinely wake in the middle of the night to hear him debating the pros and cons about whatever situation was plaguing him at the time. However, if all went well, these pills would provide passage to his first deep slumber since learning of his brother's death two days ago.

"We will be preparing for landing at Prague's Ruzyne International Airport in twenty-five minutes where the local time is 8:45 a.m. The weather is ten degrees Celsius, and the skies are overcast. Please secure your food trays ..." A flight attendant standing in the first class cabin by the cockpit door recited the same standard script being iterated across fleets of planes around the world preparing their descent. The tone in her voice conveyed a disinterest in her job as the allure of free travel had worn off years earlier.

An attractive blonde flight attendant leaned in to tap Paul's shoulder. "Sir, please wake up. You must raise your seat back. We will be landing soon."

Once safely on the ground, Paul retrieved his carry-on luggage and exited the plane. Speeding toward customs well ahead of the other passengers, he imagined he must be the lightest packed passenger on the flight. His itinerary would not have the usual touristic activities, he thought, *unless providing DNA samples to identify the body of your dead brother and cleaning out his apartment are part of a tour I don't know about.* His depressive thoughts were quickly muted by the lingering drug-induced grogginess.

After exiting customs, Paul instinctually looked around to see if someone was holding a sign saying "Benson." *Who would be holding a sign? My limo driver,* he chuckled to himself. He didn't know anyone there, and nobody knew him. He continued along the rope barriers toward the sign saying Ground Transportation.

"Paul?"

"Y-e-s?" The letters hung in midair as he stood dumbfounded at the slender, yet curvy brunette woman standing before him saying his name. Her eyes were expansive, reaching out as if she knew him. Built like a lingerie model, she moved gracefully toward him. *How did she know my name?* "Are you from the school?" he asked her.

The woman smiled and nodded. "Hi, I am Klára. We speak on phone. How is your flight?" Her voice was speeding through each sentence.

For an employee of an English language school, Paul expected her English to be better. As she stumbled over her words, he could tell she was anxious. It appeared that being confronted with a native speaker only served to increase her anxiety. However, Paul felt too lethargic to comfort her.

He looked puzzled. "How did you know I'd be here?"

"You not remember you say me your flight information?"

He felt guilty for finding her broken English sexy.

"You experience difficult times. I say you I come here today, but you no pay attention. It's okay. I here now."

"Yes, you are—and I am glad." Paul welcomed the surprise.

"This way," Klára motioned to the left. Her curves glided past his eyes, making him forget why he had gone there in the first place.

The spacious new-age style of the Ruzyne International Airport did not extend to the industrial garage structure. After all, how exciting can you make a garage?

As she led him to her car, echoes buzzed by on different levels creating a symphonic effect. She stopped at the trunk of a blue car. *Skoda*. Paul felt like he was in vacation mode. Everything was new—new brands, license plates, languages, and beautiful people. He squeezed his carry-on into the disheveled storage space and slammed it closed. Sitting in the passenger seat, he stared blankly out the window.

The little engine roared to life.

"You stay in Hotel Radcanska. Is correct?"

"Yes, that's correct."

The compact blue car lurched out of its space to join the hum of engines echoing between floors. The gears were whirring louder and louder as the car turned through the floors. In minutes, they were on Evropska, a two-lane highway leading to the city's center. Descending into a rotary, Klára began a tour of the city.

"Here is Dejvice. We also say P6, Prague Six. Many university students are being here. P6 have five universities and many country embassies. Even Czech president live here. Prague have fifteen districts."

"Which district did my brother live in?" Paul was beginning to wake up. He rubbed his eyes to have a better look around.

"P2. This is also rich district—P2 and P6." Her accent roused feelings of excitement in Paul. *So this is the foreign-language effect Steve kept talking about—they say ten words and you interpret a hundred.* In all of Steve's travels, he had learned that flirting was far easier when a partial language barrier existed—when one person didn't speak the common language well. Unobstructed by the façade erected by language, he found it possible to connect on a deeper level with the other person.

The gloomy weather hanging overhead accentuated the drabness of the Soviet-style apartment buildings lining Evropska. Feelings of Stalinist-era oppression invaded the car from every angle. Paul pointed to the characterless buildings passing by.

"Are all Czech buildings like this?" His voice couldn't hide his dislike for the homes.

"You not like our architecture?" she laughed. "Czech architecture is famous. You did not like airport? Is voted best airport in all of Europe." Klára was beginning to relax a bit, allowing her speech to slow down to form more complete sentences.

"Yeah, but it's only an airport," Paul chortled.

"Yes, and these are only apartment buildings. You wait. I show you nice architecture." Klára changed lanes and barreled into the next rotary without hesitation. Paul gripped the *holy-shit* handle with one hand and his seat belt with the other.

"So much for driver's ed classes here." Paul was definitely awake now.

"School teaches driver's ed, too," Klára answered politely, unaware of the joke.

Yeah, but did you take it?

"Look!" She pointed. "There you will see beautiful homes. This is Cubist architecture."

The street opened up, and an array of ornately decorated homes rose from the road in front of them. Each looked like a small castle featuring dynamic depths, a variety of shapes, angles, and dimensions.

Paul fell silent as the elaborate edifices enchanted him one by one. Surrounded by uniquely foreign homes, he finally felt like he was in Europe. "Okay, you win." He smiled at her.

"We are coming to P2. Do you see dancing building? Is called Dancing House."

A curved glass structure was sliding out of the building in front of them. A ten-story hourglass figure embedded in the side of the building landed on the sidewalk. Matched by the building's uneven windows sitting at different heights along each floor, the building appeared as if it was moving.

"Wow!"

"Yes, wow. Original name of building was Fred and Ginger, your Fred Astaire and Ginger Rogers. Persons call it Drunk House. Is easier to dance drunk. And window is ... are funny. Very nice restaurant is up there. What you thinking about Czech architecture now?" Her smile beamed across the car as she turned right at a KFC restaurant. "For you, Americana," she pointed and laughed. "Your hotel is on right. We to stop for few minutes and go to brother's apartment down street after." Her words reminded Paul of the purpose of his trip.

Having booked his room online, Paul already knew that Hotel Radcanska's grand architectural style as seen from the road masked the rundown interior awaiting him inside. With Klára's help, they got his room squared away before driving another three hundred meters down the road to Steve's apartment.

Chapter 3

Prague

L e Devon! I hear this hotel name," Klára said, as her blue Skoda pulled up to the entrance. "Is five-star hotel ... very famous."

Next to the opulent hotel entrance was a smaller, less pronounced doorway that read Residence Devon. A few years earlier, as the real estate boom swept across Eastern Europe, the owners of Le Devon capitalized on the trend by developing the lands behind the hotel. The equally luxurious permanent dwellings that share the hotel's amenities had been open just over a year.

Steve's apartment waited just beyond the interior sliding glass doors. Paul and Klára were greeted by a pair of security guards keeping watch over the building's exterior and courtyard from a row of closed-circuit video cameras. Klára uttered a few words in Czech, and one of the security guards handed her a set of keys as he motioned them toward the doors.

The doors opened to a brick courtyard enclosed by three modern buildings. A white Lamborghini parked in the middle of the yard acted like a magnet for Paul. He walked over and pressed his face against the glass.

"Is very nice. Now, come, this way!" Klára said, increasing her pitch and ringing the keys in her hand like she was summoning a dog.

Paul reluctantly smiled and followed. He looked back at the sports car he could only imagine owning. Behind the car, along the side of the yard, he noticed a number of police vehicles. As he approached the entrance, he could smell the odor of new construction and the distinctly sterile atmosphere of modern living.

"We look for thirteen."

"That sounds about right." Paul's voice turned down, and Klára quietly agreed.

Klára walked to the elevator, confusing Paul. *Thirteen should be on the first floor*, he thought. After Klára pressed the button, the door opened, and they entered the shiny new metal box. There it was. The first-floor button was where the second floor button should be. *Ah, right! In Europe, the first floor is the second floor in America.*

When they exited the elevator, their strides echoed in sync down the quiet hallway. "Last door on right is what guard say," she whispered as if afraid to break the silence.

The door was slightly ajar. For such a heavy door, it swung open effortlessly. A marble, spa-style bathroom could be seen immediately to the left. Passing through the short breezeway, Klára entered the living area where detectives were combing through every inch of the fifty-square meter apartment looking for clues.

Her eyes were drawn to the windows, and she let out a loud sigh. *"Magnifique!"*

The world fell away under them. The level street leading up to the complex gave no indication that it sat perched high upon a hill overlooking all of southern Prague. While the view was not the most picturesque, it had character. Each morning when the sun rose, ten kilometers of character were projected through a series of floor-to-ceiling windows, filling the apartment with natural light. At night, specks of light throughout the valley below formed a pointillistic landscape.

The man in charge spoke to Klára with an air of authority. It seemed they had met before. Dressed differently from the other officers, he carried himself in a militaristic fashion—disciplined, stern, and aggressive. Paul guessed that the lieutenant was in his early forties, slightly older than himself.

"Paul, here is Lieutenant Marek. He leads investigations for your brother's death. He does not speak English. I will translate."

Marek extended his oversized hand, which had an equally overpowering grip. Paul couldn't wait to retrieve his hand. The lieutenant pointed to a stack of journals on a wooden desk in the corner and uttered something for Klára to translate.

"These journals are strange for the English teacher. This home is strange, too. Lieutenant Marek asks how teacher lives here. Only wealthy business men live here. Many are mafia."

Mafia? This made Paul feel queasy. He explained that his brother worked as an equity research analyst for an investment management firm in Boston for many years. Despite earning a pittance next to the exorbitant Wall Street salaries, one month of Steve's base salary paid what an English teacher might hope to earn in an entire year. Add to that an annual bonus amounting to one-third of his total compensation, and it was easy to understand why Steve chose to live here. Similar apartments in Boston would cost three times what he was paying for in Prague.

Paul turned to the topic that made him uneasy. "The lieutenant said mafia."

"Yes. He asked about journals on the desk. Appointment book on desk have meetings with many mafia in Residence Devon ... what did Steve to do with mafia?"

"Meetings?" Paul could hardly contain himself.

"Who was your brother? What was he doing with mafia?" Klára followed up.

Paul could feel Marek's eyes fixated on him, trying to read his face for clues. Paul grew anxious, imagining that this might be the beginning of a cold war-style interrogation.

"I just told you who he was. How should I know what he was doing with them? Maybe he was teaching them English? Or worse—day trading."

"Day trading?" Klára asked.

"Day trading—investing in the stock market. Maybe someone lost money. Are you questioning them?"

Klára ignored his question. "Journals have pictures about body parts. He see this is fighting practice."

"Fighting practice?" Paul clarified. "You mean martial arts." His mind drifted to the times Steve would return from martial arts classes excited to try new moves on him. Paul never liked this as much as Steve did.

"Yes, martial arts. Lieutenant Marek know martial arts, but he not know this martial arts in books here."

"Are you questioning the mafia?" Incited by new information, Paul's mind couldn't move on.

Klára's voice dropped to a whisper. "Officers will to speak to mafia, but many in police working for mafia. Will not be good information source. Lieutenant Marek ask for sample your hair for DNA now."

Paul agreed and leaned forward. She plucked a few strands of hair and packed them away in a plastic bag. She wrote his name and a code on the bag, handed it to an officer, and uttered something before the officer placed it in the evidence case.

"You look like you've done that before," Paul joked.

"I not understand."

"You knew the code, and the officer took orders from you. I would think you are in charge here."

"I am modern Czech woman." She flashed a grin. "We always in charge. Lieutenant Marek ask me to get hair and tell me code."

Paul sensed that the questioning had ended for the time being and walked onto the enclosed sun porch. The heat, trapped by the glass enclosure, hit him like a warm ocean wave. He imagined Steve sitting out there for hours in his shorts letting sunlight wash over him. The view filled Paul's eyes from every direction, breathing energy into his jet-lagged body.

"Is that it?" he asked in a devastated tone, pointing to the concrete expanse monopolizing the far right side of the vista. Cars buzzing along the bridge in the distance created a relaxing, hypnotic effect.

The mood turned somber, and Klára fell silent. She nodded and looked away.

A detective entered the small room and handed Paul two of the six journals.

"What about the others?" Paul demanded.

The detective looked to Klára who translated, "Other journals are English teaching notes—grammar and similar."

"I would like to see them," Paul said, not fully trusting the officers.

Marek nodded, indicating that he understood the difficult circumstances Paul found himself in.

"Can I come again tomorrow?"

Klára began the tedious translation process again. "Lieutenant Marek says apartment open for two days more. Say to guards you come to thirteen."

Paul cringed at hearing the number again. Satisfied that nothing was being kept from him, he took the two books and one last look around the apartment before leaving.

Chapter 4

Prague

Clutching the journals, Paul followed Klára to her car. The hotel was only three hundred meters away, but his body was starting to give out, and he wasn't sure he could make the walk. They sat for a minute in silence before she turned the engine over.

Once in front of his hotel, she turned and handed him a slip of paper. "This is my mobile number. You call anytime."

"Thanks," Paul muttered.

"Number also in phone. I call you here." She held up a generic-looking phone.

Paul thanked her again and trudged his way to the front door. He turned to wave, but her car had already disappeared down the road.

After a long, hot shower, Paul collapsed into bed. Lying on his side, he began pondering the new information—*mafia, journals, detectives, bridges, Russians, thirteen ...*

The reflection of the afternoon sun off the television's faded screen woke Paul. The television and gaudy furniture it sat on reminded him of how he imagined Soviet-era luxury to be. He rolled over and began taking an inventory of his environment. The disproportionately high ceiling made him feel uncomfortable. He wondered if the room was part of a larger room that the hotel had split into three in the name of profit. His eyes followed the cheap molding around the room that divided the muted dark green wall from the ghostlike white plaster ceiling. A circular pattern in the center of the ceiling depicted where a grand chandelier must have hung when it was all one room.

Realizing he forgot to draw the curtains before falling asleep, Paul stood and walked to the window where he imagined ghosts of czars past would be haunting him all night long. Gold trim embedded in the deep maroon velvet curtains caught his eye as it gleamed in the sunlight. He took temporary pleasure in rubbing the velvet before a low rumble below his feet brought his attention to the bright red tram shooting by his window. *Tram #6.*

Paul's neck tensed up. *Fuck! Don't tell me this is going to be happening all night!* He checked his bag for the Valium pills to reassure himself.

Turning back to the room, he eyed the journals on the desk, and a rush of sadness overwhelmed him. Choking back tears, he took a seat at the desk. He fought to maintain the emotion-numbing state he had been operating under since arriving. He could not accept his brother was gone. *Let's just get through the next few days and deal with these feelings later.*

Chapter 5

Prague

He laid the two books side by side— *TCM* and *Health History. TCM? TCM? What is TCM?*

The hard-covered, college-ruled notebook was the sort of book you might use in a science lab course. Its pages were tattered and stained, having lost their strength years ago. Paul recognized it as one of Steve's journals he toted between acupuncture appointments and martial arts classes years earlier. The pentagon drawn on the inside cover was the same Paul had seen on their refrigerator. *Water, Wood, Fire, Earth, and Metal.* For the five years he lived with Steve, he had to look at this every time he opened the refrigerator door. However, this one was slightly different. *Where is the food? Isn't this the Chinese version of the food pyramid? Why isn't broccoli under Metal, or cabbage under Earth?*

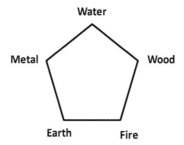

Below the diagram was written:

> The five colors blind the eye.
> The five tones deafen the ear.
> The five flavors dull the taste.

Colors, tones, flavors?

Paul turned to the first page. The heading read: *The Cycle of Creation.*

Below the heading was another pentagon—a drawing that took up half of the page. Each point contained an element with an arrow pointing to the next element, and short descriptions explained the relationships between the elements. The notes seemed well planned before being committed to paper.

The Cycle of Creation

Water

Metal enriches water (minerals)

Water feeds wood, makes it grow tall

Metal

Wood

Earth turns into metal

Wood feeds fire, makes it burn bright

Earth

Fire

Fire turns wood to ash, feeds earth

Okay, simple enough, he thought. *Eat broccoli to make Water strong. It would be nice if he told me what the hell Water means. Does broccoli make you urinate a lot? I wonder where asparagus fits in here.*

The bottom half of the page contained five smaller pentagons with the heading—*Cycles of Control*. Each pentagon showed an arrow cutting across its center from one element to another.

Cycles of Control

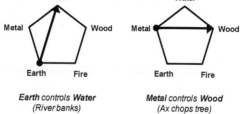

Water controls **Fire**
(Extinguish)

Wood controls **Earth**
(Roots burrow into soil)

Fire controls **Metal**
(Melts)

Earth controls **Water**
(River banks)

Metal controls **Wood**
(Ax chops tree)

It all seemed logical. But what did it really mean? No wonder the detective wanted help understanding it. Paul wanted help too.

He turned the page. *Great! More pentagons! Is this a damn geometry class?*

"Mother-Son Relationship"

Now we're moving into Oedipal Geometry! Paul was getting frustrated that the answers weren't being spoon-fed.

Lacking patience, he decided to tackle this material later at an Internet café.

He turned to the other journal. Flipping through equally worn out pages, the second journal was written like a diary, occasionally interrupted by notes and lists. He stopped at a list entitled *Symptoms*, recognizing them as a few of the symptoms that baffled Steve's doctors for years.

- Nose bleeds
- Hot flashes
- Urination
- Sleep
- Muscles / tendons

- Eyes
- Hemorrhoids
- Digestion
- Skin
- Dizzy spells

He skimmed further down until a section jumped out that would hopefully shed some light on what had happened. He noted the date of the passage. Steve had been twenty-nine years old.

My Typical Day

4/3/1997: Every morning I wake around 5:30 a.m. Groggy and sore all over, I know I didn't sleep a wink. It feels as if metal wires run through my limbs and someone is pulling on them all night long, keeping me in a constant state of tension. Well, at least I've stopped waking every two hours to run to the toilet, a phenomenon that lasted for six years!

When I stand, my first few steps are tender, like those of an old man. My muscles and tendons resemble taut violin strings that resonate a twang with every step. My knees hurt and my ankles are weak. One wrong move and something will certainly tear. It's scary, especially for someone who was used to being an athlete all his life.

Once in the shower, my feet begin to melt under the hot water, and my muscles slowly let go. However, shortly after drying off, they tense up again as if warding off something. Like a yin-yang spinning out of control, I'm overheated and chilled at the same time. All of the heat in my body begins rushing to my head, turning my feet unbearably cold. On the verge of perspiring, the mere opening of my pores makes my skin scream, an indication of how sensitive my body has become. I begin walking swiftly through the apartment. My lungs heave, and my heart pounds in an effort to cool off—a desperate attempt to prevent the onset of sweating.

Too late! An electric shock runs through my body. Sweat pours from my armpits, genitals, and backside. Chills race through every organ and my skin crawls. I grab another towel and run back to the shower.

Like clockwork, this happens shortly after I begin shaving every morning. Occasionally, it will strike while I'm on the train going to work, which really sucks. Most days are two- or three-shower days that require me to crawl back into bed, the "incubator," where I warm up. For those special occasions at work or in transit, I keep a space heater under my desk to dry undershirts, socks, and any other articles of clothing I routinely soak through. This isn't the sort of thing you ever get used to. You just learn to deal with it.

His words evoked feelings of guilt. Paul was reminded of the battles that ensued every morning over the bathroom. If he missed his opportunity to shower first, Paul had to walk on egg shells in anticipation of Steve's hot flashes. *Hurry up for Christ's sake. You're like a menopausal bitch.* He used to routinely curse at Steve for hogging the bathroom. He grew to resent his brother over time, asserting that the various maladies were merely psychosomatic.

On most mornings, I get a strange bloated sensation within a few bites of breakfast. My abdomen becomes so distended that it protrudes a few inches, and I find it difficult to breathe. It feels more like inflammation than bloating, cutting off the circulation to my feet and driving blood to my head.

Somewhere between the constant showering and breakfast, I'll need to run to the bathroom to put out a rapid-onset nosebleed before it hits my freshly pressed shirt. It comes on so fast that there is little time to react. I usually have to cup my hand below my nose as I run for the bathroom because it's gushing out like someone turned on a faucet in my nose.

When I ask doctors about this, they always tell me that it's due to cold weather and the lack of humidity. Personally, I think the fact that this happens just as often in the middle of July as it does in January seems to refute their theory. It seems related to the constipation, bloating, or inflammation, or whatever is happening down there. I wish one of these people had a clue.

Despite the excess blood in my upper torso, my face turns numbingly cold from ear to ear while waiting for the train or bus. It could be August, and my nose would feel frostbitten. My eyes are always dry and irritated, burning a path to the back of my head. My body is on some sort of nervous overdrive. When I try to look up, I can't hold a gaze, and my eyes return to the ground, or simply close. This inability to hold eye contact has proven disastrous for my interactions with women and colleagues. I'm pretty sure they think I have no confidence.

Once in the city, I make my way up State Street to Court Square. Luckily, working as an investment analyst for Gray Haired Investment Management is a pretty low stress position. I have no deadlines, very little contact with the outside world, and an office far from Mahogany Row. This place moves as quickly as grass grows. Aside from a weekly meeting, I rarely see my boss. If I died back here, it would be weeks before they'd uncover me. For an upwardly mobile young buck, this could be frustrating. Considering my daily torture ritual, this is an ideal situation.

Once at work, I enter my little sanctuary where nobody bothers me. If I had hot flashes on the train, I spend my first half-hour stripping down and standing completely naked in my office where I dry each article of clothing with the space heater. Trying to air-dry is too painful as the wet cloth against my overly sensitive skin only makes matters worse. Fortunately, my office has no windows into the hallway, and the only thing I see from my exterior window is the brick wall of the neighboring building. So far, I've made it three years without anyone walking in on me. Could you imagine having to explain something like this? Aside from that, my only other concern at work is using the bathroom.

At times, I am completely unable to urinate despite my body sending signals telling me I urgently need to go. As a result, I often run to the bathroom for seemingly no reason. I've learned to ignore many of the signals unless the "ten-minute warning" is given. During this period, my feet turn increasingly cold to the point where they feel frozen. Even the space heater won't help. Then, I know it's real. Where is the connection between needing to urinate and getting cold feet? It's not like I'm about to marry the urinal.

When I get to the bathroom, I can't go. At home, I am occasionally forced to coax my body to relax by running warm water over the glans of my penis. This sends a signal through the urethra to the prostate, relaxing it until it finally releases. Otherwise, I could be standing there for thirty minutes. My warm water solution is obviously not an option at work. Could you imagine running hot water on your cock and having your boss walk in on you? I've found it's safest to just sit during these episodes.

Next comes the problem of stopping. At times, I cannot completely void my bladder. It feels as if it's finished, but it's not! Five steps after packing everything away, urine begins seeping through my boxers. If I'm having a bad day, it penetrates through to my trousers. And, if it's a really bad day, like the date I went on at the Prudential Center, it's running down my khakis! The stain just kept growing and spreading. Needless to say, the date ended early.

Individually, any of these symptoms would be cause for alarm. Now, consider that they all happen every day and are only the tip of the iceberg. This list can go on and on. For now, take these symptoms and multiply them by seven days a week, fifty-two weeks per year, eight years (so far), and you will begin to understand what I've been going through. I walk around in a sleep-deprived state, dulling my mental capacities, rendering it impossible to identify the causes of the physical symptoms torturing me daily. The combination of my mental state, which gives way to short-term memory loss, and my symptoms make it impossible to adequately perform my work, adding stress to my already stressed out existence. This is compounded by running from one moron doctor to the next, each telling me that I am suffering from a psychosomatic disorder. Then, my friends, who don't know the full extent of my issues, tell me they know exactly what I'm going through because they've been working through some mommy and daddy issues with a shrink. Give me a fucking break.

It's difficult to put into words what this type of situation does to you—how the utter fear of not knowing what's wrong can take over your life. You spend every waking minute researching any disease that produces even the most remotely similar symptom. It's not long before you'd give anything just to know your enemy's name. Without a name—an identity—you don't know what you're trying to fight. Once you've suffered long enough without an accurate diagnosis, even the most horrific conditions begin to sound appealing. You eventually reach a point where you actually hope the doctor comes back with bad news because 'no news' no longer feels like 'good news.'

The passage went on to describe more seemingly unrelated symptoms and the mechanical solutions Steve implemented to compensate for his body's lack of functioning. His life had become a never-ending comparison between what was once normal and the path his life took. As the years passed, his benchmark for normal faded, and his efforts to lead a normal life appeared futile. Despite his life spiraling out of control, his words sounded surprisingly grounded for someone who had lost the most basic qualities of life. Paul skipped down a few paragraphs:

Ironically, I am responsible for analyzing the pharmaceutical industry. Unbeknownst to my co-workers, I've spent the past eight years as a one-man clinical trial, testing dozens of drugs to cure my various afflictions. For this opportunity, I need to thank the almighty, itchy-trigger-fingered physicians, who have enabled my trial to continue for far too long. Now, I spend my time analyzing many of the same drugs for investment purposes.

During my three years on the job, it has become clear that Western medicine doesn't have a clue what it's doing. You don't have to look too far to find cases in which modern science has disproved itself. Chocolate, once thought to cause acne and tooth decay, has no impact on acne and appears to have an impact on tooth decay equal to or less than a slice of bread. Alcohol, once thought to be bad for hypertension, is now helpful in moderate consumption. Originally, only red wine was considered beneficial for lowering cholesterol. Now, all types of alcohol are thought to be helpful. It seems that a new study regarding coffee's benefits or harmful effects is released every month, with each refuting the prior month's study. Even studies like excessive ejaculation, once linked to prostate cancer, is now thought to be beneficial as it cleanses out toxins. Personally, I'd like to know who sponsored that study and how much constitutes "excessive." Soon they will tell us that aspirin and whole wheat bread are linked to heart disease.

In my case, the doctors don't know what they are trying to cure. "Vague clusters of symptoms usually point to psychosomatic disorders ..." Could you be any more full of shit? Considering the average doctor's visit is only seventeen minutes, during which time the doctor hardly even looks up from his/her clipboard, how could they really know what's wrong? Better answers might be, "I have no idea. You should see someone who cares, might have a clue, or is willing to do his/her job and research this."

Instead, they are all too willing to prescribe the latest drugs for which the manufacturers don't understand the long-term impacts. Over the past ten years, the FDA removed sixteen drugs from the market due to safety-related concerns that included heart damage and death. Despite the many years of preclinical and clinical trials, these drugs averaged four and a half years on the shelves before their health risks could be determined. As an investment analyst, I now look at these things in terms of dollars and cents. The removal of a drug can translate into billions of dollars of lost revenues, settlement funds, litigation charges, earnings per share, and ultimately, a hit to the stock price. With so much money at stake, how can you be certain Big Pharma is protecting your interests ahead of their own?

The passage reminded Paul of his brother's weekly tirade in which he railed against the health care industry. He read a little further and decided he had had enough for the evening. His mind was saturated with dreadful images of a life of misery and pain. It was a life he witnessed, but never fully understood. *With this much, I wonder if I would have done the same thing.* Paul was beginning to think his brother might have jumped.

His stomach growled. It was time for his first Czech dinner. Rummaging through his carry-on bag, he found a fresh pair of jeans and button-down shirt among the pile of clothes he haphazardly threw together before his sudden departure from Boston. He stopped at the front desk, where a balding man wearing glasses a little too trendy for his age was reading the paper. "Hello."

The man looked up from the Czech newspaper and greeted Paul, "*Dobrý večer* ... uh, hello."

"Can you recommend a local Czech restaurant? Somewhere Czech people go ... a pub, bar ... something casual."

Paul noticed the concierge's eyes had perked up a bit and figured the graveyard shift must mean little interaction with people. "There is one nice place now open. It is little time on tram—but is good. You take tram outside of door here. You want go?"

"Sure." Paul gave him the thumbs-up.

"Tram #4 or #10. I write for you." Speaking as he was writing, the man continued, "Take tram to stop Zborovská. Turn right to Preslova Street. You find *restaurace* Smíchovský Radniční Sklípek. Best *restaurace* at 10:00 p.m. You order *vepřové koleno*."

"What is *vepzo* ...?" Paul angled his head down to look at the piece of paper as he attempted to speak the uniquely foreign sounding words.

"*Vepřové koleno* is knee of pig. Very good Czech dinner. You order with *pivo*."

"Pig's knee and *pivo—pivo*?"

"*Pivo!* Pilsner, Gambrinus ... American Budweiser! *Pivo—*" The concierge seemed to be growing excited at the thought of relaxing with a beer.

"Ah, beer!" After Steve's exaltations of Czech beer, Paul was looking forward to his first taste.

The man handed him two tram tickets and motioned as if inserting the tickets. Paul heard the train coming and thanked the man, who insisted on shaking Paul's hand before letting him go. He bolted out the door and sprinted alongside the tram car passing him by.

Once on the train, he saw a metallic silver and yellow box attached to one of the poles for passengers to hold on. He inserted a ticket, and a noise registered that the date and time had been stamped on it. The absence of graffiti and homeless passengers made Paul feel safe compared to public transportation in American cities.

His nonguided, above-ground public transportation tour began. The car descended down a long, steady decline giving way to an eclectic assortment of shops lining the streets. Most of the quaint boutiques sold locally produced home goods, jewelry, and shoes. An occasional bar, drab and sunken into a building's basement, blended in unnoticed.

A bright pink three-story brothel grabbed Paul's attention. It looked like an oasis in the middle of a string of rather ordinary establishments—a very dirty oasis. He laughed when he saw it was standing next to a fine dining establishment. Europe's acceptance of such businesses in the midst of everyday life fascinated him. *In the United States, we hide such activities in shame. Where's the shame here?*

Every block had at least one storefront with flashing neon lights. If it wasn't a brothel, it was a *herna*—a neighborhood gambling establishment long considered money laundering fronts for the Russian mafia.

As the stations passed by, a number of multinational American firms caught his eye. A large PricewaterhouseCoopers building, large enough to house a few hundred employees, was followed by an Ernst & Young building a few blocks down the road, making him feel a little more at home.

The tram entered one of the many bridges crossing the Vltava River, bringing the Prague Castle into view. Magnificently lit up against the dark night sky, its reflection shimmered in the river. The serene scene was accented by a golden glow emanating from under the arches of the Charles Bridge that connects the fortress to the Old Town.

"Zborovská," an automated voice alerted the car.

Paul pulled on the thin cord draped along the top of the windows to tell the driver he wanted to disembark. Door-to-door, the tour had lasted a short nine minutes.

Once on the street, he turned the corner and saw the restaurant's green awning. The door led to a staircase. At the bottom, he stumbled into a crowded room, which he scanned for an empty table. He spotted the only one remaining at the far end and made his way there. As he took his seat, a waitress promptly met him.

"*Pivo*?" Her monotonous tone said, *What else does one order in a Czech bar?*

"Yes, *pivo* and *vepřové koleno.*" Aware he botched the pronunciation, Paul held up the piece of paper. She took it in her hand and brought it closer to read. After nodding in a deliberate fashion, she disappeared into a back room.

The hum of voices and laughter kept Paul entertained. He could not understand a word, but enjoyed watching his neighbors engaged in their revelry. Occasionally, he heard someone he swore was speaking English only to realize it was Czech.

While getting lost in the environment, something odd happened. Two people came over, motioned to the free chairs at his table, and said something in Czech. Paul put his hand to his ear to indicate he did not understand, but they only said it louder. They proceeded to sit anyhow and carried on as if he wasn't there.

Moments later, three beers were set down on the table. In unison, all three lift their glasses, and the two included Paul in their toast. Then, they carry on in their conversation again. Paul laughed inside, figuring it was better than sitting alone.

His first impression of Czech beer was that it tasted every bit as good as Steve described. "If beer were ice cream, then Czech beer would be the banana split of beer—with a taste equally as enjoyable."

The pig's knee arrived minutes later, hanging on a metal hook suspended over what appeared to be a cutting board. Sauerkraut, horseradish, and mustard rounded out the dish. The hook was shaped like the number nine. The bottom of the nine was attached to the board, and the pork was speared by the metal curling under to form the top of the nine. The meat was tender and juicy, clearly a fattier portion of the pig for which the beer was a perfect accompaniment.

His neighbors paused for a minute and looked at his dish. "*Bon appétit.*"

"Thanks. Do you speak English?"

They shook their heads. "*Ne Angličtina.*"

"Okay." He raised his glass to them and went on eating.

Each time his beer was even slightly below half full, the waitress returned with a fresh, full glass. He wasn't sure what to make of this. He felt pressured to drink faster. After having two beers too many, he stuck out his hand to tell her, "Enough!"

Chapter 6

Prague

The next morning, Paul rose a little hung over. He had slept through the hotel's breakfast service and wasn't feeling particularly hungry. The time change and prior night's meal were working against his appetite. After showering and getting dressed, he packed his laptop bag with the two journals and set out to find an Internet café. Recalling a café on the way to Steve's apartment, he decided to wander back that way in case he wanted to visit Residence Devon again.

Vietnamese vegetable stands sprinkled throughout each neighborhood added some color to his journey. Each was a patchwork of different colored vegetable trays stacked high on the street against the shop's windows. As he walked, his eyes followed the collections of mosaics embedded in the sidewalk. Small square bricks formed the same black-and-white patterns over and over, leading him to the Bohemian Brew. Now only steps from Steve's apartment, he wondered if his brother had been a frequent customer.

The café's eclectic charm sat in its partial subterranean setting with windows large enough to make Paul feel like he was part of the pedestrian traffic. The café's assortment of books covering the walls reminded him of a library. A woman behind the counter looked up briefly from her magazine to acknowledge Paul's presence. *A naughty librarian in this city of sin?* Paul mused as his thoughts wandered back to the sheer number of brothels he passed on the tram the night before. He took a seat at one of the empty tables and removed the journals from his bag before placing his order at the counter.

The young woman, one of the many university students living nearby, delivered a frothy latte adorned with cinnamon. He returned to the diary hoping to find something that would provide insights into his brother's psyche or situation. *Was it depression? How could it not be? But what about the mafia? Was he experimenting with Chinese herbs? After all, herbs are drugs. Steve used to say that 25 percent of pharmaceuticals are derived from herbs.*

He turned to where he left off, eight years into Steve's crisis.

> 6/15/1997—The progress of my symptoms has resembled the process of a shoe breaking down. It happens so gradually that you don't realize it's even happening. As your posture becomes compromised, pain begins setting into different areas of your body as slowly as the shoe wears out—your back, hips, knees, ankles, etc. This goes unnoticed for a period because the human body can adapt to tolerate substantial amounts of pain. However, after enough time passes, the pain grows to become unbearable.

Most people only come to realize that the shoe is the cause when they buy a new pair and feel the difference. Most of us are very bad at reading the signals of our own bodies and take action only after damage has already begun.

The worst of my symptoms set in gradually over the first six months, at which point they reached that unbearable state. As time wore on, new referred symptoms sprung up, compounding the initial problems. This made it difficult to isolate the true causes. Eventually, you forget what your normal state of health was even like.

Looking at the shoe, you can't tell which part started breaking down first. Was it the heel? Had I replaced the heel, would that have stopped the rest from falling apart? You consider your gait and the surfaces you have been walking on. You decide to seek out a doctor for answers. He comes to the brilliant conclusion that you simply need to think happier thoughts while walking.

Unsatisfied with his conclusion, you seek out a second opinion. You take your worn out shoes, smarting shins, and fallen arches to another clinic. A flustered doctor, overbooked with too many patients, rushes into the room. He briefly looks up to shake your hand and then buries his head into his clipboard. He doesn't bother to see you are holding the shoe. He only reads "shin splints" and hands you a bottle of pills. "Take two pills daily—one in the morning and one at night." Before you can ask what the pills are for, he has already rushed out the door to his next appointment.

My favorite line from the TV show *House* is "choose your specialist and you choose your disease." In this world of specialization, most doctors are unable to see beyond their specialty. As such, they are unable to diagnose a cluster of vague symptoms that connect different areas of the body. With limited time per patient, they throw a bottle of pills at you, recommend surgery, or say your problems are psychosomatic.

Desperate for a cure, it's easy to see why patients often overmedicate on pharmaceuticals and herbs.

Anyhow, psychosomatic disorder is never a diagnosis the patient wants to hear. Nobody wants to hear that it might be some flaw in his or her personality. People want immediate relief, something psychotherapy typically doesn't provide. When considering what I've been going through, how could I not have substantially elevated stress levels? So which came first, the chicken or the egg?

Paul's mood grew somber as he was reminded of their first two years living together in Boston. He had referred to this period as the *storm before the calm*. He made the mistake of agreeing with one of the doctor's psychosomatic diagnoses, driving them further apart at times. Something had definitely changed in his brother over time. One minute, he was completely calm and relaxed. Then, the slightest stressor might send him into a rage, losing total control. Afraid to confront Steve in the midst of slamming cabinet doors, yelling, and flying objects, Paul would exit the scene to let things blow over.

While most of these symptoms are debilitating in their own right, even when combined, they are still only the tip of the iceberg. The worst of it has been losing my ability to have sex at the age of twenty-one—the prime of my life.

Something happens to a man's psyche when faced with the prospect of never having sex again. He comes to realize that every action he's taken in life is somehow related to getting laid. Take that away and you take away his purpose in life.

Even at the age of twenty-one, it was readily obvious. Having developed physically at a young age, reaching puberty years ahead of my peers, my psyche was deeply rooted in my physical and sexual being. Losing that side of me, a side that comprised a large part of how I saw myself, was devastating. At first, when I found myself alone, I would burst into tears for seemingly no reason. However, a place deep within the darkness of my psyche knew exactly why.

Most people will tell you they already know that "men only think about sex." At this point, it's a cliché. While they are correct, they usually say this in reference to specific actions that scream "sex." For example, you might hear this said about a guy who sleeps around or cheats. However, this typically focuses on the pleasure derived and stops short of describing how all consuming sex is for a man. Sometimes I wonder if most men are even aware of the amount of time and effort they really devote to finding sex.

Consider something as simple as going for a coffee. Watch a man entering a café, especially one where there are attractive women sitting, and you will notice that everything he does is related to sex. If given options, watch where he chooses to sit. How does he position his body? In what tone of voice does he order his coffee? Who does he choose to make eye contact with and how often? How much does he tip the cashier?

I bet if you conducted a study in which you observed the tipping habits of male customers, you'd find that higher tips were left when an attractive female customer was standing behind him.

These subconscious choices are all rooted in sex and tell you exactly how he feels about himself. You can apply this to almost every setting in which you put a man where there are women close by.

Now, if you can't have sex, why bother sitting near the attractive woman? Why open your body up to her in hopes of engaging her? Why leave a larger tip than is warranted?

Paul paused to think about how much of a tip he had left the girl at the counter minutes earlier. *This is Europe—people don't leave tips*, he reassured himself about the paltry 0.37 Czech Crowns.

I find it interesting how many women take offense to the notion that all of men's actions are based upon sex. Even men I know have taken offense. However, they usually only do it when women are standing by, in an attempt to appear as if they have much more depth than the statement implies. In short, they are angling to get laid. People confuse this drive to have sex with a lack of depth, cheapening the courtship. In fact, from my own experiences, I can tell you that the opposite is true. Desire to have sex makes a man come alive. A man will make bold and romantic gestures that are full of creativity if sex is even a remote possibility. What's the point when you remove the ability to have sex? A man's interest and depth are intertwined with sex. Without it, he will literally feel dead to the world, as I have felt for the past eight years. Feigning such actions without the ability to have sex has been a monumental task, something that was effortless when all systems were "go."

The best way to describe what it's like to lose your ability is to liken yourself to a computer. Your operating system contains a function called "procreation." Without this function, your CPU will not run properly. The PC will only start and run basic operations in an inefficient manner. Often, it gets caught in infinite loops and crashes while trying to boot up. The frequent crashing makes you lose confidence in your system. However, your operating system contains other functions that keep attempting to connect to other devices and load new software. This adds to your frustration because you know it's not possible, but you can't stop it from trying. Since it's the only system you have, you constantly run system tests and bring it to the repair center. The repair guys can't find any problems. So they tell you to simply think happier thoughts when turning it on.

You quickly realize that your system is destined for a toxic landfill in China and wonder how many more times you will try to reboot it before terminating it.

Despite living together for five years, Paul can't believe how well his brother hid this side of his life.

Oddly enough, if you are a man entering a café who is unable to have sex, you still feign confidence while ordering and select a seat near an attractive woman, despite knowing that there's no real possibility for you. The entire time, you feel like you are butting your head against the wall because you can't stop looking to procreate, leading to a frustrating cycle. Once on a date, you're not sure why you are there. After all, you can't have sex. Your frustration is augmented by parents and friends who get on your case to settle down. Feelings of isolation increase because you can't tell anyone. Not only is it embarrassing, but it is something that none of your friends in their twenties or thirties can understand. You no longer feel compatible with the world you knew. Intense amounts of depression and anger consume you. Desperation to find a cure sets in, occasionally leading you to very risky behavior.

The only bright side to each date is the opportunity it represents to test out your equipment and collect additional data points. I was an early explorer of the Cougar nation for obvious reasons. First off, they were easier to get into bed. Also, I figured older women would show more compassion for what I was going through. I was wrong. Women take a man's inability to perform far too personally when it has nothing to do with the woman. After all, if I didn't want to sleep with her, I wouldn't have ended up in bed with her. The "it's not you, it's me" line never worked for me, despite actually being true. No matter how much I tried to explain it, they would take a difficult situation and make it worse.

Often, the feelings happening in my lower abdomen have been too vague to describe. Other times, there are more specific feelings, such as my PC muscle becoming inflamed; feeling like it was blocking my ability to squeeze down there. When I am able to have sex, my nostrils become inflamed, chills fill my body, and I sweat profusely—making it fun for nobody.

In the past eight years, I've been to bed with more women out of desperation than I care to count, creating one emotional roller coaster ride after another. Interestingly, I didn't sleep with any of them. To be more accurate, I couldn't sleep with any of them. To make matters worse was that all of this activity had turned me into a full-blown germ-a-phobe.

Once my problems started, I desperately sought out opportunities to test my equipment. Ironically, each opportunity placed me directly in harm's way. It soon became clear that the fear of never having sex again was far greater than the fear of contracting an STD. Reestablishing one's purpose in life supersedes all other fears.

Isolated, depressed, angry, desperate, and now freaking out about what I might have caught the night before, my life has become pretty fucked up. Psychosomatic disorder? Sure, why the fuck not?

So far, I've worked with three shrinks. All three have said that I do not exhibit signs of clinical depression. However, when they looked at my health history, it clearly points to a psychosomatic disorder.

My health history traces back to three events that happened over a six month period. The fact that my symptoms set in gradually over time, and it's been eight years since this period, has made it difficult for me to identify the underlying causes of each symptom. The first event was a whiplash injury I sustained during ju-jitsu class. This made it difficult to sleep for many months. After six months, the pain in my neck had mostly subsided, aside from occasional periods of stiffness. X-rays and MRIs performed on my neck showed no signs of damage. The second was a one-night stand with an older woman who was outside of my safe college environment, someone for whom I had no context. This happened shortly after reading up on the realities of STDs. Despite being protected, I still freaked out. The last event was the combination of stressors related to graduating college and entering the real world. I found the interview process to be nerve-racking, intensified by a rapidly increasing sleep deficit from the injury. To compensate, I became a coffee and chocolate junkie, which only made it more difficult to sleep and exacerbated my stress levels. I'll admit that two of the situations point to psychosomatic manifestations.

At one point, one of my shrinks suggested that I join a support group and talk about my problems with other men who were going through this. I thought it was a good idea and signed up. Upon entering the room, it became clear that I was going to be their youngest member. Most of the men were in their sixties and had difficulty discussing their problems. Interestingly, no matter how old they were, they all confirmed this loss of identity, a loss of purpose in life. Even if they were married and had kids, they still felt dead to the world. Now, imagine this happening at the age of twenty-one. Aside from a few brief encounters with women, you are dead before you've even had a chance to live. Confused, scared, and desperate, you see all of your dreams disappear, and suicide becomes a very real option. Not a day passes when I don't think about it. I don't want to die. I just don't want to live like this—robbed of my soul and then tortured each day to remind me of what little I have to look forward to. It really comes down to how much more of this I can take before I snap and do something drastic.

Paul knew about the hot flashes, eye pain, bloody noses, and sleep issues. However, Steve's sexual issues were news to him. In fact, he might have thought the opposite based upon the plethora of dates Steve had gone on each week. Looking back on it, there was an air of desperation about it. Steve rarely told tales of conquest that contained the borderline misogynistic guy talk typically accompanying most post-date recaps of men in their twenties. Instead, Steve's tales were filled with sad undertone of frustration and disgust for both himself and his date. He never reported any sexual issues, only mismatched personalities, misleading photos, and freeloaders expecting a nice dinner from a stranger they met online. Nonetheless, he continued scouring online dating Web sites to enroll the next test subject in his own ongoing personal clinical trial. Occasionally, he would return early in the morning and wake Paul by pacing back and forth on the linoleum floor and banging the kitchen cabinet doors in search of junk food to alleviate his stress. Attempts to get Steve to talk about it were deflected. Looking back on these episodes, Paul saw that his brother was indirectly screaming for help. He wondered if he had tried hard enough to help, or was he only interested in getting back to sleep.

Chapter 7

Prague

V ibrations radiated from Paul's bag, moving it across the table. He lifted the flap to find the silver disposable flip phone Klára had given him.

"Hello." He tried to subdue the excitement in his voice. Aware that his current state of mind was rendering him more susceptible to such feelings, he didn't dwell on the initial feelings of guilt. *I'm in a strange land, and I don't know a soul here. Hell, I'm trying to piece together my brother's death.*

"Hello, Paul. Here is Klára. How are you today?" Her upbeat voice projected a childlike innocence that permeated Paul's being. "You will can go to apartment?"

Noticing that she occasionally forgets the articles in her sentences, among other grammatical mistakes, he corrected her. "The apartment. Yes, I would like that."

"Lieutenant Marek will be there. He wants know progress of journals."

"Okay, I will be ready in a few hours."

"Two hours?" Klára sounded puzzled. Faceless conversations proved more difficult for her.

"Sure, two hours is good. I will meet you at the apartment at two o'clock. I am at the Bohemian Brew. Do you know it?"

"Yes, two hours, two o'clock, I meet you at Bohemian Brew. Tak." She hung up abruptly, leaving Paul confused.

Realizing it was noon and he should eat something, Paul returned to the counter to scan the English version of the menu. His thoughts drifted to calculating an appropriate tip.

After taking his seat, he resumed Steve's journey of sexual exploits gone wrong. Narrative after narrative, many dozens in total, began and ended the same way. Drinks and appetizers turned into a physical encounter that sounded rather ordinary. Once lip locked and tongue-tied, the feel of his date's breasts pressing against him sent a current of erotic excitement racing around his body. With his erection now rigid and firmly pressing into her, she would start gyrating from the excitement as they removed each other's clothing.

She was soon staring eye to eye with his member, gently running her fingers along it, watching it spring back into the air as she experimented with his natural hydraulic system. It was solid, strong, and ready for action. It seemed like all systems were "go."

Anticipating a lengthy session with a younger lover, the older woman typically initiated the move from the couch into the bedroom. This change in position triggered some vague changes within. *Fuck!* He was losing it. Hurried, he would begin fumbling with the condom, but it was too late. It was over.

From somewhere in the depths of his abdomen, PC muscle, or prostate, he would receive signals of inflammation.

Noticing the dejected look on his face accompanying the descent to half mast, she would try to salvage the situation by grabbing it and pulling it toward her. She would then utter some perfunctory dirty talk that only made things worse by adding fuel to his fear of disease, making him jump back to say, "Whoa! Not without a condom." He would then try to smooth things over. "I'm sorry. I'm just not feeling very well right now. My stomach is bothering me."

Internalizing that younger men no longer find her attractive, she would shut down emotionally, gather her clothing, and leave the room. Steve would then return home only to masturbate without any problems. In the end, he often agreed that the symptoms pointed to a psychosomatic issue. However, he was convinced that nobody knew his body like he did, and the feelings he was experiencing told him that something else was at play.

After a handful of these stories, Paul skipped ahead a few sections in search of a period when things appeared to change for the better in Steve's life. Around Steve's fourth year at the investments firm, he started dating someone seriously. The beginning of the relationship had a rocky start, which now made more sense to Paul.

It was around the same time when Steve had given up on Western medicine, exchanging it for yoga classes at the local YMCA. By this point, he had already visited over eighty different physicians around the Boston area. Each had their own diagnosis accompanied by a toxic script. If his problems were in fact psychosomatic, running from doctor to doctor was not helping matters. Practicing yoga allowed him to de-stress and focus more on his degenerating body.

Steve did with yoga what he had done with all the other health care modalities that showed promise; he dived headlong into it. He began practicing morning, noon, and night, often closing his door at work to crank out a few sun salutations. Over time, he developed a closer connection with his body. The combination of deep breathing and meditation allowed him to achieve deeper stretches, feeling as if he were gradually pulling the fascia apart and releasing tension built up around the organs harboring these vague sensations. However, like all of the prior modalities, the benefits from yoga reached a plateau, and many of his symptoms returned, but with less severity.

Paul noted that the end of Steve's relationships often coincided with the plateaus he encountered with each health care modality. *Was each relationship only a chance to test out the new health care he was receiving? Or were the improvements in his health helping him enter into more successful relationships? Well, define successful.* While this period was the most stable Paul had seen his brother in years, Steve was attracting people with rather negative energy.

As the journal went on, it described a never-ending cycle of plateaus. Each new health care modality he pursued would eventually stop short of reaching a full state of health, at which point he would move onto another—often trying more than one at a time. While in yoga class, Steve overheard the teacher talking about a Chinese doctor located in Brighton, a neighborhood of Boston. He jotted down the doctor's name and made an appointment.

Steve's journal described the experience.

Today I went to the Chinese pharmacy in Brighton. It smelled horrible. Upon opening the door, you're hit in the face by a thick, musty smell. In the back, they prepare various herbal teas in these large cauldronlike pots. It's a throwback to the Middle Ages. The left wall of the pharmacy was lined with drawers containing loose herbs. The right side had rows of packaged herbal remedies, mostly pills and liquids imported from China. I walked to the back of the store and took a seat with about twelve other patients. The store seemed dirty and rundown. It wouldn't have surprised me to see chickens running through the waiting area.

When it was my turn to see the doctor, he led me back to his office. He carried himself with the serenity of a monk. After taking a seat, he asked if I had ever been to a Chinese doctor before.

"No," I replied.

"Please roll up your sleeves and place your wrists here." He pointed to a small pad. I laid my hands over it with my palms rotated toward the ceiling. "Just relax," he said. This guy was relaxed enough for the two of us.

He proceeded to take the pulse of my left hand. He lined up his three fingers along my radial artery and pushed in. He then moved to two fingers, and then one. He then switched back to three, then two, and then three. He continued prodding my artery for a few minutes without any apparent order to his fingering or placement on my wrist. His head was resting in his other hand, blocking his eyes. So I knew he wasn't gathering information in any other ways. Occasionally, he would pause to take notes, but he never looked up the entire time. After three minutes, he switched to my right pulse and repeated the process for an equal amount of time. When it was all done, he asked me to stick out my tongue. In total, he only looked at me for less than a minute and then proceeded to give me his diagnosis.

"You have asthma."

"Yes." Asthma! From my pulse? How the hell did he know that from my pulse?

"You do not sleep enough."

I nodded.

"You have a large ball of gas in your belly."

Indeed! I felt like I could have fueled a natural gas bus for a month. My abdomen was hard as a rock, and not like a six pack—more like a one pack—a giant one pack of gas.

"You must use the bathroom to urinate. Would you like to go now?"

Afraid of missing my turn, I had been holding it in for an hour while waiting. How did he know these things?

"You eat too many sweets to stay awake. Spleen is weak, and liver is hot. You eat too much chocolate."

Paul laughed aloud. Steve was a self-proclaimed chocoholic, an addiction he picked up while living in Austria. Each year, he would receive multiple shipments from friends still living there. It was common to see him eating a bar for breakfast.

"Your right knee hurts."

I just laughed. I couldn't believe how much this guy knew about me from my freaking pulse.

"Your neck hurts and your right shoulder hurts."

"Ah ha!" I stuck my finger up in the air. Finally! He got one wrong. I told him about my neck injury ages ago, but neither my neck nor shoulder hurt.

"Okay, pulse says your neck and shoulder hurt. So be careful of your right shoulder."

I told him about the prostate condition that my urologist diagnosed me with, the so-called leading expert, a world-renowned physician who had proven about as useless as all the others.

"No, no prostate condition."

"He seemed pretty confident that I have a prostate condition."

"But you do not have a prostate condition." The Chinese doctor tried to sound confident, too, but he just wasn't as convincing.

I asked if he would make me a tea for the prostate or not. He finally agreed but still persisted that it's not the cause of my problems. He suggested I try acupuncture instead.

I asked him for a specific diagnosis, but his response just sounded foolish. "You have excess liver fire and yin deficiency."

Great! What the hell am I supposed to do with that?

Chapter 8

Eleven months prior to meeting the Chinese doctor

Steve had been watching an episode of *60 Minutes* with his parents that profiled a doctor testing the latest treatment for erectile dysfunction on Gulf War veterans. Naturally, Steve was glued to the television. When the episode finished, he snuck away to write the doctor. In his e-mail, Steve explained his cluster of symptoms and health history. The doctor responded a few days later with hopeful news, "One of the leading experts in the field, Alan Silberman, lives in Boston." Relieved to hear that, Steve made an appointment. After all, a referral from a leading researcher profiled on *60 Minutes* was pretty valuable.

Impressed with Dr. Silberman's credentials, Steve had entered the doctor's office with renewed hope that someone might actually be able to explain to him what was happening inside of his body. While waiting, he read the plaques outlining the doctor's various medical school accomplishments. A faculty member at one of Boston's premier medical schools, Doctor Silberman specialized in physiologic investigation of sexual dysfunction in both men and women. He held director-level positions at numerous medical charities specializing in sexual dysfunction and authored hundreds of articles on the subject, as well as a few books. Steve had high expectations.

Doctor Silberman, a graying man in his midfifties, stood four inches taller than Steve. When he entered the office, he carried himself with a high degree of self-importance. Having waited three months for the appointment, Steve was eager to get started on a cure. He jumped right into his debilitating daily routine of chills and hot flashes, eye pain, digestive problems, urinary hesitation, voiding issues, etc. He then expanded on the more vague symptoms—his inflamed prostate area, clear discharge, urethral pain, and impotence.

Dr. Silberman grabbed his script pad and with a giddy voice asked, "Do you want Viagra?"

Disappointment swept down Steve's face as his eyebrows rose in disbelief. He raised his voice and spoke in a tone that ridiculed the doctor's lack of effort. "I'm only twenty-nine years old. Do you really think it's appropriate for someone my age to be on a drug like that? There is clearly something wrong, and I figured you could find out what it is. Are you telling me you don't know what's going on?"

The thought of being challenged by a layperson irritated Silberman, who took an authoritative tone. "I have plenty of twenty-nine year olds on Viagra."

"I'm sorry, but is that supposed to be a valid reason? As I already said, I don't think it's an appropriate drug for someone my age. Nor is it appropriate for me to be on that drug just because you have other people my age on it. Everything was working fine down there. Then, one day, nothing was working. Before these symptoms started, I was having sex with my girlfriend for four to five hours straight, every night. I was so horny, I'd even come home after and jerk off. I could go forever and was going broke on condoms. Could I have worn it out?"

"First off, you wouldn't have worn it out, even at the rate you claim you were going." Resentful of being challenge, the doctor's tone grew increasingly dismissive. "It can take a beating, no pun intended. Secondly, I've been doing this work for over twenty years. I'm pretty sure I know what I'm doing."

This was not Steve's first encounter with an obstinate physician who took too little time to render an appropriate diagnosis. He had already wasted enough time with incompetent doctors who ushered him out of their offices before he had a chance to ask his questions.

In anticipation of this appointment, Steve had buried himself in medical texts for a month. He had read about every possible disease state that exhibited his symptoms and entered the meeting with a list of three possible diagnoses written on his notepad. He was looking to see if the so-called leading urological expert would pull one of them out of his hat.

Aware that he had waited three months for this initial appointment with Silberman, Steve decided to take a conciliatory tone and press for a definite diagnosis. "Let's start over. I think you would agree that Viagra would only cure one of the ten symptoms I've described. We've not discussed what could be causing the dysfunction or the other nine symptoms I'm presenting."

"Fine, let's go over your symptoms again," Silberman said with a curt tone, annoyed that his patient was not taking his advice at face value and was now leading the meeting.

Steve picked up his notepad. His voice mimicked that of a game show host. "What causes chills and hot flashes, inflammation in the prostate area, clear discharge from the urethra, pain in the urethra—as if something is tearing in there—urinary urgency, hesitation, and voiding issues—and impotence?" He kept the symptoms limited to those a urologist deals with.

Pressing an imaginary buzzer, Dr. Silberman screamed, "Prostatitis!"

Steve was relieved that the doctor had guessed the first diagnosis written at the top of his notepad, especially since he had already made up his mind well before arriving to receive treatment for prostatitis.

According to the Mayo Clinic's Web site, prostatitis is a bacterial infection in the prostate that could cause inflammation in that region, especially between the scrotum and rectum. It fit almost every symptom, including urinary urgency, hesitation, difficulty voiding, pain when urinating and ejaculating, chills, fever, and abdominal pain. The only symptom the diagnosis did not address was impotence. Steve figured if he could solve eight of the nine symptoms, the ninth might take care of itself.

Doctor Silberman ran a battery of tests, including both urinalysis and PSA tests. Despite both coming back negative, the overconfident doctor now wanted to prove that he could cure Steve's problems. He wasn't going to be shown up by some twenty-nine-year-old pissant.

"Your PSA is low, which is good. The urinalysis showed no signs of bacteria. However, false negatives are common. Your digital rectal exam also showed little inflammation. Normally, I'd say you are fine. However, since we don't have an accurate diagnosis and all of your symptoms point to prostatitis, that is what we will treat. I suggest we start you with a shotgun approach. We'll throw everything at it."

He grabbed the prescription pad again and began writing scripts for Hytrin, Propecia, Flomax, and Floxin. Hytrin, a blood pressure medication, and Flomax, a muscle relaxant, were prescribed to relax the muscles around the prostate to allow urine to flow more easily. Propecia, an alpha blocker, inhibits an enzyme that converts testosterone into another hormone that makes the prostate grow. Lastly, Floxin, an antibiotic, was prescribed to fight the infection he never found.

So why was Steve sitting in a Chinese doctor's office eight months later?

Floxin was only the first of six antibiotics to be prescribed over an eight-month period. Each was progressively stronger, wreaking havoc on Steve's intestinal flora, the good bacteria that helps the body synthesize and assimilate food. They also caused a number of side effects that included vomiting and skin rashes. When he read that the standard prescribing period for prostatitis was only six weeks, he lashed out at Silberman, calling him irresponsible.

While all of his symptoms, even sexual symptoms, had improved somewhat with Western medicine, he was still unable to consistently have sex. He felt the relief was coming at too high of a price when considering the drugs and their side effects. He was wracking his brain day and night to understand why he could only have sex in certain positions, and typically only for short periods during which he had to work diligently at not disturbing the balance to keep things going.

He couldn't tell what it was about transitioning into other positions that created these feelings in his abdomen. He knew he was reaching another plateau and wasn't willing to take the Viagra that Silberman kept pushing. Steve was convinced that his current drug regimen was only masking his symptoms. He believed something more could be done.

Certain his problems were physical, Steve was led to yoga. Even if it didn't cure the primary symptoms, he believed it would help with the constant physical soreness he felt all over from his lack of sleep.

Within a few classes, he was hooked on the immediacy of the relief it brought him. Yoga soon became his new religion, helping to wean him off the drugs in only a couple of weeks. It allowed him to maintain the same level of health he had while on the drugs, minus the side effects. Around the time yoga's positive effects had reached a plateau was when he overheard his yoga instructor describing the Chinese doctor. He decided it was worth a shot.

When he told Silberman about the Chinese doctor's conclusions, Silberman laughed him out of the office, ridiculing Eastern medicine as nothing more than witchcraft and hocus pocus. Steve felt foolish and angry at Silberman's narrow-mindedness.

However, years of not knowing what was wrong had made Steve desperate for a diagnosis. While the Chinese doctor's description of Steve's symptoms was impressive, he never actually provided a diagnosis that made sense. Finally having one he could believe in—Silberman's—Steve wasn't about to change quarterbacks in the middle of the down. *Excess liver fire* and *yin deficiency* were not diagnoses that Steve could get behind, let alone understand. Other than telling him he had to urinate, the Chinese doctor missed the most important urogenital symptom, impotence.

Who are you going to believe, the leading expert in erectile dysfunction or a back alley herbalist?

A few days after persuading the Chinese doctor to prepare a tea for the prostate, Steve picked up his three-week supply of the herbal concoction. Each dose was individually packaged in a clear plastic pouch. The contents looked like muddy water and smelled even worse. He was instructed to heat the contents and drink one packet in the morning and another at night.

The foul-smelling mixture's gritty consistency and putrid taste made his tongue shrivel and taste buds revolt. In the beginning, he tried holding his nose to get it down, but it was so awful that he had to experiment with flavoring additives, sugar, and alcohol. He wasn't sure he would be able to stomach two of them every day, and for three weeks at that. However, by the end of the third week, Steve was calmly sipping the tea in front of the television as his brother looked on in disgust. They both wondered if he had done permanent damage to his taste buds.

When he had exhausted the last of his pouches, Steve felt let down by the results. Ready to give up on Chinese medicine, he noticed his shoulder began hurting. The herbalist's caution registered in his mind, prompting him to make another appointment. He thought it seemed pretty coincidental that his shoulder was in pain right as he finished the last packet of tea. When he met the herbalist, he was convinced to give acupuncture a try.

I was lying on the table and the herbalist's sister entered the room. She was every bit as calm as her brother. After performing the same pulse trick, she instructed me to roll up my sleeves and pant legs. She explained that needles in my foot will help my shoulder. "Sure, that makes sense," I said sarcastically, but I don't think she got it. When the needles were inserted, some gave me an electrical sensation. A few were so intense that they had to be removed immediately.

She returned to the room every ten minutes to twist the needles, which produced more of the electrical sensation. As the session went on, I felt my body letting go. My mind was clear, and I was close to falling asleep.

This was the most relief I've experienced in years. It's clearly powerful stuff, and I need to learn more about how she's doing it.

The positive effects of the treatments lasted only a couple days, requiring Steve to return a few times per week. On weekends, this was fine. However, making the trips on workdays was proving difficult. The travel time alone to go between Boston's financial district and the pharmacy consumed his entire lunch hour. While the results were consistent enough, he had to find a new doctor, someone closer to work.

Steve decided to call Lu, an old high school friend. Originally from China, Lu's parents owned a shop in Chinatown. Steve explained he wasn't feeling well for quite some time, selectively omitting his sexual symptoms, and that he was in search of an acupuncturist. If anyone would know of a reputable acupuncturist, it was Lu's mother. She was dialed into the local community.

A day later, Steve received a call from Lu's mother with the name, number, and address of their family doctor. "Doctor Lee is my very good friend. We just spoke, and he is waiting for you to call. He will take extra special care of you as a personal favor to me. Please feel better soon."

By this point, Steve had visited with over ninety Western doctors, continuing to see other doctors while working with Silberman. He couldn't find two physicians to agree on any one physiological cause. Many wouldn't provide a second opinion once they learned that Silberman was his first. The only consensus reached was that he was experiencing psychosomatic manifestations, which was still an unacceptable conclusion to Steve.

Doctor Lee performed the same pulse diagnosis and tongue examination as the doctor in Brighton. When he finished, he said, "Steven, you have excess liver heat and yin deficiency. Fire and water not linking." It was the same poetically perplexing diagnosis that made no sense to Steve. However, what did make sense was that two doctors came to the same conclusion using the same diagnostic technique. This was a first, and quickly sold him on Chinese medicine.

"Have you ever treated this before?" Steve asked eagerly.

"Many times," Doctor Lee replied calmly. "Steven, we get started. I take very good care of you until you have no more problems. You have questions, you ask, I answer. Okay?"

2/17/01: It's been three months, and Doctor Lee finally cracked. I don't think he believed I would actually take him up on his promise to answer my questions. If he knew that I've accumulated a library of Traditional Chinese Medicine (TCM) books that cover topics from acupuncture and herbs to qigong and martial arts, he might not have made that promise.

We meet three times per week—Monday, Wednesday, and Friday—every week. Each time I try asking him questions about what he's doing, he ends the sessions the same way—a pat on the back that feels more like a shove out the door, and, "Okay Steven, see you Friday—See you Wednesday—See you Monday—Just don't ask me a freakin' question about TCM."

Today, I had enough. He tried the pat maneuver, and I held my ground. "Doctor Lee, you promised. You said, if I have any questions, you would answer."

How do you say, "Oh shit" in Chinese? His face fell flat when he realized I wasn't going to budge.

"One moment." He left the office, and I heard the clinic door lock. He reentered the office and locked that door, too!

A chill ran up my spine. I wasn't sure what I had gotten into—some sort of secret society or something. Despite his slight stature, I know he studies tai chi and could probably take out a small army.

"What is your question, Steven?"

I asked him about the microcosmic orbit, a meditation technique. I asked if you bring your energy up the front of your body and down the back, or up your back and down your front. I kept getting confused about this because some books didn't specify it very clearly, while others said one or the other.

I could see he was growing increasingly nervous as the words spilled from my mouth. "Who's your master? Who teach you this?" He said it as if I had revealed some sacred ritual.

According to Chinese lore, TCM was a closely guarded secret only being passed down from father to son. This is understandable when you consider that Chinese medicine was the basis of many martial arts practices. Someone who understands the five elements will understand how to knock an opponent out or even kill him by striking different combinations of points. Most combinations require two or three points. However, sometimes only one point is needed.

On nights when Steve returned from ju-jitsu class, Paul would hide out in his room. Steve was a teacher by nature, compelled to show others every interesting new thing he learned. It didn't matter if it was ju-jitsu, Chinese medicine, or news about the stock market. You name it, Steve would want to share it. Joint locks, arm bars, and choke holds, however, were not things most people want to learn by example, with them being the example.

> Before people had guns, martial arts were necessary to protect your family and property. As such, the secrets were closely guarded. Today, martial arts are widely available. However, I would guess that most people studying them have no idea that their kata routines are actually sequences of strikes to pressure points rooted in Chinese medicine. What looks like a block is often a strike to a pressure point. While most practitioners may know a few individual points, I doubt most understand the medical theory behind the combinations. From my experiences, most Chinese doctors from China are reluctant to share their knowledge.

Despite all of the things Steve tried to show Paul, he never even hinted that this side of martial arts existed.

> 3/12/01: After each session, Dr. Lee writes a script—a full page of Chinese characters detailing the herbs I'll be drinking for the next two days. I go to the pharmacy down the street from his office on Harrison Ave and hand it to one of the women behind the counter. She lays out a few sheets of folding paper and three of the employees begin pulling herbs from different drawers. They cross paths, bumping into each other as they ferry herbs between the

drawers and counter. At the counter, they measure and dump the herbs onto the different sheets of paper before being folded into neat little packages.

Now that I'm researching the properties of the different herbs he's prescribing, my visits to the pharmacy have grown longer. I spend half an hour or so perusing the packaged Chinese products on the pharmacy's shelves or questioning the people behind the counter. At first, they would not speak with me. They were very skeptical of "round eye." I feel like the token white guy in Chinatown.

Over time, I've become friends with one woman behind the counter, Yin-su. Every time I am in there, she laughs at me for drinking the tea. "Chinese tea tastes horrible—that's how you know it's real medicine." She was surprised when I told her that the tea doesn't bother me anymore. I guess I've had so much of it now that I'm used to it. I gotta say that I feel sorry for Paul because the smell lingers in our apartment for hours.

Paul nodded as the words conjured up nauseating memories of the odor. The power of his mind played a trick on him, making the next bite of his sandwich taste sour, as if he was expecting to eat something that tasted like the tea.

Last week, I had an eye-opening experience. While waiting in the pharmacy, I went over to talk with Yin-su, and this old guy came over. I had never seen him before. He just stood there, looking me up and down while she and I were talking. After a minute of creeping me out, he looked up and said a few sentences to her in Chinese. She looked at me and translated. "He says you have excess liver heat and yin deficiency." Seriously? WTF? How does every

Chinese person know I have excess liver heat and yin deficiency? Or do they go around saying that to everyone?

I asked how he knew, and she continued translating. He began pointing to different parts of my hands, face, and hair. Each body part told him something different about the flow of energy within my body. For example, he pointed to my thumbnail and said it was too red, and that the lunula (white portion) was too small. To him, this said fire was overpowering water, indicating an unbalanced relationship between my heart and kidneys that led to excess liver heat. The small lunula suggested that my metal and water (lungs and kidneys) were weak, contributing to yin deficiency. Additionally, the size differential between the lunulae on the right and left hands indicated some sort of water imbalance. Next, he pointed to the portion of my palm below the thumb. The skin was speckled red and white, confirming liver-related issues, or excess liver heat. Finally, he pointed to my graying coarse hair, stating that it confirmed a weakening of water, or kidneys. This was exactly what the other doctors said. This guy was able to read all of this in under a minute.

"Who is this guy?" I asked.

She said he is a Chinese doctor who works in the back of the pharmacy. He only sees Chinese patients due to language and legal reasons. I asked how much he charges. She answered, "Five dollars."

I've got to say that this was my most impressive experience with Chinese medicine yet. Now I've got three diagnoses, all saying the same thing. This is incredible. I've been back to the pharmacy three times now, and he's come over to chat with us every time.

Chapter 9

Prague

H allo!" Klára startled Paul, shaking him out of his trancelike concentration.

He uncurled from the hunched-over position his body had collapsed into while reading the journal and took a deep breath.

"Ready?" Klára asked. "We will walk."

Paul gathered his things and followed her up the stairs. She asked about his first night. He described the pig's knee and steady flow of beer.

"This is very popular Czech pub," she added. "Tonight, you and I will go to dinner. What you think?"

"Sure. I'd like that."

"Okay, we go to Old Town where we see many tourists."

They passed by the guard's desk, and the doors slid apart, granting them access to the well-fortified courtyard. Paul noticed that the white Lamborghini was absent from today's scenery. As they walked toward Steve's building, a view of the distant city flashed between the buildings. Once inside, they climbed the flight of stairs leading to the desolate hallway, a grim reminder that he was not on vacation. Having spent the day reading his brother's journals and hearing Steve's voice inside his head made the reality of the situation more difficult to swallow, especially when he saw the police rummaging through the scene again and the bridge in the background. Paul started to choke up.

Lieutenant Marek was standing on the porch, holding two pieces of paper. His head moved attentively between them, studying their contents. Hearing the officers greet Klára and Paul, he spun around. Marek motioned them onto the porch and began talking impatiently with Klára. He was trying to explain the papers, but Paul could see that Marek was moving too quickly through them, waving them wildly as he jumped between them. In Marek's mind, she wasn't supposed to understand, only translate. Frustration grew between them as Klára tried explaining that she cannot translate what she does not understand.

"What's he talking about?" Paul jumped in sensing something was amiss.

Flustered by her encounter with Marek, she snatched the papers out of his hand and returned to speaking in broken English. "This lieutenant's paper, from home. This Steve's paper from book. Lieutenant photocopy. Lieutenant make fighting practice at home many years."

"Martial arts." Paul corrected her as he motioned with his hand to tell her to slow down and compose herself.

"Yes, martial arts practice. He say me it look familiar, but many more points here on Steve's page. Many points with notes.

Many Chinese letters. I think he interest more in brother's fighting martial practice. Maybe not much interest in case because lieutenant thinking is simple case. Two possibilities. Mafia kill brother. Or brother depressed."

Marek interrupted her, talking over her more aggressively than before, forcing her to recoil. When he finished, she turned back to Paul. "He believe Steve depressed. Detectives speaking with mafia in building, but he no think it will matter."

Paul interjected, "What about the calendar with the appointments? The mafia appointments?"

"Lieutenant sends officers to research this more. Lieutenant ask about brother's journals. Asking what you learn. Asking more about martial fighting practice."

Paul explained that one journal was a diary and the other contained his notes on Chinese medicine. "Steve developed some health problems that are explained in the journals. However, it seems that things were getting better. I have not finished the journal."

Klára continued translating. "Lieutenant wants to know what kind of problems?"

"I am not sure." Paul did not want to divulge too much information until he had a better picture of his brother's situation. "There were many physical problems—eyes, stomach, skin, sleep, etc. It seemed that acupuncture was helping him. These diagrams the lieutenant is pointing are related to acupuncture. Is it possible to speak with an acupuncturist here?"

"Yes, I can make this appointment," Klára said.

"Tell the lieutenant that I am not finished with the journals. I will be done in the next day or so. At that time, I'll have more information about my brother's problems."

Paul took a few minutes to have a look around while the lieutenant talked with Klára. He walked slowly across the hardwood floors running his fingers along the cookie-cutter furniture, likely purchased at one of the Western big-box stores steadily taking over the world. In the bedroom, a pile of his brother's clothes lay upon the bed. A corkboard displayed postcards from the different cities and attractions Steve had visited before arriving in Prague—Athens, Santorini, Mykonos, Rome, Budapest, Berlin, and Bratislava. In the distance, the whistle from a locomotive departing its station could be faintly heard.

Paul exited the bedroom to peruse the kitchenette, equipped with stainless steel appliances. The refrigerator and cabinets were well stocked with organic ingredients, various grains, and a full range of culinary supplies. Over time, Steve had discovered that many foods exacerbated his symptoms, forcing him to eat most of his meals at home, a necessary chore to avoid unwanted ingredients. Aside from a few dishes soaking in the sink, Paul didn't see any signs of depression.

He called out to Klára, "Can you bring the lieutenant over here?"

"What do you find?"

"Nothing."

"Nothing?" Klára sounded confused.

"That's the point. The refrigerator and cabinets are full of good quality foods. There's not a drop of alcohol here. People suffering from depression typically drink in excess and eat a lot of junk food. Look over here. One night's worth of dishes. Someone who is depressed might have weeks of dishes piled up. I just want to make sure he has taken this into account before he concludes that the mafia was not involved."

"Okay, I tell him." She lowered her voice to a whisper. "Problem is, if mafia involved, officers here may not want help."

"I understand. What about the lieutenant? Does he want to help?"

"Is difficult to know. He is very interested in journals. Maybe for fun. Maybe for solving case. We to understand after speaking with acupuncturist. I go now to call acupuncturist for you."

Paul continued probing the apartment. He wheeled around an abandoned television sitting on a wooden stand in the corner of the room. While the set looked new, he figured it had never been used since his brother was unable to understand Czech. Continuing into the breezeway, Paul sifted through the closets, flipping through an assortment of spring and winter coats. Shoes for all seasons covered the closet floor.

He moved to the entryway and took in the view of the most luxurious room in the apartment, the spa-style bathroom. Just beyond the door to the hallway, Paul could hear Klára.

"I know what you are planning, and it scares me. Are you sure you can handle this?"

He held his breath. *Was that Klára speaking English fluently? Planning? Planning what? And with whom?* He stood still, wondering if his mind was playing tricks on him as it did at the pub.

Chapter 10

Prague

Klára poked her head in the door. "Ready? We going now." *Broken English,* Paul's racing heart slowed. After hearing that the police might not be interested in pursuing the mafia leads and unsure of the lieutenant's motives, Paul was feeling on edge.

They exited the Devon complex and made their way to Klára's car parked a half a kilometer away. Paul concluded his mind was playing tricks on him, which was good because he wasn't about to give up having his own tour guide for the evening. She opened the door, dropped the file she was carrying into the backseat, and slammed the door.

"We take metro."

Paul was a little disappointed. He liked being chauffeured around the city. She led the way down Belehradska Street to the metro station, I.P. Pavlova, named after the famous Russian

Nobel Prize winner who first described classical conditioning—programming a dog's salivary reflex response to unrelated stimuli. She handed him a ticket to pass through the gates. Once on the other side, they stepped onto the escalator. The precipitous drop came quickly, leading Paul to clutch the railing.

"Our trains are very deep in ground. They are for war time. So escalators are fast and steep." Prague is home to one of Europe's longest escalators, Namesti Miru. Approximately one hundred meters in length, it takes roughly two minutes to travel.

They could hear trains pulling into the station from opposite directions, and they were still twenty meters from the bottom.

"Quick, we run!" Klára went scurrying down the escalator with Paul right behind her. "Left train!" she called out.

They boarded the crowded train with plenty of time to spare. Klára brought Paul to the end of the car to avoid the throngs of passengers sandwiched tightly in the middle. A sequence of xylophone tones indicated the doors were closing, prompting Paul to grab the red pole attached to the wall and dig his feet into the sandpaper-like floor. An automated voice announced the next station, and the train gradually accelerated, producing a high pitch sound that resembled a jet engine.

Paul's eyes darted through the train, capturing images of the assortment of people. He enjoyed people watching, often sitting at Boston-area cafes for hours, observing the comings and goings. He was fascinated by the number of tall blonde women standing throughout the train. Standing 5'7", he wondered if they liked shorter men.

The train began to slow and Klára tapped him. "We go off now. This is Muzeum stop." When they reached the top of the stairs, Klára pointed up the hill. "National museum is there in back of us." The museum's magnificent dome lit up the fading sky behind it. "We are in New Town now. Here is Wenceslas Square. The man on horse there is St. Wenceslas. Do you know St. Wenceslas?"

Paul smirked and started humming the tune to "Good King Wenceslas."

"We walk now to Old Town."

Paul simply nodded and followed her lead. His senses were quickly overloaded with stimuli. Hearty aromas from the fresh pizzas displayed in the window of the Half & Half café called to his stomach. His eyes were blinded by the Czech glass stores displaying ornate vases and jewelry. His ears were distracted by the various accents and languages of the tourists around him. He did his best to keep pace with Klára.

At the bottom of the boulevard, they approached a large pedestrian intersection. Klára turned to Paul and said, "This street is na Příkopě. Many years past, this street was water around castle."

"Ah, a moat."

"Yes, three streets—na Příkopě, Revoluční, and Národni—make moat. We enter Old Town now."

The road narrowed significantly as they entered a cobblestone, pedestrian only part of town. A hodgepodge of Renaissance and Baroque style buildings accented the crooked road. People sat outside under heat lamps enjoying their dinners, talking, and laughing. They continued straight for five minutes when Klára dashed into an organic grocery store.

"Come! We take short route through store. Is easiest way to find favorite restaurant of mine."

The door at the back of the store opened into a darkened alley. *A restaurant? Back here?* Paul became nervous again as he saw Klára disappear down the street. He followed cautiously, looking over his shoulder. The alley opened up to a broader street, and Restaurace U Zirku appeared.

"See! Pig's knee and English menu!" Klára was pointing to the chalkboard menu standing outside of the restaurant as she waited for him to catch up. Indeed, it was written in English, catering to the two and a half million tourists that visit Prague each year. "In Prague, men enter restaurant first. Is Czech custom. You can know tourists because they let women in first."

"Okay," Paul said hesitantly.

"*Dobrý večer*," the hostess greeted them. Klára then took the lead to let the hostess know she was Czech in order to avoid getting ripped off. Unsuspecting tourists clogging Old Town every summer were often overcharged through a series of tactics that pad their bills—bogus taxes, beers that were never ordered, and delivering expensive imported bottled water instead of the local bottled water that costs half the price. When a group of tourists is drunk enough, they usually never notice or complain. The hostess led them into another room.

Klára's eyes told Paul she was happy to show him her wonderful city. "Tonight, after dinner, we go to famous bar for foreigners. Are you hungry?"

"Very! What do you recommend?" Paul preferred dining with a local, even if it were in the touristy section of town. He felt experiences with locals gave him the real flavor of the country.

"You eat pig's knee yesterday. I recommend you can try beef goulash with dumplings. Goulash. Do you know goulash?"

Paul scanned the menu for her suggestions.

"Goulash is from Hungary. Dumplings is traditional Czech food—same like bread. Is fast."

Paul liked the sound of that.

"Good. I will order pig's knee. You try and compare to yesterday's pig's knee."

The waitress came to take their orders. When Klára finished ordering, she looked at Paul. "Tonight we drink wine. Is season of *burcak*."

"Bur...sack?"

"Yes, it mean young wine. Only two months in fall can man drink *burcak*. You will like. Tell me what you learn about Steve. Do you learn new things?"

Paul nodded and began elaborating on the topics he touched upon earlier at the apartment, focusing on the amount of stress it caused Steve to not know a diagnosis. He told her about the multitude of doctors his brother had visited over the past decade for a myriad of vague symptoms. He painted a picture of someone who felt failed by Western medicine. Despite finding hope in Chinese medicine, there was a definite overtone of anger directed toward the Western doctors he had seen.

Klára listened patiently, asking an occasional question to clarify words she did not understand. Paul liked playing teacher. It offered him a sense of authority he wasn't provided with working as a staff accountant.

The waitress placed the pitcher of wine between them, and a fizzing noise began rising from inside the carafe. Paul looked inside to see bubbles popping along the surface of the opaque orange colored liquid.

"Burcak make this noise. Czech wine is made in Moravia." As Paul poured two glasses of wine, she explained that Moravia is located in the eastern part of the country, producing over 90 percent of Czech wine.

"*Na zdraví* ... Cheers!" Klára held up her glass.

"Oh, that is good." The sweet fizz danced around his tongue. "It's like alcoholic juice."

"See, you like!" Klára mused.

"Okay, enough about my problems. Tell me about yourself."

Klára took a deep breath before launching into her story. Her words fumbled over each other as she described how she ended up at the language school. While completing an MBA program at a local university, she took a job as an intern with the school helping to design their marketing campaign. After finishing her studies, the economy took a nosedive, and she was left with few options. Her goal of pursuing a career in international marketing was put on hold. Since she was not involved in the day-to-day operations of the school, she had time to help Paul, for which he thanked her.

The waitress returned with the food. Paul's goulash was nothing like the ground meat version he had while visiting his brother in Austria years earlier. The heat from the plate warmed his face. Half of the dish contained eight large chunks of beef covered in a brown creamy sauce. The meat looked tender, as if it had been stewing for hours and would break apart with a light touch from his fork. The other half was covered by a stack of spongy bread, spread across the plate the way a black jack dealer fans a deck of playing cards across the table. The edge of the stack bordering the meat was soaking up the overflow of sauce.

Klára's pig's knee was presented on a regular platter, lacking the medieval look and feel of that served to Paul the night before. Nonetheless, it looked succulent. She was already cutting a portion off to give him. When he offered her some from his plate, she declined.

"I cannot my plate eat. Is too much food. Careful, *burcak* is strong. How you feel?"

"Great." His shoulders were no longer locked next to his ears from the tension that built up while reading Steve's journals. His mind, once saturated with depressing thoughts, felt free. He felt like he was on a date—well, a quasi-date with a beautiful foreign woman—the kind he would never meet in Boston. In fact, the last time he was on a date was many months, and she had never made this much effort.

Then, he remembered why they were both there. *Maybe she wouldn't be here under normal circumstances.* He took a look around and realized that most of the women sitting around him were equally beautiful and that Klára was simply average for Prague.

"Are all women in Prague beautiful? Every one of them looks like they stepped out of a magazine."

"Yes," she smiled. "We have most beauty contests in all of Europe. Lots of competition to be woman here. What you think for me? Am I beautiful?"

If Paul's face were not already red from the wine, his blushing would have been more noticeable. "Yes, of course."

She smiled and tilted her head down as she gazed up at him. "Thank you."

As dinner wore on, their light banter volleyed back and forth. Her enthusiasm to know more about Paul's life in the United States drew him in deeper. She taught him a few Czech words and described customs he might find unique to Eastern Europe. Eventually, she brought the conversation back to the journals.

"Do you know what other journal is? Many body parts with dots and lines. The Chinese writing. It looks very complicated."

Paul looked up, unsure how to explain his brother's metamorphosis into Chinese medicine that might make her understand. "How long can you sit in stillness?"

"I do not understand. What is stillness?"

Chapter 11

Prague

W hile sitting in the café, this question had leapt off the page at Paul, reminding him of the night Steve posed the same question to him. It always served as a turning point in Paul's mind—the calm that followed the storm.

How long can you sit in stillness?

Paul explained how he had arrived home earlier than Steve and started preparing a fifteen-minute meal out of the cookbook his mother had given him for Christmas one year. Once it was ready, he sat in front of the TV to eat when he suddenly sensed someone standing behind him. Nobody had greeted him when he arrived, and he hadn't heard anyone enter the house.

"I just assumed I was home alone. Naturally, my adrenaline began pumping. I grabbed the knife next to me and spun around." Sauce ran down Paul's knife as he held it up to demonstrate for Klára.

"Who was it?" she sat forward in anticipation.

"Steve."

Paul described how his brother had been standing there for at least a minute, his eyes relaxed, almost trancelike, and he was smiling ever so slightly. He looked more composed than Paul had seen him look in years.

"Then, the wise ass said, 'Boo,'" Paul imitated his brother's understated tone. "I yelled, 'Bastard! I almost killed you!' He pointed to the dull knife in my hand and said, 'How? Were you going to butter me to death?'"

"Butter?"

"Never mind." He realized she was confused. "Then, he asked me, 'How long can you sit in stillness?' I read that in his journal today, and it reminded me of this experience."

Paul explained that his brother had been sitting in his room for two hours with the goal of not thinking. Eager to share his experiences, Steve described how the human mind spins when it's not distracted by talking, reading, watching television, listening to music, etc. To stop this never ending stream of chatter is like trying to stop a force of nature.

"I tried this, and he was right. At first, your mind just can't stop thinking. It's kind of funny because you sit back and watch a comedy play out. There's one part of your mind that's calm, and it watches the other part go crazy."

Steve had been practicing this on the train to work, literally training his mind to not think. He had been consistently making it for twenty-five minutes without a thought. On this day, he left work early to go home and try for a longer period.

"I think I am understanding stillness now. Is like meditation, correct?"

"Yes. At first you select a word to think every time your mind goes running off. It could be something as simple as 'relax.' After a few weeks, he said he didn't need to use a word anymore. I was never that disciplined, and I drive to work. It's difficult to drive and not think. Anyhow, it is kind of interesting. It made me look at things a little differently. I mean, how often do you actually stop thinking and give your mind a break?"

"Never!" Klára burst out with laughter. The wine was having its effect.

As Paul continued describing his brother's metamorphosis, he recounted how Steve's desktop medical and drug reference books were replaced by books about Eastern medicine and philosophy. Yoga had replaced soccer and weight training, and he had resumed his martial arts training—studying softer styles similar to tai chi.

With a lot of persistence, Steve had found a few teachers in Boston's Chinatown who had taken him under their wings. He began spending five days a week there learning herbs, qigong, and acupuncture. It was about this time that Paul noticed Steve's daily philosophical questions started. Over time, this thoroughly annoyed Paul. Tired after a long day, he just wanted to relax.

"I didn't want to think about not thinking, or debate the pros and cons of not speaking. I used to tell him that was exactly why I watched television, to not think or speak. If it wasn't philosophy, it was being his guinea pig on how to efficiently inflict the most pain or how my diet would eventually cause me all sorts of diseases. Anyhow, it doesn't matter anymore. I can't believe he's gone." Paul turned away to fight off tears.

"It's okay. It's okay." Klára took his hand and tried to comfort him from across the table.

Ignorant of the table's atmosphere, the waitress dropped the bill in front of Paul as she zipped past. Klára reached for it, but Paul beat her to it. She reached for her wallet, but he stopped her. Opening the bill, he calculated the conversion to be less than $30. It was quite a bargain for two people to dine in the center of the touristic section of a city. He dropped his credit card into the bill sleeve and placed it at the edge of the table with the card slightly visible.

"Thank you. I will buy drinks at the club. On the way, we walk you to touristic sites."

Paul continued describing Steve's emotional transition. For as long as Paul could recall, Steve resembled an atom whose electrons were spiraling out of control into its core. Then, one day, he had the serenity of a Taoist monk. The process had been so gradual that Paul never really took notice. He didn't know if this meant his symptoms had disappeared or if he became more adept at dealing with them. The fact that Steve had started dating someone seriously made Paul believe that the symptoms must have disappeared. *Did this mean he was finally able to have sex again?* He was still unsure.

"My brother was becoming Chinese. I used to call him the 'Medicine Man.' Within a few months of finding his new teachers, our cabinets were full of herbs. He began experimenting and did some things I didn't think were possible."

"What things?"

"He went on a special diet in which he lost thirty pounds in less than four weeks. Do you know how much that is?"

"No. How much in kilos please?"

Paul paused to make the calculation. "It is roughly thirteen and a half kilos."

"What? How he do that?"

The Pentagon! Paul thought back to the pentagon on the refrigerator with the foods.

"He had rules for eating. For example, he always started with the densest part of the meal first, like meat, or nuts, because these are the most difficult for your stomach to digest. He ended with the foods that are easiest to digest—vegetables and fruits. He never drank within a half hour before or after he ate. And, I remember him always saying, 'You must eat with the season.'"

"Eat with the season?"

"Yes, you only eat foods that are grown in that season. So foods that are grown in the summer would not be eaten in the winter. He would say, 'They grow in the summer for a reason. They give you the proper energy for that season.' It was always about 'energy.' Anyhow, those are only a few rules. He had dozens, and they all seemed to be related to the pentagon."

"What do you mean? Pentagon?"

Paul opened the journal to show her. "This is what I'm trying to understand from the journals. This is why we need to find an acupuncturist. This pentagon may be the key to it all."

The waitress returned with two credit card receipts. Being in a touristic area, Paul decided to leave a tip on par with what he might leave in Boston. After signing the slip, he pondered if he had done it because he was in a touristy part of town or because he was with Klára. He was feeling buzzed from the *burcak* and did not care either way. As they left, Klára led Paul through the organic grocery store again.

Once back on the main pedestrian way, Klára said, "We walk back to the moat. Is this correct word?"

"Yes," he laughed. He was more impressed that she remembered the article.

"Is possible your brother teach at companies here—on this road."

Na Příkopě, also a cobblestone pedestrian way, was much wider than the other streets, reflecting its use as a moat centuries earlier. Paul began paying closer attention to the storefronts, observing the larger banking institutions along the way, places where he imagined his brother might have taught. *This is the life. Teaching sounds like an easy gig when you only have four students and are surrounded by beautiful women all day. Why didn't I do this?*

Chapter 12

Prague

Klára led Paul to the Náměstí Republiky metro station, a yellow line train. Signs hanging in the terminal showed the different colored lines crisscrossing throughout the city. They exchanged trains at Mustek and rode the green line out to a station called Flora, located inside of a shopping mall.

"We get off now."

"Where are we?"

"Flora." At the top of the escalator, Klára veered to the right. "This way."

They made their way to street level and exited the mall onto Vinohradska Street. Klára led Paul across the street and down another alley.

"You like taking me into some pretty dark streets. Where exactly are we going?"

"This is best bar for all foreign men," she quipped.

"Really, in a seedy back alley?" *She's taking me to a brothel,* he thought. "That's not necessary. I'm not into that sort of stuff."

"Beautiful women? I see you looking at all women in Prague. Now, we find you one. Maybe even two."

Despite living in what Paul considered to be one of the most difficult social scenes in the United States, Boston, his straight-laced personality would never allow him to engage in such activities.

"No, no, I'm not into paying women for sex."

She started laughing. "Pay for sex. That not necessary in Prague for handsome man like you."

Comments like that made Paul want to stop and kiss her. While he had enough courage to do so, courtesy of the young wine, he didn't want to be presumptuous. After all, she was taking him to a bar to meet other women. He still didn't know if she had a boyfriend, and the dirty alley wasn't exactly a romantic setting.

"We go to Millennium Club. This is club for Czech women that like meet foreign men. You will be very popular."

Steve had written Paul about the Millennium Club, describing the scene as, "Shooting fish in a barrel, except you're one of the fish. You just sit back and wait to be shot." Steve had learned of the Millennium Club from his then-Czech-girlfriend's co-worker. It was not exactly what she wanted him to tell Steve the night they all got together for drinks. Shortly thereafter, he broke up with her to explore another side of Prague. On most weekend nights, he could be found sitting at the bar enjoying himself.

The alley opened up to a commercial passage separating two buildings. On one side was a modern gym, featuring a row of shiny new treadmills and elliptical machines. On the other side, there were a number of shops, including a restaurant.

"Come, we go in." She skipped ahead to grab the door to the restaurant. "Remember, in Czech, men first."

A buxom blonde hostess greeted Paul. "*Dobrý večer.*" Her smile drew his eyes up to her face, saving him from the prolonged embarrassment of staring at her chest.

"Uh, hello?"

"Pardon, good evening, sir. This way please." The hostess naturally assumed he was alone, just a drop in the steady stream of foreign men passing through their doors every night.

Are you sure this isn't a brothel? Paul thought.

She turned back to check on him and realized he wasn't alone. "Oh, pardon me. Are you looking for the club? Or are you two joining us for dinner?"

Klára stepped forward to take over the conversation. The two women had a good laugh at Paul's first visit. The word "brothel" was woven into the continuous flow of Czech passing between them. Each time he heard it, they paused for a moment to laugh.

The hostess stepped back, as if to size him up. "Welcome to Prague. I am sure you will enjoy yourself sir." He now felt less guilty for having honed in on her well-advertised cleavage.

Paul descended the spiral staircase careful holding the railing as he looked across a bar that was close to capacity. The small dance floor off to the left was moving like a kaleidoscope of bodies. Klára took a seat at the bar while Paul stood. The bartender came over, and Klára ordered two *Be-tons*.

"*Be-ton?*"

"*Be-ton* is Becherovka—Czech herb liquor—and tonic. You will like."

The bartender sat the drinks down, and Klára threw a two hundred Crown note on the bar. Paul calculated it to be equivalent to ten U.S. dollars and thought, *Cheap for two drinks at a nice establishment, especially one where beautiful women go to hunt for men.*

"*Na zdraví!*"

Two blonde women wearing form-fitted dresses next to them chimed in, "*Na zdraví!*" Paul's eyes locked on the oversized breasts busting out of their dresses. From the minute they arrived, Paul saw them eyeing him as if Klára wasn't even there. While he was flattered, it made him uncomfortable because he had never been in such a situation.

"Where are you from?" One of them asked.

Drunk and not conscious of his actions, Paul was soon ignoring Klára to make conversation with his two new friends. Once she finished her drink, Klára leaned in to say, "You take tram 16 to I.P. Pavlova. Do not take taxi. Be safe. Go home to hotel with woman. Less safe is woman's apartment. Maybe men or mafia there."

He thought her comments were premature. This was uncharted territory for him, a dream of something unattainable in his world. Women like this did not exist in the Boston he knew. If they did, there was no way they would ever have shown him this much attention, let alone two of them while he's sitting with a third. Now, he could better appreciate his brother's e-mail.

Suddenly conscious to the idea of Klára leaving, Paul shouted, "Wait! You're leaving?"

"Yes, I work in morning. You have two new friends here. Is okay. We talk tomorrow about acupuncture meeting."

"Okay. Thanks for tonight."

Five minutes later, Paul was on the dance floor with one of the blondes. A little too drunk to dance, he more or less stood there trying not to fall over as she grinded up against him. Not quite sure how he ended up on the dance floor or how he chose which woman to dance with, he had had enough teasing. He ran his fingers up the back of her neck, weaving them into her hair. She came forward and started kissing him.

A few minutes later, she stopped his advances to say, "I am married. Only small fun."

Married! Small fun? Where am I?

"If you like, you can dance with Marcella. She is single."

What kind of sharing do they teach here in kindergarten?

She waved to her friend to pick up where she was leaving off. However, it would only be in his dreams as Marcella was already kissing another foreign guy who had taken Paul's place at the bar.

He figured it was just as well. It was already midnight. If he was going to meet the acupuncturist tomorrow, he wanted to be well rested. He gave her one last kiss and excused himself. After retrieving his coat from the coat check at the bottom of the spiral staircase, he made his way to the tram stop.

Chapter 13

Boston

A resounding thud registered as the metal door to the east garage of the Massachusetts Medical Center slammed shut. The noise startled a frustrated patient searching for her car in the enormous parking structure.

After a long day of surgeries, too tired to change out of his scrubs, the weary doctor trudged his way through the garage. Row after row, the weight of the day lifted, and thoughts of each surgery faded like the dimly lit gray metal door behind him. He gave a reluctant smile and wave to the woman as she closed her car door and sped off.

His black Mercedes SL500 was still where he left it fourteen hours earlier, the last parking spot of the faculty section. Memories of his final prostate surgery had been replaced by rumblings of hunger for the dinner his wife would have waiting for him. He approached the rear of the car with his keys drawn.

The trunk sprung open, and a flash of light and noise ricocheted down the row of cars, signaling that the alarm was disabled.

Dropping his briefcase into the trunk, the doctor abruptly collapsed under his left knee. A shooting pain shattered its way up his back and into his head. He fell forward, clutching the trunk for support. His adrenaline peaked, dampening all thoughts and fine motor skills. Unable to think clearly, he was unsure what was happening to him. He never saw the hooded man who had appeared from behind the support beam across the aisle. A swift kick to the back of the doctor's knee had lit up his *water* meridian, the energy channel running from his small toe, up his back, over his head, and to his eyebrow.

The hooded man's breathing remained slow and steady, matching the calm tranquility of his eyes. He moved gracefully with the doctor, following him down toward the trunk. Combinations of pressure points flashed across his still mind until he found a match—*water extinguishes fire*. His arms moved forward in a circular motion. His leather-gloved hands converged on the doctor's neck at a slight upward angle, striking the *fire* meridians with the pinkie-ridge side of his palms. The doctor's energy surged into his head before everything went dark.

With the doctor unconscious and slumping over the edge of the trunk, the assailant swiftly handcuffed him and drove three acupuncture needles into his captive's neck and scalp to assure a peaceful ride.

Less than a minute after having stepped into the light, the hooded man sat calmly in the driver's seat of Doctor Silberman's Mercedes. The minimum-wage security guard, passing hours of mind-numbing boredom with online backgammon, was oblivious to the events that unfolded on the monitors next to him.

With his unconscious package under wraps, the assailant backed out and proceeded down the exit ramp. The gate's sensor read the transponder on Silberman's windshield, and the wooden plank lifted.

The Mercedes sped along the desolate streets of Boston's financial district. The digital clock display read seven thirty p.m. The city's hustle and bustle was long gone, rolling out of town on the last rush hour commuter train to the suburbs.

Chapter 14

Boston

Doctor Silberman began to stir in the trunk, quickly quelled by the sharp pain inflicted by the needles in his neck. The most he could muster was a faint groan.

"There, there doctor. We will be home soon." The doctor barely made out his assailant's muffled voice from the driver's seat over the constant deafening noise produced by the tires gripping the asphalt.

The doctor attempted piecing together the route his assailant was taking. He tried visualizing each turn, and identifying each noise outside the car. However, having been unconscious during the initial five minutes of the journey left him disoriented.

A sudden bump in the road followed by a metallic sound beneath the tires led the doctor to believe they had crossed onto one of the large metal plates used to cover construction sites. What he couldn't see was that the car had crossed onto the Summer Street Bridge, and was leading them into the Seaport district. Within minutes, the corporate landscape outside of the car quickly faded and was soon replaced by industrial structures—a sign they were venturing into South Boston.

The doctor's shock had worn off. While the needles were placed in sedating points, they had the opposite effect when he tried to move. With the handcuffs pinning his arms behind his back, he couldn't figure out what the man had done to his neck, or why the pain became unbearable when he squirmed. He did his best to remain still, which was difficult in a car bounding down the road at forty miles per hour.

The car pulled into a dirt parking lot. Silberman could hear gravel scattering beneath the tires as they slowed to a stop. He heard the car door open, followed by a chain-link fence closing and locking in the distance. He had no idea where he was. The sound of gravel grinding under each footstep grew louder until the remote key sprung the trunk open. A distant, yet familiar face stared down at him, but the doctor couldn't place it. Never at a loss for words, he attempted to scream, but the pain from the needles cut him short. "Who the hell—"

The stranger reached around the doctor's neck and plucked the three needles. He held them up for the doctor to see before tossing them to the ground.

"What the fuck are those? You stuck me with those? Are you fucking crazy?" His blood was boiling now as concerns of disease and sanitation crossed his mind. Realizing his assailant was of much shorter stature than him, the former college athlete decided he could take the man when he got out of the trunk, despite being handcuffed.

"Up, up." The man motioned for him to sit up. He grabbed the doctor's arm to drag him out of the trunk.

When Silberman's feet touched the ground, he lunged at his assailant, attempting to bury his head into the man's chest. Still holding Silberman's arm, the assailant took a step back and slid his free hand up the doctor's chest to his neck. Using the bones along the side of his wrist, he applied pressure to the vagus nerve running down the side of the doctor's throat. As he rotated his wrist upward, grinding it in, Silberman's body weakened, and the man easily guided the doctor's body to the side, crashing him into the ground.

Silberman's face was bloody from landing on gravel, and his heart was pounding. He started kicking spastically to push away from the man.

"Where do you think you are going? Stand up and come with me or I will make you."

"Fuck you! Uncuff me and we'll see if you can make me."

"All right."

The man circled the doctor faster than Silberman could spin on the ground to fend off the coming attack. Grabbing the doctor's head, the assailant rotated it, pressing firmly into pressure points that forced the doctor to comply. Silberman flipped onto his stomach to stay ahead of the pain.

The assailant gripped the doctor's pinkie and ring fingers, bending them backward, just shy of their breaking points. The doctor screamed in pain. His shallow breathing increased as he begged for it to stop. The assailant pulled on the doctor's shoulder until Silberman came around to a seated position. He then applied pressure to the doctor's fingers while still holding his shoulder. Silberman shot to his feet, dancing on his toes.

"I thought you said you were going to uncuff me!"

"No, I said I was going to make you."

Silberman saw the three-story sandstone-colored brick building at the end of the parking lot where he was being marched toward. Boards covering the windows, dumpsters full of refuse, and fresh salt air told him that it was one of the gutted abandoned factories somewhere along the water front. The closest buildings were three hundred meters away. Screaming for help would have been useless, especially at this time of night.

Realizing that he might not come out of that building alive, he tried slowing down the march. "Where are you taking me? What do you want with me? Who are you?" His efforts were met with increasing pain that kept him moving along.

"We will get to all of that."

"People are going to notice I'm gone."

"That's been taken care of."

Chapter 15

Boston

By the time Doctor Silberman had reached the top of the metal stairs, his backside was drenched with sweat. His heart was racing as the fear of the unknown bombarded his mind with grim thoughts. *Keep calm. Keep calm. If he wanted to kill me, I'd already be dead. Just stay alert. Look for weapons.*

His assailant opened the heavy metal door before them. A brightly lit modern spacious loft-style abode revealed itself. The smell of freshly coated hardwood floors reached Silberman's nose as his eyes inspected the 3,500 square foot area. It was a sharp contrast from the crumbling exterior. The area looked like a hybrid of an apartment, doctor's office, and gymnasium. Lab equipment could be seen through one of the doors across the main room, and free weights sat in the corner next to the entrance.

In the middle of the room, a platform stood a meter off the floor. The structure looked like a boxing ring. However, there were no ropes or posts, just a perfect canvas-covered plane hovering above the glistening new hardwood floor. The right wall housed a kitchen area, complete with new stainless steel appliances, cabinets, granite counter tops—and knives. Silberman's pupils dilated at the sight of the knife block, but there was nothing he could do. The other two walls contained doors to additional rooms.

The doctor was directed toward the first room on the left. It looked like a standard doctor's office, equipped with an examination table, swivel stool, side chair for the patient, and a mobile medical cart. Medical posters hung on the wall detailing the vascular and urological systems of the human body. Next to the posters, fake diplomas were hung. When the doctor saw an army cot and toilet in the corner, the reality of his situation set in.

"Welcome to your new home, Doctor."

"I don't understand. Do you want me to treat patients here?"

"You are the patient."

With his pinkie and ring fingers torqued, the doctor's fire channels continued sending messages through his body. The captor collapsed the doctor's knee in, bringing Silberman's head to a more accessible height. Clapping his hands together, he caught the front and back of Silberman's head, striking wood and water points sending the doctor lifelessly to the floor.

After sitting Silberman upright in the chair, the man strapped him in and left the room. He closed the heavy metal door behind him and stood there for a minute looking back at his hostage through a sliding panel cut into the door.

A look of satisfaction came across his face as years of preparation were finally paying off. He gripped the circular steering wheel handle in the center of the door and turned it, securing the door with a series of deadbolts. Simultaneously, a spring-loaded mechanism released eight rows of protective sharpened spikes that protruded into the room to deter any attempt to kick down the door.

Chapter 16

Prague

Tram 16 pulled into I.P. Pavlova at 12:15 a.m. Paul staggered down the normally humming street, now quiet and dark. Once inside the hotel, the sight of another person breathed life into the man at the desk.

"How was vepřové koleno? You like?"

"Yes, very good. Thank you for your suggestion."

"Where you come from now?"

Paul hesitated, wondering if the concierge knew about the bar's reputation. "The Millennium Club."

The man smirked and said, "Why you come home alone?"

Apparently, he does. Paul just shook his head and went up to his room.

It dawned on him that he had yet to call his parents. He took the phone from the nightstand and sat on the edge of his bed. His mother answered. Usually a nervous wreck, she was calmly numb in her disbelief. He could hear the kitchen television on in the background as she was preparing dinner. She asked about his flight and hotel.

"My hotel is right down the street from where Steve was living."

"Don't talk about your brother in the past tense." She was unable to deal with the thought of losing one of her sons.

"Okay, okay. Since I arrived, I have met with the police twice at his apartment. A woman from the school, Klára, has been helping to translate. The police found a number of his journals and asked for my help to understand their contents."

"What kind of journals?"

"You know—his martial arts and Chinese medicine books, and a diary. I spent the entire day reading at a café by his apartment before going back there for a second time. I just returned from dinner with Klára, the woman the school sent to assist me."

In the background, Paul could hear the evening news on his mother's television.

"Unbelievable," she muttered.

"What?"

"This doctor. The guy has a wife and two kids. One night after work, he just takes off and goes to the airport. Apparently, he had some kind of drug addiction and checked himself into a rehab clinic in Arizona without telling anyone. They found his car and phone at the airport. The only way they knew was because he finally had the sense to have the clinic director call his wife. Apparently, once admitted, you aren't allowed any contact with the outside world. He could be in there for months."

"What's the guy's name?"

"Silber-something. It sounds familiar. Your brother saw practically every doctor in this city. I'm sure he saw this imbecile, too."

"Silberman?" Paul asked.

"I think that's it."

"I read about him in the journal. I think 'idiot' was the exact wording he used. Silberman is the urologist Steve worked with for about a year. The guy kept prescribing him drug after drug, mainly antibiotics."

"I told your brother not to take those pills. They made him sick."

"I know. It sounded like the guy really didn't have a handle on Steve's problems, yet persisted with treatments. I also think Steve was pretty susceptible to believing just about any diagnosis at that point," Paul added.

"Have the police learned anything yet?"

Paul decided it was best not to tell his mother about the appointments with the mafia or the lack of interest in pursuing that avenue. "I have a meeting with an acupuncturist tomorrow to review some things in these journals. Who knows? Maybe Steve was experimenting with herbs again. However, I didn't see any in the apartment today. The police think it was depression."

Chapter 17

Prague

Morning came quickly, leaving Paul's head in a slight fog. Unable to fully wake up, he threw on his clothes from the night before and wandered down to breakfast. The other travelers looked on as the American in their midst stacked his tray high with a gluttonous pile of cold cuts, cheeses, rolls, eggs, yogurt, coffee, and some watered-down orange-colored drink supposed to pass itself off as orange juice. He took a seat at a table and felt his *burcak* hangover subside within a few bites of food.

A vibration emanated from his pocket. He poked around to locate his phone. "1 New Message. Acupuncturist @ 9:30. I come to you at 9:00." He cleared the message to see the time—"8:45 a.m." His neighbors eyed him with disdain as he shoveled yogurt and eggs indiscriminately into his mouth while slurping the coffee. He made a sandwich from the rolls and cold cuts, wrapped it in a napkin, and stashed it in his pocket. Deciding not to touch the orange potion, he raced out of the breakfast room to get ready.

The night concierge, finishing up his shift, waved to Paul as he ran up the stairs. Figuring he was in Europe, Paul decided not to shower. *When in Rome...*

Klára arrived right on time. She put her phone down after typing out a message and began reading a magazine.

"I would have come sooner," Paul said as he hurried down the stairs, "but I had to return to the room for the journals."

"Good. How was two girls last night?"

"Married!"

"And? Did you have good time?"

"It was great, but I left shortly after you. That *burcak* is strong."

"Yes, is my favorite. Okay, my car is outside. Ready? Acupuncturist is in Andel. This is P5."

"P5?" Paul asked.

"Near pig's knee restaurant from first night."

"Right!"

He closed the door to the Skoda, and a new tour began, this time during daylight hours when the stores were open and teeming with people. He preferred the view from the height of the tram, which was less dizzying. Klára zigzagged around cars as she sped down the corridor. The signs of the familiar major American firms were a blur in the passenger side mirror.

The blue car zipped over the bridge bringing the castle into full view. In the daytime, it lost some of its splendor as it was no longer accented by the warmth of the lights. Tourists were swarming along the Charles Bridge, taking pictures with the baroque statues marking the bridge. The statues, thirty in all, had been erected some three hundred years after construction of the bridge started.

Once in Andel center, a modern shopping area demarking the heart of Prague 5, Klára turned left. "Oktoberfest!" She pointed to a small outdoor market in front of the Andel metro stop on the right. Wooden kiosks serving beer, fire pits roasting sausages, and children's rides stood in front of a number of trendy shops.

She turned left down a side street. "We drive by Steve's school. My school, too, there on left. Do you see?"

Through a partially opened gate on the street, he saw a yellow building at the back end of a courtyard. The school's sign hung over the sidewalk.

The car slowed and turned right down a one-way street lined with parking spaces on the left. They passed under a bridge with a gigantic Czech beer bottle painted on the side. A hand holding the bottle came over the side of the bridge, making it look more lifelike.

Klára pulled into one of the free parking spaces on the left and said, "*Tak!*"

"Taag?"

"*Tak.* It means 'so.' We are now here."

The plaster side of the building was peeling, and plaster was strewn about the sidewalk. They came to the door of the old decrepit building, two kilometers from the school. The sign on the door read "Doktor Huang—Licencovaný Akupunkturista." They rang the buzzer and waited for a moment in silence before a slender elderly Asian woman greeted them. Her hair was jet black, like that of a woman in her twenties. Her thin wrinkled lips cracked a smile. "Doctor waiting for you."

Klára addressed Paul's question before he had a chance to ask it. "Doctor and wife speak no Czech, only Chinese and

English. I do not know if good English. You may be lucky today."

"Hello, hello. Welcome." The doctor greeted them as they entered the courtyard. "How may I help you today?"

Paul had to restrain from laughing at the doctor's thick Chinese accent. It reminded him of the times Steve would imitate his teachers in Boston when conveying the secrets of life to their young grasshopper.

The old man was eager to help. His happy demeanor exploded with excitement. "You are Steve's brother."

"You know Steve?" Klára asked.

"Yes, he is a teacher here." The old man pointed toward the corner of the courtyard, as if the school were only a hundred feet away. "You look like brother of Steve."

"I am. How do you know Steve?" Paul already knew the answer to his question. Steve couldn't go anywhere without stopping into the local Chinese community and kicking the tires.

"He comes here every week. Sometimes to buy needles, sometimes herbs, sometimes we simply talk. He is a very smart boy." To the old man, anyone under the age of fifty was a boy.

Paul was relieved to hear the doctor was proficient in English. "What would you talk about?"

"Sometimes he gives me English lessons ... we discuss politics, philosophy, and medicine. He likes talking about medicine. He really does not like Western medical system though." Paul shook his head in agreement. "Then, we usually end with qigong practice."

"Qigong?" Klára sounded perplexed.

"Qigong. It is the same like tai chi. Tai chi is only one type of qigong. There are thousands of qigong. Everybody only know tai chi."

"Would you teach Steve qigong?" Paul asked.

The man started laughing excessively, holding his belly. "Steve teaches me qigong. My father was qigong master in China. But Steve already learn in Boston many teachings my father teach me. Is there problem with Steve?"

"Steve died." Paul hesitated. "He was found under the—"

"Nusle Bridge." Klára finished his sentence.

"The police are investigating if he jumped or was murdered," Paul added.

"No, Steve didn't jump," the old man said with a calm certainty. "He was always very happy boy. He could not jump. He could not be murdered." The old man's confidence in his last statement begged it to be questioned.

"What do you mean, he could not be murdered?" Paul asked.

"His qigong is very strong. Strong mind and body. He even beat me one or two times." The doctor smiled.

Normally, Paul might have laughed. However, he had heard Steve's stories of little old men, half his height, throwing him around the dojo like a rag doll.

Klára couldn't contain her skepticism. "What you mean? You fight Steve?"

"Yes. No. Not fight. We practice together. Come, I will show you." He looked at Paul. "Push me."

God, not this stuff again. They are all looking for practice partners because they keep breaking their last one. Paul stepped forward and sighed. "Fine."

He placed his hands on the old man's shoulders. The doctor dropped his center of gravity, firmly planting his feet on the ground.

"Okay, you push."

Paul leaned into the old man, who was as sturdy as a brick wall. Paul was now straining, unable to budge him even an inch.

"You may begin pushing now." The old man laughed.

Barely perceptible to the eye, the doctor pivoted slightly, shifting his weight backward and to the side. Paul leaned into his front foot to stabilize himself as if he were standing on a train that came to an abrupt stop. As he struggled to regain his balance, pushing backward, the old man stepped in and sent Paul flying with a flick of his wrist. Paul landed three meters away sprawled out on the ground. To an observer, the motion was so subtle that it looked like the old man simply flicked his wrist and sent Paul into the air with some magical power.

"Whoa!" Klára exclaimed.

The old man turned and bowed. "This is qigong practice. Understand energy, use little effort to throw Steve's brother there. This is simple example, but I must make many years of practice to do this. Steve was natural with qigong. He understood these concepts quickly. Even beat me. I already said that."

Paul collected himself and returned to the group holding up the journal for the doctor to see. "We are here to discuss this. Have you seen this before?"

"No. What is this?"

"It's one of Steve's journals on Chinese medicine. Can you help us understand it?"

"Of course. We go into my office." He barked an order at his wife in Chinese. Like a stereotypical old couple fighting, she screamed something back, threw her hand at him, and disappeared into the building to fetch the pot of tea. "Wife will bring tea."

Chapter 18

Prague

The doctor led Paul and Klára into the main building at the rear of the courtyard. They walked down a dimly lit dirty hallway with cracked walls and hanging lights that looked like fire hazards. The unsanitary patient rooms they passed made Paul wonder how health could be found in such a contaminated environment.

Doctor Huang's office was the largest room in the building. Stacks of Chinese newspapers littered the corners, and the walls were adorned with anatomical diagrams—each detailing different energy channels. The doctor pulled out a few folding chairs for his guests to sit.

"I have read some of this journal, and it all seems to be based upon this." Paul opened the book and pointed to the large pentagon on the inside flap.

"Ah, you ask about the five elements?"

"What is it?" Klára asked.

"Five elements are everywhere. This is how Chinese think of the relationships in nature." The doctor pointed to each element one at a time. "Water feeds wood, wood grows tall. Wood feeds fire, fire grows strong. Fire burns wood, turns wood to ash, becomes part of earth."

As the doctor continued reciting the formula, Paul bypassed the pentagons, skipping ahead a few chapters. Each of the first five chapters was devoted to an element in the pentagon. Paul landed on *water*.

"Here it is. Water. See here. What is he talking about?"

Each chapter started with a list of items specific to that element. The list contained medical items, including organs, acupuncture points, herbs, and pulse descriptions. The lists also extended beyond the realm of medicine to include sounds, directions on a compass, colors, seasons, emotions, tastes, and foods. Additional notes Steve had scribbled could be found next to each list.

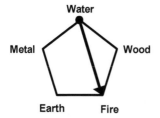

For 2,000+ years, the Chinese have known that too much salt is bad for your heart.

Paul pointed to the note and said, "Amazing if it's true."

"It is true. For thousands of years, Chinese people have described the world in five elements. Everything in the world belongs to these categories—water, wood, fire, earth, and metal. We live life thinking in terms of the five elements. For example, wife pours a cup of tea. This is water and earth."

"Mud?" Paul asked sarcastically, thinking about the muddy-looking medicinal concoctions his brother had created every night when living together.

The doctor looked annoyed, as he expected more from Steve's brother. "In the pentagon, each element helps the next. Water feeds wood, wood feeds fire. Do you understand this?"

"Yes," Paul and Klára said in unison.

"Okay. Now look at this smaller pentagon. Do you see the arrow that points from water to fire in the center?"

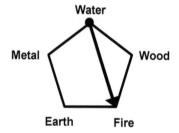

"Yes."

"What is the relationship? Friends? Do they feed each other?"

Klára jumped in, "Water stop fire."

"Very good, water makes fire weak. Water *controls* fire. Now, what does earth control? Where does the arrow go?"

Paul pointed to another small pentagon and answered with a hint of uncertainty, "Water?"

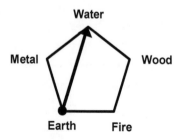

"Yes, earth controls water. We think of a simple example from nature—a river. A river is water. But the sides of the river are earth. Earth controls the river's direction, earth controls water. Now, in the cup of tea, which is water and which is earth?"

Klára's face showed her excitement at having made the connection. "Tea is water and cup is earth."

"That's great, but how do we use this?" Paul saw the connection, too, but it was far too elementary to impress him.

The doctor pointed to the pentagon. "This system helps us understand the laws of nature. Everything belongs to water, wood, fire, earth, and metal. Understand how they help or control and you understand nature. This knowledge is power. Understand?"

"Okay." Paul was skeptical. "So how does this mean that the Chinese have known for thousands of years that too much salt is bad for your heart?"

"Everything belongs to an element. What are the organs for water?" The doctor pointed to another pentagon hanging on his wall that listed organs below each element.

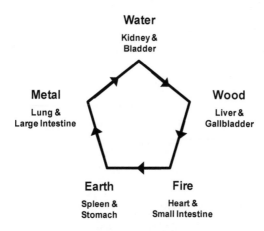

Water
Kidney &
Bladder

Metal
Lung &
Large Intestine

Wood
Liver &
Gallbladder

Earth
Spleen &
Stomach

Fire
Heart &
Small Intestine

"Kidney and bladder," Klára answered, pointing to the diagram above the doctor's head.

"Good. What is taste of water? You see in book, there." The doctor pointed to the middle of the page in Steve's journal.

Taste of Water: Salt

"It's no accident that kidneys are water organs. Kidneys clean water in blood. What happen to your blood when you eat salt?"

"You retain water," Paul answered.

"Look on page. Look at arrow. What does water control?"

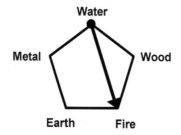

"Fire!" Klára grew more enthused.

"What organs are related to fire?" The doctor looked at Klára.

"Heart!" She pointed to the diagram again.

"Very good. The taste of water is salt. This is logical because the world is covered in salt water. Eat salt and you make water strong, and blood becomes heavy. Now, it is difficult for your heart to move heavy blood. Strong water controls fire. Too much salt and you weaken fire. Salt is bad for your heart."

It became readily apparent to Paul why Steve was drawn to Chinese medicine—its simplicity. It must have been a welcome change from the HMOs and specialists he detested so much, their tests, and the procedures, drugs, and lack of concrete diagnoses that followed.

"Okay, okay. I get it now. Everything on these pages is related to water? The color of water is black? Water's season is winter? Its weather is cold? The direction is north? Kidney, bladder, bones, hair, fear, ears, hearing, putrid—all water?"

"Yes," the doctor nodded. "My father taught me a simple way to remember. In the north, winter is very cold, so cold that your bones hurt. In winter, water freezes and becomes black— black ice on road. In winter, life is very quiet. When there is an accident on black ice, noise travels far." He pointed to his ear. "Look, ears look like kidneys. Loud noise give you fear, and you pee your pants. Bladder problem, water problem." The doctor bent over in his chair laughing.

The look on Klára's face told Paul she didn't understand the joke, but she laughed nonetheless.

The doctor composed himself and continued, "Chinese doctors consider all things on page when treating patient—color, smell, sounds, emotions, body parts, and more. When patient has water problems, he will be cold, have black color, easy to frighten, sensitive to noise, and have problems with urinating and sex. These observations have been made consistently over thousands of years."

Paul's face showed he registered the connection between the fablelike lesson and the chapters for each element on the pentagon.

"Five elements are in all areas of Chinese culture ... martial arts, feng shui, food ... even sex. This is why China has one billion people." The doctor's face lit up with laughter again.

With the doctor's last comment, it dawned on Paul that there was another reason Steve might have been so consumed with Eastern culture. With over one billion people in both China and India, and books like the *Kama Sutra*, they surely understood a thing or two about sex. *What better place to look for answers to his problems?* He flipped a few pages deeper into the book.

"Okay, so this is all simpler than I thought. However, I don't know what these pages are. Can you explain this?" Paul pointed to two pages facing each other. On the left page, there were a number of Chinese characters written in a list format. The right page contained acupuncture points written next to pentagons depicting different arrow combinations.

The doctor looked at the left page. "Ah. Here Steve write formulas for tea."

"Tea?" Klára asked.

"*Medicína*," the doctor answered in his limited Czech as he held the page closer to inspect the formulas. A puzzled look crossed his face.

"What's wrong?" Paul asked.

The doctor paused for a minute and looked up. "These are not correct teas, not to heal water problems."

"What do you mean?"

"This tea," the doctor pointed to the first group of Chinese characters. "This makes fire stronger—it will overpower water. The next tea below makes earth strong, to control water." He began flipping through the chapters to read the formulas for wood, metal, fire, and earth. A look of despair came over him as it became clear that Steve might have become sick using these herbal formulas. "All of the teas here are poison to drink—make person sick in very specific ways—even kill them. For example, this one makes fire strong, not allow you to sleep, make emotion problems, and many physical problems. I don't understand."

Paul felt his heart twisting in his stomach. "Are you saying that these teas could have made Steve emotionally unstable? Is it possible?"

"Yes, is possible. But I only sell Steve ginseng, cordyceps, and herbs for food." The doctor became defensive. "I never sold Steve herbs in these formulas here. It's not possible that Steve killed himself." He paused for a minute to find his words. "Chinese medicine brings cures slowly. Change tea every two or three days because the body changes with time. So the tea must change, too. Your body is different today than last week." The doctor pointed to the book. "These teas are not slow. These teas are very fast, like Western drugs. Fast changes make big problems, make illness. Steve knows this."

The doctor's comments brought Paul's thoughts back a few years to an investment decision Steve used to talk about. When he began studying Chinese medicine, Steve began looking at the pharmaceutical industry differently. Using the same logic described by the doctor, Steve had recommended selling the firm's entire holdings in pharmaceutical companies that profited from lifestyle drugs. These were drugs taken regularly to treat conditions such as high cholesterol, impotence, osteoporosis, pain, hair loss, acne, etc. Patients are required to take many of these drugs daily, while others might be taken once a month, or even once a year. A drug that metabolizes in your body over an entire year just didn't make sense to Steve. *You are different today than you were last week.* So why take the same drug over and over?

As a result of selling their holdings, Gray Haired Investment Management avoided taking substantial losses on Merck's stock when Vioxx, a Cox-2 inhibitor pain medication, was found to cause heart disease. To Steve, anyone well versed in Chinese medicine, who also understood that the Cox-2 enzyme is expressed in the kidney (water), might have concluded that a drug affecting water could in turn affect the heart (fire)—and that prolonged usage of such a drug might cause a problem with one of the two elements.

Paul's mind returned to the discussions. Searching for better news, he interrupted the doctor, "What about the other page? The points?"

"These points are for martial arts." The doctor held up a white plastic acupuncture doll covered with what looked like a connect-the-dots game. His finger followed methodically along the different point channels. "Each organ has two energy channels along the body, one on the left side and one on the right. We have symmetry. In this combination, he starts with earth. Look." He pointed to the pentagon in the journal. "Earth controls water. Which organs are related to the earth element?"

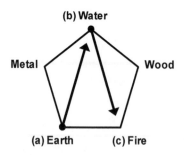

"Spleen and stomach." Klára pointed to the pentagon above the doctor's head again.

"Good. These channels run down the front of your body, down to your toes. Next, he strikes a point on a water energy channel." His finger traced the channels as he spoke. He moved from the spleen and stomach meridians to the kidneys and bladder, or water meridians. "Finally, he strikes a point along the fire energy meridian and the person goes down." He pretended to strike the doll and then slammed it to the desk, startling Klára.

"Can you start with any element?" Paul pointed to metal.

"Yes." The doctor pointed to another diagram on the wall. "Cycle of Destruction. This is simple system to learn. You can see different combinations here. Each element controls another. Strike elements using order shown here in picture—water, fire, metal, wood, and earth." His hand traced the star in the middle of the pentagon. "Begin with any element and follow lines in middle. I show you some combinations."

Cycle of Destruction
- *Metal chops wood*
- *Wood (roots) dig into earth*
- *Earth stops water (river banks)*
- *Water extinguishes fire*
- *Fire melts metal*

"That's okay!" Paul pushed his chair away from the doctor, expecting to be used for target practice again.

"No, I show on chart," the doctor laughed.

The doctor went on to describe how energy must move smoothly from one element (organ) to the next. If the flow is disrupted, the person will become sick, rendered unconscious, or worse, dead. He explained that the Cycle of Destruction is only one system, and that many other point combinations exist that you cannot find in books. However, simply knowing the Cycle of Destruction is not enough. A student must learn the specific points to strike, the angle to strike, and type of strike that triggers a specific point. The secrets of *dim mak*, or death touch, had been kept closely guarded since before the time of

Christ. Traditionally, they were passed down from father to son or teacher to student. Only students showing strong moral character were given access to this knowledge. However, in the early 1900s, the secrets began to leak out of China.

What appeared simple on the surface became increasingly complex for both Paul and Klára. The doctor explained that some qigong practitioners believe point combinations should be selected based upon the season or time of day, and it is important to include both yin and yang energy channels in each sequence. For each element, there is a yin organ and a yang organ. For example, of the water organs, the kidney is a yin organ, which means bladder is the yang organ. Also, one side of the body is considered yin and the other is yang. Each layer added more rules exhibiting the same symmetrical imagery. While not scientific, the concepts had a definite logic to them.

Paul and Klára were feeling inundated with each new round of information and decided they had found the answers they were seeking. Not certain whether or not to believe the doctor, Paul concluded that Steve may have been using herbs in an incorrect fashion. He thought, *while Steve understood the logic, he could have applied it incorrectly. Steve could have been buying the herbs elsewhere if he didn't want the doctor to know about his problems. Or he could have brought them from Boston. Lord knows he had enough of that stuff floating around.*

They thanked the doctor, who offered his services if they had additional questions.

Chapter 19

Boston

Doctor Silberman woke two hours later in a groggy state. Restrained to a chair a little too small for his body, he had slept with his head dangling only inches from his thighs. His neck was sore and temples throbbing. He struggled to straighten himself and realized it would be impossible to break free.

Craning his neck, he surveyed the room. *Medical cart—maybe there are surgical sharps inside.* With his ankles bound to the legs of the chair, the doctor summoned all of his strength to push his way across the room using only his toes. He began biting the handles in an attempt to open the drawers, but soon realized they were locked.

He heard the panel in the door behind him slide open and strained to turn around.

"I see you've come to. How are we feeling?"

The door unlocked, simultaneously withdrawing the spikes, and opened slowly. The man entered wearing a white doctor's coat and carrying a clipboard. He walked over to the doctor, who now cowered away in anticipation of being struck.

"You are wasting your time. The cart is empty." He grabbed the arm of the chair and swung the doctor around to stare menacingly into his eyes. "Do you remember me?"

"Ben—Bens—"

"Benson. That's right. The one you couldn't cure. Probably one of many you couldn't cure."

"Right, now I remember. You're that impotent little fuck who kept coming to my office every week for a year, harassing me to fix your wanker." Used to being in control, Silberman couldn't stop his need to lash out and dominate the conversation. "So let me guess. You finally took Viagra, took too much, got priapism, and ended up blowing up your cock. Now, what—you're gonna get even by torturing me because I couldn't fix it before?"

"Well, I'm glad you can finally admit you couldn't fix my wanker," Steve said calmly. "That's a big admission coming from someone so willing to throw every drug imaginable at it instead of admitting defeat."

"It was psychosomatic! Nobody was gonna fix it! You needed a shrink—which you're clearly demonstrating right now!"

Steve became visibly irritated. He overpowered Silberman's voice, "Nobody else would even attempt to fix it! It was as if you had called every other urologist in the city to kill any chance of getting a second opinion. Once they found out you were involved, they were all too scared of saying something contrary to your opinion!"

An arrogant smile came across Silberman's face.

"Go ahead, keep smiling. By morning, that smile's gonna be upside down. I can promise you that. A few things about you stuck in my mind even years after finding a cure for my problems, which were physically based, mind you."

"Physically based?" He paused for a minute. "Right, prostatitis. Now, I remember. We gave you the shotgun treatment. That was the standard treatment at the time for nonbacterial prostatitis."

"Sure, for someone who is sixty-five years old! I was twenty-nine!" Despite years of meditation, Steve's self-centering techniques were no match for the pent-up anger and frustration that his psyche unleashed. "You pumped me full of toxic shit—a shotgun of toxic shit!" Steve bloodied Silverman's face, matching punch after punch with the names he called out for each of the eighteen drugs Silberman prescribed over the year they worked together. When he finished, he said, "There was never anything wrong with the prostate. And why would you prescribe antibiotics for nonbacterial prostatitis, especially when you just said it was all psychosomatic?"

"You were desperate," Silberman cried out. Now, he too seemed desperate—desperate to get away from another barrage of knuckles and elbows. He spoke quickly. "You came in my office with more knowledge of the prostate and sexual dysfunction than most of my residents have after their third year of medical school. You demanded some sort of treatment. We ran tests, looked at the symptoms, and came to the most logical conclusion. Don't you remember? Do you think you were the only one? Half of my patients have completely vague symptoms, and all demand me to prescribe something!"

Steve took a seat in front of the doctor, interlaced his fingers in his lap, and started tapping his thumbs methodically. "Sure, I remember. The 'patient population doctors dread seeing come through the door.' We were the group for whom you don't have a clue what's wrong—'a vague cluster of symptoms' is what you called us, meant to be some sort of joke you tossed about with colleagues. Here's a novel idea. How about saying, 'I don't have a clue,' right from the beginning instead of turning us into your own private clinical trial? But you couldn't. You were a bit too taken with all of your awards, books, speaking engagements, and kickbacks from drug companies. Your ego was bigger than this office."

"You even told me which drugs you wanted!" Silberman yelled.

"That's supposed to be a reason for you to prescribe something? Because the patient wants it?" Steve's eyes peered through Silberman. "Basically, that just makes you a drug dealer, pushing whatever Big Pharma asks you to. Since every other commercial on television is for sexual dysfunction or incontinence, I would imagine every patient coming through your doors has a drug in mind. What an easy job you must have—business must be good."

In recent years, Silberman's job had actually become increasingly stressful since direct-to-consumer advertising and the Internet *empowered* patients. Every patient thought he had the answers, testing Silberman at each turn.

Steve continued his lecture. "I don't care how desperate I was—which I'll admit to. It was your job to make appropriate decisions. I can tell you that offering Viagra to a twenty-nine-year-old with my symptom profile was not an appropriate decision. Had I taken it, I might have actually gotten priapism and done permanent damage down there."

Steve stood up and circled the doctor before pulling the swivel stool up alongside Silberman.

"So let me tell you why you are here, doctor."

"It's about time." Silberman grew defiant.

"You are going to have the unique privilege of joining our little club you so aptly named. You too will become one of the vague cluster of symptoms. When I'm done with you, you will know exactly how it feels to have your body fall apart in a matter of weeks. You'll have 'vague' unexplainable symptoms that range from irritating to excruciating. And the best part about it is that you won't have a clue why. Your only way out of this nightmare—your only path to freedom—will be to find the very cure you failed to find years earlier. I'll let you treat yourself. Trust me, you'll try desperately because at times the pain will be so unbearable that you'll wish you were dead—your fate should you fail again."

"Why are you doing this?" His voice trembled.

"Let's just say it's your continuing education credits for the year. Even the leading expert in urology needs some continuing education. How can you honestly treat a disease if you have never actually experienced it? What makes you qualified to be an expert if you've never actually suffered the pain, humiliation, and complete and utter lack of sensation down there? So just think of it as me making you a better urologist." Steve paused for a minute. "In fact, you should look at it as if I'm doing you a favor. When I'm through with you, you won't be able to have sex at all—among many other issues. Now, if you can cure yourself, you should feel that you've earned your place as the leading expert in male sexual dysfunction. However, if you can't, you really shouldn't be practicing. Wouldn't you agree?"

A surge of fear engulfed Silberman's cerebral cortex, leaving his mind swimming in a dense fog of frantic thoughts. He never thought he'd lose his potency this early in life. If that day came, he always figured the drugs would be there. He could simply write himself a prescription. Sure, he'd experimented with the drugs he prescribed, convincing himself that this helped him better understand his patients. But whom was he kidding? He didn't need the drugs. And who wants to use them if you don't have to?

"What's going to happen if I can't find a cure?" Silberman's voice quivered.

"In that case, I can't let you leave here to poison more people. That would be irresponsible. Don't you think?"

Steve walked out of the room only to return a minute later twirling a knife in his hand. His eyes conveyed an alarming distance, rendering Silberman speechless. He had retrieved the boning knife from the wooden knife block in the kitchen. Its vulcanized rubber handle gave it a comfortable nonslip grip, perfect for cutting meat from the bone, and its freshly sharpened six-inch blade shined of newness.

"So here's what we're gonna do for tonight's entertainment before sending you to bed." Steadying his grip on the knife, Steve approached the doctor from his left.

"No, no, no—what are you gonna do with that?" Silberman stammered.

"I'm going to make a point. I saw you eyeing these when we arrived." He reached across the doctor who started shrieking until he saw that Steve only intended to cut his right hand loose. He then stepped back and held up a key in one hand and the knife in his other. "This is the key to the front door. I'll put it here in my front pant pocket. You may take this knife and cut yourself free. Get the key and you can go free."

Steve dropped the knife on the floor in front of Silberman and exited the room. He walked to the corner of the platform and ascended the five stairs leading to the top. Silberman looked on in astonishment. He couldn't tell if this was a trick of some sort.

"Hurry. The offer expires in a minute." Steve removed his lab coat, threw it off the far side of the platform, and waited.

Silberman's hand shot down to grab the knife. The sharp blade passed cleanly through the restraints. Lightheaded from being beaten and sitting hunched over for hours, he rose gingerly. Holding the doorjamb for support, he staggered into the main room. Gripping the knife in his right hand, he climbed the stairs contemplating how he was going to use the steel blade on the man standing between him and his freedom.

The doctor found his footing and began taking cautious swipes as he circled his much smaller opponent. It was the first time he had stood eye to eye with Steve and realized he was substantially larger. Thinking he could overpower his opponent, his fears initially subsided.

However, with each swipe, Steve never seemed to move. He maintained the same position—his open palms, close to his body at shoulder height, facing Silberman. He positioned himself effortlessly to avoid each fear-laden slash with little more than a step to either side, bob of the head, or rotation of the shoulders—always reappearing in the same position, flustering the doctor.

Silberman knew he must act quickly as his opponent was much younger and in better shape. He didn't think he could outlast Steve if the fight dragged on. One wrong move and his opportunity would be lost.

As his nerves settled down, Silberman decided it was time. He started slashing wildly, however, each slash missed. Breathing heavier, Silberman retreated to the opposite corner to catch his breath, but Steve maintained the same distance, never giving him a chance to rest.

Silberman became increasingly anxious that his time was coming to an end. Without adequate time to rest or think clearly, he drew the knife back next to his waist, took a deep breath, and readied himself to plunge the steel blade into his opponent. Before he could gather enough energy to lunge forward, Steve had stepped in to close the distance. Using his left hand, Steve trapped the knife hand against the doctor's body, stopping Silberman's energy dead in its tracks. His right forearm caught the side of the doctor's neck, lighting up multiple pressure points. Silberman experienced a sudden drop in blood pressure and lost his balance. Stepping between the doctor's legs, Steve trapped the doctor's foot and drove his knee into the side of the doctor's leg, forcing him to the ground in a controlled fashion.

Steve stood over Silberman, dropping his knees onto the doctor's ribs and head, pinning him down to maintain a position of control. As Silberman curled into a fetus position to avoid additional attacks, he could feel his knife hand being tied up in a painful joint lock that forced the release of the knife. Steve grabbed the knife, trapping Silberman's fingers against the handle, rotating them backward to continue maintaining control through pain.

In the midst of Silberman's wailing, Steve calmly stated, "I only played out this little game to prove a point. You will be wasting your time if you try to challenge me. Do we understand each other?"

"Clearly!" Silberman screamed, indicating that his finger couldn't take anymore.

Steve let go and walked over to the kitchen to put the knife back in the wooden block. Silberman laid there on the mat feeling helpless, barely able to move.

"You said your prostate was not the problem. If not, then what was?"

"After leaving your care, I spent the next eight years in Chinatown, working closely with a number of doctors. Chinese doctors. You know, the doctors you ridiculed as charlatans. It was those doctors who figured out what was really happening."

Chapter 20

Prague

Paul woke with another Be-ton-induced headache. He and Klára had painted Prague's Old Town red the night before, visiting the famous Sex Museum and Astronomical Clock. They had dined in the shadow of the St. Nicholas Church, an eighteenth-century baroque masterpiece that serves as the centerpiece of the Old Town Square. Classical music streaming from its ten thousand pipes had serenaded their meal.

With the music still playing in his ears, Paul was eager to get back to the task of completing the journals. He could see the end in sight and figured the notes would read more smoothly since his meeting with Doctor Huang. He grabbed a quick bite with his fellow travelers and exited the hotel. Walking along Belehradska, his thoughts were clearer now that he had overcome his jetlag. The stronger connection he was developing with Klára helped improve his mood, as did having more definitive answers about his brother, even though they were not the answers he was hoping for.

He arrived at the Bohemian Brew and descended the stairs. The woman behind the counter smiled, making him feel like a regular.

"Latte?" she asked.

Paul smiled and nodded as he took a seat. He laid out the journals side by side and continued with the diary, thumbing to where he had left off.

4/21/05—Finally! One hundred and forty doctors later and I've found someone who actually knows what the hell is going on.

Paul's eyes were now glued to the page. He looked back at the date. *Two years ago. He had been better for two years?*

A few weeks ago, I was strolling home from work gazing absently through the windows of neighborhood bars when an attractive blonde woman caught my eye. I decided to stop in and take a seat near her figuring I could strike up a conversation.

As usual, the discussion turned to acupuncture. Maybe it's because she was a nurse. Maybe I'm just that predictable. Anyhow, part way through the conversation, she turned to me and said, "Have you been to Tom Tam?" She started raving about his style of acupuncture. Having been in Chinatown for eight years now, I thought I had met every doctor there. Naturally, I was skeptical at first, but decided to keep an open mind. A few days later, I made an appointment.

It was a completely different experience from the other Chinese doctors. There was no pulse diagnosis or tongue examination. He only asked for a list of my symptoms. When I finished, he said, "It's your neck."

"So from impotence, hot flashes, digestive problems, sleep issues, eye pain, nose bleeds, vertigo, and urinary issues, you get my 'neck.' How? I don't understand. My neck doesn't hurt," I replied. "I had whiplash years ago, but it's healed. The leading orthopedic specialists and neurosurgeons tell me that my MRIs and X-rays confirm nothing is wrong there." By this point, I had seen seven Chinese doctors who all told me the same diagnoses—excess liver heat and yin deficiency. I had expected a similar diagnosis.

Seeing I didn't believe him, he walked over, put his hand around my neck, and pressed in with his thumb. I shot off the table and landed on the floor screaming in agony. "What the hell was that?"

"See? Your neck."

I was shocked because as far as I had known, my neck didn't hurt.

He then asked me to take off my shirt and lie face down on the table. He slid his fingers down my spine until he reached the middle of my shoulder blades. He pressed into a point roughly half an inch to the side of my spine, which proved to be as tender as my neck. "Do you feel?"

"Yes," I groaned loudly.

"This is the point for hot flashes." His hand slid a little further down to the middle of my back and pressed into another sensitive point. "This is the point for digestion."

He only used a handful of needles, maybe eight in total. He placed them in my scalp, neck, the tender points along my spine, and my Spleen 6 point (just above my ankles). Before he had even left the room, I felt like someone had drugged me. I felt more relaxed than I had in years. Every muscle let go as I drifted off to sleep. This was something I could never do during the daytime—and it was only 9:00 a.m.! It was by far the most amazing acupuncture session I've ever had. I felt completely cured in one session.

A feeling of relief swept through Paul, who had grown weary trudging through his brother's chronicles of torture and needed to hear something positive from all of this. The journal went on to describe how the benefits only lasted a couple of days, forcing Steve to return every few days and drop another $80 each time. As time passed, however, the effects began lasting longer and longer.

Having found someone who knew the answers, Steve tried to pump him for information. However, Doctor Tam was not forthcoming during the sessions, which annoyed Steve. The most he said was, "Ah, you know traditional Chinese medicine. TCM is a very beautiful philosophy. You see I don't do pulse diagnosis or even look at your tongue. What we do here is TCM 2.0, Pentium chip inside. TCM is still using a 386 processor." Working with a few hundred patients each week, Tam did not have time to sit and explain his system.

Additionally, he did not think Steve was very sick. "Here, we see very sick people. You are not sick. You should go to Doctor Lee. You are wasting my time. There are people with real problems that need my help."

Steve had shot back, "I went to Doctor Lee for over two years—three times a week. Before him, I spent six years working with six other acupuncturists. After all the herbs and acupuncture, I'm broke and still not better. You are the eighth acupuncturist."

After a few weeks, Steve noticed that Doctor Tam's patient base consisted primarily of cancer patients who had heard of him through friends or the Internet. Steve was surprised when he saw a nurse from Massachusetts General Hospital wheeling in a patient to receive treatments. He later learned that the Dana-Farber Cancer Institute had initiated a survey study of the benefits of Tam's Tong Ren therapy. Local area news stations had also begun covering the success rates of his patients. Steve didn't understand how he was just learning of Doctor Tam now.

Curious about Doctor Tam's system, Steve bought his book on Tong Ren healing. He learned that Tam was reviving the lost art of huatuojiaji, an ancient acupuncture style developed by a famous doctor named Hua Tuo who lived during the Eastern Han Dynasty (206 BC–220 AD) and Three Kingdoms Period. Similar to the wide variety of martial art styles, there are also many styles of acupuncture. Unfortunately, Doctor Hua Tuo's unique style was lost as the result of a political feud. Books detailing his methods were burned, and the doctor was killed. As a result, huatuojiaji, his form of acupuncture, was lost.

In searching the Internet, Steve found many stories of Hua Tuo's legendary healing abilities. While there were many inconsistencies in both the stories and dates, Tam's version of huatuojiaji did for Steve what all the ancient lore claimed Hua Tuo was capable of in his time. Tam had combined what little was known about huatuojiaji with Tui Na, qigong, chiropractics, TCM energy points, and an understanding of anatomy from the West.

Steve found Tam's approach interesting because it agreed with how he understood the differences between Eastern and Western approaches to health. Steve often likened medicine to a clock. The West can tell you everything that goes into making a clock—the hands, gears, springs, batteries, etc. However, despite all of this detailed knowledge, they cannot read the time. The East can read and adjust the time, but they cannot tell you much about the moving parts inside the clock.

Tam was bridging this gap by combining the West's understanding of anatomy with the East's understanding of energy.

Chapter 21

Prague

After several months of treatment and completing Tam's book, it had become clear to Steve why he had been having so many symptoms. He was happy to finally have the answers he was so desperately seeking. However, he wondered why it took seeing 140 doctors to find someone who could figure it out. After all, many of these doctors were so-called leading experts who only wasted his time and money.

The remainder of Steve's journal provided a summary of his journey.

In total, I've spent close to $100,000 of my own money to find a cure. If I add the amount paid by insurance, the number tops $300,000. Since insurance companies negotiate discounts with health care providers, searching for a cure without the benefit of insurance and the associated discount would have cost well over $600,000.

On the Western front, my payments went to deductibles and co-payments for doctor visits, drugs, procedures, and tests. I've gone through numerous primary care physicians and worked with multiple urologists, cardiologists, neurologists, pulmonologists, psychologists, endocrinologists, dermatologists, orthopedists, physical therapists, ENTs, osteopaths, and even a proctologist. Every doctor included at least three appointments. There was the initial appointment, followed by an appointment to run tests, and then follow up appointments to review the results and prescribe any drugs. When drugs were prescribed, they often required additional appointments to check for liver or kidney damage.

Switching to alternative medicine was equally as expensive since most of it was paid for out of my own pocket. Along the way, I met with multiple acupuncturists, chiropractors, qigong instructors, massage therapists, yoga instructors, muscle testers, naturopaths, and ayurvedic practitioners. In addition to the cost of appointments and classes, I've accumulated a library of health-related books and spent thousands of dollars on unproven dietary supplements every year.

By the end of his journey, Steve had become turned off by many healthcare professionals he met. While he acknowledged that most people on both sides of the aisle had good intentions, he was embittered by both the process and an equal number of God complexes.

Most Western physicians never spent enough time to understand what was actually happening. Instead, they were too busy pretending to have all of the answers. With the average doctor's appointment being less than twenty minutes, I felt like a part moving along a conveyor belt. If an answer was not readily obvious, it seemed like my PCP was quick to outsource me to a specialist. If that didn't work, I was sent to another and so on. Eventually I changed PCPs. However, no doctor actually performed any real research on my behalf. Most probably forgot about my problems as quickly as I walked out of their office. In fact, anytime I've tried to dig deeper, they often became dismissive and referred to my issues as psychosomatic.

On the alternative side, many doctors overstepped their bounds by recommending treatments for which they were not qualified, had little research to support, or never actually used with other patients. Some also used less-than-reputable tactics to bully patients into buying their supplements.

Steve knew that entering the realm of alternative medicine had the inherent risk of consuming his fair share of snake oil. It took a few years of performing his own research to understand which herbs and practices were safe and productive. When he met a practitioner who prescribed something inappropriate, he was not shy about calling him or her out on it. He also learned that most supplements recommended could be found at specialty merchants like the VitaminShoppe and were of equal quality and cheaper.

Snake oil comes in two forms. It's not just what you consume. It's also the advice and lessons people offer that they might not be qualified to provide. Everyone wants to play doctor or master, and this comes at great risk to the patient and legal risk to the practitioner.

I have come across countless examples:

1) Go into any health supplement stores and you'll find clerks who go far beyond selling herbs. They make recommendations, health claims, and specify dosages. In my opinion, this is a ticking liability time bomb for retailers that hire a bunch of wannabes to play doctor or pharmacist.

2) There was the massage therapist performing visceral massage who concluded that I had Candida, a systemic yeast infection, after massaging my abdomen for a few minutes. Brilliantly, she recommended I take a yeast-based product to kill off the yeast. Now, does this really make sense? When I asked if she had ever taken it or had patients on it, she replied that she had only heard that it was a good product.

3) There were the two yoga instructors at a center in North Carolina. One had watched a two-hour video on qigong, and the other had attended a weekend seminar on Kundalini yoga. Each decided to introduce these energy practices into their classes. Such practices take years to learn when taught by a master and can be dangerous if taught incorrectly, causing a range of physical and psychological problems. In both classes, I chose to perform my own energy practice, different from the class, because I could tell the teachers didn't understand the basic principles. At the end of one of the classes, the teacher cornered me to ask why I didn't participate. When asked about her training in such arts, she became hostile—not very yogic. How likely

is it that someone in her class could be desperately seeking a cure to an ailment and take that incorrect routine home to practice for months on end, exacerbating their problems?

4) Lastly, there are the countless martial arts instructors who have never been properly trained in dim mak, or more importantly, revival techniques needed after they knock someone out. Yet they use their students, who have put their trust in them, as guinea pigs to practice such dangerous techniques. They don't even understand that the long-term side effects can be far worse than the initial attack.

It seemed like every few months, I encountered someone teaching or offering something he or she wasn't qualified to teach or offer. Unfortunately, most students and patients are not well informed enough to know the difference.

Steve's experiences left him jaded. His journal described how he retreated from taking mass classes that catered to the American fitness fad. He continued pursuing the Eastern arts for their intended benefits, but he only sought out the most reputable teachers who often operated out of back-alley, low-budget facilities. He perfected his knowledge of medicine, martial arts, and yoga with a religious fervor.

Having finally found a cure, the conclusion of his journal left Paul with additional hope.

Over the years, I've had to learn to control many of my physical issues and the pain that went along with them by entering deep, prolonged periods of meditation. I would walk through most days in a quasimeditative state, constantly focused on regulating my energy everywhere I went. With such an enormous distraction removed, my newfound freedom allows me to easily access the deeper recesses of my mind. The additional computing power has left me hyperaware, automatically gathering and processing a myriad of stimuli without realizing it's happening. I recall details of people and places I wasn't even aware I was observing. My mind reaches conclusions to complex problems so swiftly that it feels more like a gut reaction. Yet I am able to break down the logic in the same way a chess player effortlessly sees a dozen moves in advance. My mind now centers itself as if it was on autopilot.

Life brings you what you need, not what you want.

Learning to remain detached became my key to staying sane. It allowed me to believe that all of this was happening for a reason—that it was all part of some greater plan and was no accidental journey. However, something is missing from the equation. With my progress and newfound clarity, I should feel happy to be alive once again, not merely subsisting. Yet I feel cheated by the system. If knowledge is supposed to be the reward, it feels anticlimactic, hollow, and empty. It leaves me wanting for something more—something that justifies this miserable journey filled with torture and humiliation.

If the world is truly a dynamic interplay between yin and yang, or equal opposites, then what is the opposite of this?

Chapter 22

Prague

After closing the journal, a grin came over Paul's face. He could not sit still after coming to the realization that his brother had been cured for two years. Deep down, he never fully believed that Steve was capable of committing suicide. The clarity in his writing told Paul that he was not depressed. He was certainly irritated, but not depressed. It didn't make sense that he could have been the jumper. *Do they even have the correct body?* Doctor Huang's comments now held greater meaning for Paul. He needed to tell someone, so he picked up the phone to call Klára.

Twenty minutes later, he saw the top half of the blue Skoda pull up from where he sat. He grabbed his bag and exited the café.

"Hello." She greeted him with a kiss on the cheek after he closed the door.

"Ah, I like that."

"This customary for Europe. I only shake hands with Americans, but you different."

"I see," Paul replied.

"*Tak*, we go to Hradčany for lunch. Do you go before?"

"Hrad-chany?"

"Yes. This is castle neighborhood."

"No, I've not been to the castle." Paul said enthusiastically. "I've only seen it from the road."

"*Tak*. You in better mood today." Klára noticed the smile on his face. "Relax and enjoy ride. You tell me at lunch. Okay?"

Paul nodded.

The car descended toward the Dancing House, where Klára took a right and drove along the river. The cars merged like a funnel into one lane and passed between the tram tracks and the extravagant baroque homes lining the Vltava River. Paul was mesmerized by the buildings. Each was an intricate collage of high windows and ornate balconies. Colors, contrasts, lavish moldings, and a full cast of statues led up to a symphony of spires. Volumes of detail filled Paul's eyes to the point where he found it difficult to discern where each home began and ended.

The Charles Bridge was sporadically visible through the trees and traffic on the other side of the road. He could see a group of heavyset tourists, likely a church group, lining up at one of the statues.

"What's the statue with the gold ring around its head? Do you see all the tourists lining up?"

"That is St. John of Nepomuk. There is legend. Make a wish and touch statue, and your wish comes true. If you believe, we will touch it."

"Okay."

Another group, a much younger contingent of women, was posing provocatively with the statue of Saint Christopher as they laughed and snapped photographs. *Sorority girls*, Paul thought.

High above the bridge sat the Prague Castle. Klára started her tour. "Prague Castle is one of largest castles in Europe." She went on to describe that it covered roughly six football fields and dated back to the ninth century. Every major European architectural style is represented in the various buildings within the castle grounds. There was the baroque Basilica of St. George, the oldest church within the castle's walls. She pointed to the gothic spires. "This is St. Vitus Cathedral. This building started in 1344 and only finished in 1920s—almost six hundred years!"

As the road drew closer to the Charles Bridge, the Skoda entered a baroque corridor that resembled an old carriage lane passing under two large arches hollowed out of the building in front of them. Cars were passing under what was once somebody's living room. On the other side of the underpass, throngs of tourists were pressed up against the roadside waiting to cross to the bridge.

Parking was going to be difficult in the tourist section of town. Their eyes were darting back and forth, searching up and down side streets. Klára spotted a car exiting its parking spot on a side street across from the Four Seasons Hotel and darted up the street only to realize she was going the wrong way on a one-way street. The car quickly rolled through a three-point turn, and she pulled safely into the space.

They exited the side street and walked toward the bridge. Joining the other tourists, they crossed the street and passed under the Old Town Bridge Tower, the entrance to the Charles Bridge. The tower was widely considered to be the most beautiful gothic bridge tower in all of Europe. Coats of arms from the different regions of Bohemia decorated the sixty-four-meter-high late gothic tower. Three statues were displayed above the coats of arms. Saint Vitus, the patron saint of Bohemia, was in the center, with King Charles IV and King Wenceslas IV located on his left and right, respectively.

Klára and Paul wandered along the bridge, weaving between tourists stopped at the different statues. Klára explained that each of the thirty statues commemorated a different patron saint. Paul slowed down to look at a collection of sepia-toned photographs of the bridge that reminded him of the first time he saw it at night from the tram.

As they approached the statue of St. John of Nepomuk, Paul saw he was going to have to squeeze in between the other tourists to get his hand on the statue to make a wish.

"Go make wish, but do not tell it."

Paul kept one hand on his wallet as he wedged his way through the mire of heavyset tour groups from various Western countries. His free hand landed on the bronze relief at the base of the statue, touching the head of a knight. He closed his eyes and made a wish. As fast as he had squeezed into the group, he was popped back out by the growing pressure of cellulite-infused bodies cramming together.

Passing under the second Bridge Tower on the other side of the river, the street emptied into a cobblestone area called Malá Strana, or "Little Side." In medieval times, this area was home to the German population of Prague. Now, it is the summertime home to tourists walking the mosaic-embedded sidewalks and eating at outdoor bistros visible through archways hanging over the sidewalk.

Klára turned Paul to the left and directed him away from the tourist traffic. Once they reached the corner, she pointed to the Crème Caffe Il Balcone, her favorite place in this part of town. After settling into one of the outdoor tables, a waiter came to take their orders.

"You are in good mood today, Paul. Tell me what you read. I also have news, but for later."

"Steve's journal! I've completed it. There is no way he could have committed suicide. He found the cure to his ailments two years ago. I just don't think he—"

Klára placed her hand on Paul's arm to stop him. He could see the disheartened look on her face. "Paul, I am very sorry. DNA tests come today. The body is of Steve. Lieutenant Marek say it to me it is mafia. He never have burning body jumping before. It all is logic, and DNA now say is true."

Paul felt his chest tighten. Unable to catch his breath, he tried to speak but choked on every word he forced out. His eyes began filling with water until a tear broke through. A trickle turned into a steady stream cascading down his cheeks, and he began sobbing uncontrollably. Klára's attempt to protect herself from such a display by selecting a public place to break the news failed as the contrast between renewed hope and certainty proved too much for Paul.

The waiter arrived with the food and looked unsure of what to do. He just stood there looking on while holding the tray. Klára motioned for him to set the plates down, which he promptly did and retreated inside. Tourists at nearby tables watched as Klára attempted to console Paul. Eventually, she waved the waiter back, handed him three hundred Czech Crowns and asked to have the food wrapped to go.

"I am sorry. I was thinking you already understand he is gone. I take you to hotel now." Her eyes expressed genuine sorrow for bringing him to such a public place.

"It's okay. I'm sorry for this. Give me a minute. I will be fine." Paul wiped the tears from his eyes.

The waiter returned with the bag and left it on the table.

"Okay. We go to car now?"

"No, no. I don't want to go back to the hotel just yet. I'd like to walk around a bit. I can't eat at the moment. But if you are hungry, please have something to eat."

"I not able to eat now when I see you hurt. I know where we go." A smile came across her face. "Come!" Her childlike exuberance, emphasized by a slight tug on his hand, made Paul think they were about to skip to their destination. However, his energy had already drained from his body, and her efforts to boost his spirits were lost on him.

She led him south along the street until they reached another bridge crossing the Vltava. They walked to the middle of the bridge where the stone wall lining the bridge opened up to a wide set of stairs that led them down to a grassy island. Walking to the far end of the island, they sat on benches looking out at the baroque homes that had captivated Paul on the drive down. They ate lunch in silence. Barely conscious of the food he put in his mouth, Paul spent the time staring through blurry eyes at the cityscape across the river. Klára's words blended into the background noise of rustling leaves and babbling water passing by.

"I will prepare to return to the U.S. tomorrow. When will it be possible to collect my brother's belongings?" Paul had grown cold. He wanted nothing more to do with this country. It had robbed him of his brother, and he suddenly felt uneasy about being there.

"Is possible to go to apartment tonight. We go now." Klára reached over to take his hand.

Chapter 23

Three weeks later in Boston

Natural sunlight poured into the warehouse from the skylight above highlighting the newness of the renovations. Having just completed his morning yoga routine, Steve sat on the platform meditating in lotus position while receiving the warmth of the sun.

Every morning began with the same routine. From a standing position, Steve would swing his arms freely like a helicopter twisting at the waist with his feet planted firmly in the mat. At the full extension of the twist, when he was looking behind himself, the momentum of his arms would wrap them up against his body, landing strikes to key pressure points on his chest and back. He would then reverse direction to strike the other side. This twisting routine gently squeezed the blood out of his organs and jump-started his energy flowing to his limbs. Once his body was loosened up, he would start with his neck and work his way down, rotating each joint ten times in both directions. This opened up his body further by stimulating key pressure points located near each joint. Lastly, he would use his fist to tap softly along each energy channel in his arms and legs to send energy to each organ.

Once warmed up, he engaged in some core strengthening exercises, performed a quick yoga routine, and ended with thirty minutes of meditation or qigong.

When he rose from the mat, he could hear the doctor moving about in his room. It was breakfast time. After preparing something simple for himself, he started on the doctor's breakfast—a more involved affair.

It is said about traditional Chinese food that if it's prepared correctly, it can heal the body like medicine. The traditional Chinese food this refers to is the food you might see older Chinese immigrants eating in Chinatown. However, if it is prepared incorrectly, like the fast-food equivalent altered for the Western palate, it will leave the body vulnerable to disease.

Considering the average person eats three or more times a day, Steve understood that a person's diet has significant influence over their physical well-being. From his work with Chinese medicine, he also knew that diet and herbs can bring about dramatic psychological changes, such as anxiety (fire), fear (water), anger (wood), depression (wood), and sharp swings in emotions (fire) that could be used to heighten symptoms. This is why diet was one of the three ways he planned to alter Silberman's health to bring about the desired changes.

Thus far, all of Silberman's meals have had three things in common. They are all high in fat, sugar, and stimulants. Consuming high quantities of fat makes the liver work harder, requiring wood to use more energy. When wood works hard, it creates heat, making it dry and brittle. As a result, a person whose liver is taxed is quicker to snap and get angry. In addition, an overburdened liver (wood) draws energy from water, the element that feeds it. Consuming high quantities of sugar makes the pancreas work harder, drawing more energy to earth. Too much earth overpowers water, restraining it and making a person fearful. Excessive amounts of stimulants make the heart work harder, creating a raging fire that burns wood too quickly, feeds earth too fast, and melts metal. As a result, a person with this diet is likely be more susceptible to heightened level of anxiety and experience greater mood swings between anger, depression, and fear.

For added measure, each meal contained herbs to accentuate the effects of the food.

Once finished, Steve opened the door to release the doctor.

"You know the drill," he said as he walked up to the platform.

Silberman emerged from the room hobbling toward the platform. He could smell the plate of scrambled eggs waiting for him—two eggs with two additional yolks were scrambled with heavy cream to create a rich, fluffy delight. A bowl of sugar-laden cereal sat next to a bottled blend of whole milk and cream. A warm muffin laced with herbs and lathered with butter sat on a small plate. A tall black coffee supplemented with additional caffeine and other herbal extracts completed his breakfast.

In order to get breakfast, Silberman had to climb the platform and work for it. This was a requirement for each meal. As the weeks wore on, the doctor's emotional state deteriorated further. He felt helpless, afraid, and angry. Each time the door opened, he knew pain stood on the other side. If he wanted to keep eating, he had to pay a price. It was explained to him that if he didn't come for food, he would receive the beating and no food. So he might as well stretch his legs a bit and eat.

However, stretching his legs was getting more difficult as his knees had begun hurting days earlier.

Additionally, Silberman was exhausted from waking sporadically throughout the night. His room was equipped with a set of strobe lights embedded in the walls that were controlled by a timer. Every two hours between midnight and 4:00 a.m., his eyes were pounded by a blitzkrieg of rapid flashes just long enough to wake him up. By the time he was semiconscious, the lights had already stopped their intrusion into his slumber.

At first, he was unaware of what was causing him to wake. He figured it was the stress of the situation. However, within a few days, his body fell into the rhythm of waking every few hours. This was partly a function of the lights and partly due to being worn down by stress, caffeine, and herbs. Eventually, he woke before the lights went off. When he realized the source of his waking, he flew off the handle, picking up the medical cart and throwing it against one of the walls. It missed the lights, which were behind protective grates. The noise woke Steve, who laughed when he realized Silberman had figured it out.

Unable to sleep consistently, his body was unable to repair itself, accounting for his weakened knees, exhaustion, and flushed face. His body was losing yin energy; he was becoming yin deficient. The Chinese believe the world is made up of the dynamic coexistence of yin and yang energies. When looking at a yin yang diagram, the white portion represents rising energy, or yang energy—expansive, active, strong, and hot. The black portion represents falling energy or yin energy. Yin energy is the energy that keeps us grounded—contracting, passive, yielding, and cold. It helps us sleep restfully at night.

Steve often related the relationship between yin and yang energy to a grain of brown rice. A grain of brown rice is made up of two main parts—the endosperm and bran. The endosperm, or white rice, gives you a sudden and temporary spike in your blood sugar. This is yang energy—quick and sudden bursts that can fizzle as fast as they start. The bran portion of brown rice represents yin energy. It contains vitamin B, which helps regulate the energy from the endosperm, stretching out the yang energy over a longer period, keeping you grounded. As a result, you do not receive the dramatic spike in blood sugar that taxes your body's ability to produce insulin. As such, you do not crash after and crave more food. This is one reason why it is recommended that we eat whole grains, to obtain both yin and yang nutrients.

The doctor's yin energy was being used up quickly due to his lack of sleep, emotional stress, and poor diet. As a result, there wasn't enough yin energy to keep his yang energy in balance. His body was now waking in the middle of the night of its own accord. He was overheated, experiencing mild night sweats. Irritated and fidgety, he could not calm his mind, leaving him with no clear train of thought. In the mornings, his mind was in a fog until he had something to eat, but the relief never lasted more than an hour.

Silberman reached the corner of the platform. Dark bags had formed under his eyes that looked more like a full set of luggage. His face was red with anger over his lack of sleep. He brushed his disheveled hair back revealing a set of bitter, yet discouraged eyes. The doctor was conflicted with emotions as he walked toward the center of the platform. He wanted to kill his captor. He was livid that a man of his stature was being subjected to such humiliation. He wanted desperately to prove he was better, but he couldn't. Each time he scaled the stairs, he was gripped with the fear of what pressure point attacks awaited him. The pain was unlike anything he had experienced before. His captor had complete control over the situation, over his pain, and over his life. This was not something to which the doctor was accustomed.

To Steve, each session on the platform was used to target the energy channels he was already taxing with his culinary terrorism. It was also his opportunity to keep his skills from rusting. He would tell the doctor, "Nothing trains the senses like having a live opponent with nothing to lose and everything to gain." On occasion, he went overboard and was required to revive the doctor when the strikes had flatlined him.

Silberman bent over and ran at Steve like a linebacker on the football field. Gliding backward with the doctor, Steve's palms ricocheted off pressure points on Silberman's head, slowing his momentum. Steve passed to the side of the doctor and landed a quick swat to his lower back. Silberman's legs gave out, and Steve sauntered to the corner to give him space to get up.

"Up, up!" Steve yelled.

Silberman no longer knew what to do. Over the weeks, he had tried grappling, boxing, and even his best efforts at a dropkick. Whenever he got close, his attacks were picked apart point by point. Any limb that came into Steve's space was attacked, trapped, controlled, and contorted in some way as to effortlessly inflict extraordinary pain. This provided little incentive for Silberman to get up from the mat, let alone throw a fist he knew he wouldn't get back.

Steve walked over to stand next to Silberman who flailed in an attempt to take him down with a scissor-kick. Steve dropped down to one knee, landing it on the kidney meridian running down the inside of the doctor's calf—the yin water channel. Silberman grabbed his leg and screamed until his voice went hoarse.

"See? That's what you get for your lack of effort. Okay, breakfast time," Steve said cheerfully, taking delight in the doctor's pain. He walked off the mat without breaking a sweat.

After each meal, Silberman was strapped to his cot where Steve performed acupuncture on him.

"The interesting thing about acupuncture, doctor, is that the needles I insert now will not only affect the organ I'm working on at this moment, but they will also affect a different organ in twelve hours. So this is truly around-the-clock care."

"Care? This is what you call it? Goddamn care?"

"What would you call it?"

"Torture! It's goddamn torture!" The veins in Silberman's forehead were throbbing.

"It's no different than how you treat your patients. Every Tuesday when you performed surgery, you cut them open in an area of the body where nerves run every which way. You have no idea what damage you might do down there each time you make an incision. At least, this way I'm not making incisions."

"I try to help people! You're trying to kill me!"

"If I wanted to kill you, I wouldn't have gone to this much effort. I know it doesn't seem like it, but I am trying to help you," Steve said with a smile. "All of this is truly for your benefit."

Silberman began shivering.

"Are you cold?"

"I'm freezing! What the hell did you do to me?" Goosebumps were forming on Silberman's arms.

"So a minute ago, you were feeling hot from our workout and breakfast, and now you feel cold. Is that right?"

"Workout? You call that a friggin' workout?"

"Well, for me it's good practice. Anyhow, everything we are doing has a reason. Please answer the question."

"Yes, I was hot and now I'm cold. What the hell is going on? Make it stop!"

"That is your yin waning. You have too much heat and now—"

"Too much heat? But I'm freezing!"

"Yes, too much heat. Heat causes expansion. It cuts off your circulation, and now you are cold. It's actually quite simple. I'm sure you are familiar with a yin yang, right?

"Yes."

"It's the relationship between yin and yang energy. When you move too far in one direction, or one energy, it gives way to the other. Too much heat gives way to cold. Your heat is rising. Your face is red and feet are cold. The interesting part is that your hands are red and probably freezing, too."

"They are like ice cubes!"

Steve placed his fingers on the doctor's radial artery. "Your pulse is beating like a racehorse. So with red hands and plenty of circulation, your hands are still cold. Sorry, 'like ice cubes.' Can your Western medicine please explain that one?"

Chapter 24

Two months later

I t was 2:00 a.m. when Doctor Silberman had just returned to bed after using the toilet. He lay there thinking about a lecture he had attended years earlier at a symposium in New York on the body's ability to cope with stress. The presenter likened the body to a manual transmission car. When the body is running at a normal stress level, this is equivalent to a car running in third gear. When stress sets in, the body shifts into fourth gear to deal with the stressor before returning to equilibrium, or third gear. On vacation, the body temporarily drops down to second gear. Upon returning to a normal routine, work and family pressures, the body returns to third gear.

However, when the body experiences stress over a prolonged period, it gets stuck in fourth gear. Soon, fourth gear becomes its normal operating mode. With all new stresses, the body races to fifth gear to cope. When on vacation, it temporarily downshifts to third gear. With a new resting state of fourth gear, the body is revving higher than it used to, taxing the mind and wearing out its organs faster.

For weeks, Silberman had been redlining in fifth gear. His torture had moved well beyond a dietary and physical focus. Periodically, pictures of his children were delivered without any note or indication as to what they meant. Additionally, Steve had befriended the doctor's wife, Dorothy, through their local Rotary club where she was a regular member. On occasion, he played recordings of their conversations at the weekly meetings.

All of these actions were purposefully left vague to make Silberman's mind spin endlessly about the possibilities that could extend well beyond the warehouse walls, far out of the doctor's control. Introducing psychological warfare was a natural way to weaken water, with the associated emotion of fear. After all, Steve had dealt with excessive amounts of fear during his journeys that were made light of by various physicians. If he was going to replicate his problems, they needed to be equal in magnitude and dimension.

Starting a few weeks ago, Silberman's body had locked into a continual state of tension. He began experiencing problems sleeping due to an overactive bladder. He was now waking every two hours to run to the toilet. On this occasion, he stood waiting to go for ten minutes before his body let go and cooperated. As he squeezed out the last drop, a chill raced through his body that he had not been able to identify or shake. His prostate area felt inflamed, making it increasingly difficult to get that last drop out. Silberman wondered if he was suffering from some sort of infection.

Each time he climbed back into bed, it took him forty minutes to fall asleep. Feeling cold and clammy, he would spend fifteen minutes rubbing his legs together under the covers to generate enough warmth to relax. When it got really bad, he would run his feet under hot water in the sink, one foot at a time. By the time he fell asleep, his body would wake him to use the toilet again.

When morning came, Silberman's body ached from the constant lack of sleep. He was having difficulty keeping his eyes open for very long because they hurt. He couldn't tell if the problem stemmed from being tired or something else. His mind sat in a deep fog, semi-alert and irritated, making it difficult to understand what was happening to him. He was quick to snap, which he was often made to regret. He wanted to take action, but felt a deep level of weakness that robbed him to his soul.

The doctor's condition eventually deteriorated to a state where torture was no longer necessary. Without an accurate understanding of his condition and proper treatment, his symptoms would persist indefinitely. The doctor was no longer required to come to the platform before each meal. Instead, he was given the floor to do as he liked. Steve allowed him to walk around the room inspecting the free weights, lab equipment, and even the kitchen.

Silberman was warned that any attempt to grab a knife or other utensils would be met with severe consequences. Despite the warning, the temptation got the better of him, and he quickly found the knife he tried to conceal pressed against his throat. Steve promptly dragged him to the platform for a special practice session.

The slot in his door opened.

"How are we feeling today, Dr. Silberman?"

"Fuck you!" Silberman sat shivering under his coarse woolen blanket. Every morning, he complained about new symptoms plaguing him. "I need medical care. Just drop me off at an emergency room. I won't tell anyone about this place. I promise. Just let me get something to take care of this."

"What would you take? What exactly is wrong as you see it? I want your expert diagnosis."

"Well, I'm not going to spout off any of that crap about earth, wind, and fire, or some other '70s music group you keep babbling about!"

"No, doctor, just your expert Western opinion will do."

"Fine! Well, I can't take a piss properly for starters! And I'm goddamn cold all the time."

"Those are symptoms. I want your diagnosis, your leading expert diagnosis."

"Fine. Urinary hesitancy might point to a prostate issue, especially when combined with urgency. There! Are you happy? Or it might be bladder stones, an infection that has narrowed the urethra, or even prostate cancer. That's why I need to get to a hospital. It's probably an infection from those goddamn needles you're using. Who the hell knows where you got those things? I can't know until I run some tests."

"Does it hurt when you urinate?"

"Sometimes!"

"What does that feel like? Is it a burning or tearing sensation?"

"What? Oh, so you're my PCP now? Just get me to a trained Western medical doctor, you crazy freak."

"Burning or tearing, doctor?" Steve asked patiently.

"Tearing!"

"Why not diabetes, damaged bladder, or nerve damage? They also have these symptoms. Have you tried to have sex?"

"With who? Oh right, all the beauties walking around this insane asylum."

"Do you find yourself waking with erections, or do you feel dead down there?"

Silberman suddenly fell silent. He realized he could not recall the last time he had experienced an erection. A man typically experiences multiple erections throughout the night without being conscious of them. If he has not ejaculated in a long time, waking with an erection becomes more likely. "Dead," he answered.

"I told you that you would experience exactly what your patients experience." Steve's matter-of-fact tone left the doctor's mind stewing in the bad news after he closed the slot. He started desperately playing with himself to see if he could get a rise out of it. His complete lack of feeling and success brought him to tears.

Steve returned twenty minutes later holding the doctor's prescription pad taken from his briefcase.

"So what's the conclusion doctor? Do you know what you have?"

"No, I don't know what it is, probably an infection."

"There are some rubber gloves over there. Would you like to give yourself a digital rectal exam?" A sarcastic grin spread across Steve's face. Silberman shot a nasty look back at Steve, who replied, "Well, I'm certainly not going to do it."

Steve handed the doctor his script pad through the slot.

"What's this?"

"It's your opportunity to cure yourself. Go ahead, prescribe yourself some drugs, and I'll have them filled."

The doctor took the pad and thought for a few minutes before scribbling a series of illegible prescriptions.

Viagra—50 mg per day x 30 days
Avodart—0.5 mg per day x 30 days

Flomax—0.4 mg per day x 30 days
Floxin—400 mg 2x per day x 45 days

Steve read through the scripts. He held up the Viagra script and said, "I didn't use it, so you won't either. It's time to use those deductive skills of yours." He crumpled the paper and threw it over his shoulder before closing the slot.

Chapter 25

Three weeks later

Doctor Silberman woke to a loud commotion outside of his door. He heard an unfamiliar voice. Another man was in the main room, and he was yelling at Steve.

Silberman realized this may be his only chance to free himself.

"Hello! Hello! Can you hear me? This crazy's got me locked up in here! Help!" Silberman was screaming at the top of his lungs.

On the other side of the door, Steve was indoctrinating his new patient, a pudgy Japanese-American man dressed in a white lab coat. The new patient stood a few inches shorter than Steve and was struggling to stay a step ahead of the wrist lock Steve was enforcing.

"You have someone else in there? What is this place?"

From behind the closed door, he could hear Silberman yell, "It's hell! Run!"

"Dr. Yoshida, you were a big disappointment as a primary care physician. So I have brought you here to redeem yourself."

Yoshida flipped onto his back to temporarily release himself from the wristlock, telling Steve that he had studied some form of martial arts in the past.

"Very good, Doctor!" Steve applauded as he transitioned into another wristlock. "Up! Up!" He lifted Yoshida by applying pain through the wristlock and directed him toward the platform. "My last opponent was no challenge. Let's hope you will put up more of a fight. However, if your martial arts are anything like your medical skills, I'm afraid you won't be much better."

Dr. Yoshida had served as Steve's PCP for a number of years based upon what turned out to be a poor recommendation from a friend. Looking back on it, an endocrinologist who specialized in treating geriatric patients might not have been the best choice for a PCP. In fact, Steve thought Yoshida never should have been accepting younger patients at all. After reading about a $300,000 Medicare fraud case involving Yoshida, he knew it was time to find a new PCP.

Once he had guided Yoshida up to the platform, Steve swept the doctor's leg and drove him into the mat. Yoshida's eyes glazed over for a few seconds as the ceiling spun above him. He was slow to get up.

"Do you remember how many referrals you wrote for me? You sent me on a wild goose chase before you even took five minutes to review my problems for yourself. I was working with a PCP and still receiving disjointed care!"

Distracted by his own anger, Steve moved in without realizing that the doctor was feigning injury. When he got within striking distance, Yoshida launched a kick into Steve's gut, sending him flying. He landed on the mat, short of breath and gasping for air. *Let the pain pass. Breathe slowly. Breathe through your nose.* He quickly calmed his mind and the muscles surrounding his throat, chest, and abdomen.

Looking up at the skylight, a flying knee-drop fell from above. Steve reacted quickly, rolling to the side to avoid the blow. He sprung to his feet and backed away. Steve was a little flustered and needed a minute to center his mind. However, Yoshida wasn't going to give him that time.

Yoshida ran off the platform and headed into the kitchen area. Sensing he was losing control of the situation, Steve followed to put an end to this. Yoshida ran past the stove and made for the knife block. He drew the serrated knife and turned back only to meet a stainless steel pot cover cutting through the air like a Frisbee. It smashed him in the nose, and blood began pouring down his face. He stood clutching his nose and waving the knife erratically as he screamed in pain. Steve closed the gap, attacking Yoshida's knife hand to rid him of the weapon. Once Steve was in control of the knife, he landed a blow to the side of Yoshida's chin that left him unconscious.

The activity in the main room fell silent. Silberman sat for a few minutes trying to piece together the events. When he heard the sound of a body being dragged into the adjacent room, feelings of despair quashed all hope.

Chapter 26

Boston

Doctor Yoshida came to and found himself strapped to a chair in a room that looked like a replica of his Chestnut Street office. It had the same sterile atmosphere, cold furnishings, posters, plaques, and equipment as the office holding Silberman.

The bandage covering his broken nose partially obstructed his view. The pain had spread into his sinuses making his eyes sensitive to the light, forcing him to squint as he inspected his surroundings.

The door opened, and Steve entered.

"How's the nose doing, Dr. Yoshida? I didn't want to have to do that to you, but you left me no choice in the matter."

"No choice? You are holding me here against my will!" he retorted in a nasally voice.

"Do you know why you are here?"

"No!"

"You are here because of your utter lack of competence as a PCP. On eleven separate occasions, you farmed out my treatment to specialists before you actually took five minutes of your own time to investigate my symptom cluster for yourself. When you did, the best you came up with was to hook me up to an EKG machine. Think about it. You even gave me a referral to another endocrinologist. You're a goddamn endocrinologist! Doesn't that seem a bit strange? It was as if you weren't even paying attention to what was going on in your own office."

"So I'm a terrible doctor. So what? You could have chosen another PCP. Is that any reason to abduct someone? What do you plan to do with us? Kill us?"

"That depends upon you."

"What does that mean?"

"The man in the next room is very sick. I've made him that way over the past four months. Now, I've brought you here to cure him."

"To cure him? Have you thought about just letting him go?"

"I could, but his symptoms would not improve. In fact, they will likely deteriorate further. He's been trying to cure himself, but it's not working. That's why I've brought you here."

"Cure himself? What do you mean?"

"He's a doctor like you. Now, the only way you and he will go free is if you two can figure out what's wrong and nurse him back to health. Until you've found a cure, you will be brought one step closer to his condition with each passing day. Do you understand?"

"His condition? What is his condition?" The doctor's voice trembled.

"You'll find out soon enough. Do you understand what I've told you?"

Yoshida nodded.

"Good. We will start his treatments in a week. Now, let's take care of those raccoon eyes." Steve pulled a handful of individually packed, sterilized needles from his lab coat pocket and inserted them around Yoshida's eyes and nose before leaving the room.

Yoshida felt his sinuses relax and the swelling around his engorged nose ease up. It reminded him of how his grandfather used to care for him as a child back in Japan. However, with the death of his father shortly after his family immigrated to the United States, the body of knowledge that had passed from father to son for centuries had been lost with the disruption in his family's lineage. With medicine in his blood, he had decided to move into Western medicine.

Steve returned twenty minutes later to remove the needles and offer Yoshida the same opportunity initially provided to Silberman. He dropped the boning knife in front of Yoshida, placed the key to the loft in his front pant pocket, and made his way to the platform. Yoshida cut himself free and leapt to the platform eager to claim his freedom.

He began slashing his way toward Steve as a skilled knife fighter might. The blade carved its way diagonally through the air, starting from each shoulder and cutting toward the opposite hip. Then, the knife reversed direction moving from hip to opposite shoulder. It happened so fast that the six-inch steel blade was a blur.

Steve remained centered, still, and calm, as he waited for Yoshida to approach. He looked past the doctor's arms, staying focused on the core of Yoshida's body—the positioning of his shoulders, hips, and feet. If he did not let the arms distract him, Steve could read his opponent's energy, momentum, and balance. The slashing was only a distraction, meant to kill by a thousand cuts. If used correctly, it would set up an opponent for the real blow, a sudden plunge to the belly, chest, or other key body part.

When Steve saw the doctor load his energy for the plunge, he immediately stepped in to deflect the knife hand with the ridge of his forearm before it gathered momentum. As the doctor followed through with his right foot, Steve swept it, dragging it a little further than the doctor intended to step. Yoshida's front foot came out from under him, and he crashed to the mat.

Still holding the knife, the doctor jumped up. Despite being winded, he began slashing in a controlled fashion again, trying to set himself up for another opportunity. Upset that he did not control the weapon after the first encounter, Steve decided not to give Yoshida that opportunity. He timed the doctor's movements and stepped in after a downward slash. Trapping the doctor's arm across his own body, Steve stepped behind Yoshida. He reached up and caught the doctor by his broken nose as he swept Yoshida's legs again, sending him into the mat. Steve maintained control over the doctor's knife hand this time. He quickly applied pressure to his wrist, forcing Yoshida to release the knife. Using an arm bar, he guided the doctor onto his stomach before retrieving the knife.

Steve threw the knife off of the platform and let Yoshida up. It felt nice to have some real practice, and Steve wanted more.

"I see you've studied a hard style. Karate?"

"Yes, karate. My family tradition."

"Looks like you are out of practice," Steve observed. "One more time?"

Yoshida assumed a traditional wide fighting stance, typical among most hard forms. Steve stood nonchalantly with one foot only slightly in front of the other. His palms facing his opponent as if pleading for help—certainly not the look of a fighter.

Yoshida moved in with a front snap kick, commonly used to enter an opponent's space and set him up for another strike. Steve matched the harder style, snapping his knee up and into the inside of the doctor's calf, striking along the earth meridian—spleen. As Steve put his foot down, he stepped in to land a blow on the doctor's water meridian running down the abdomen. *Earth controls water,* automatically registered across his mind. The doctor recoiled in pain, preventing Steve from landing the third blow along the fire meridian, which would have knocked the doctor out.

Yoshida straightened himself out in the corner before returning to the center of the platform. He turned his body sideways and telegraphed the thrusting side kick he was about to unleash. Steve stepped out of the way to let it pass him by. Now standing directly behind the doctor, Steve struck Yoshida's lower back with an open palm to a point called the Gate of Life. He followed up with a combination of strikes to the neck and head, and the doctor fell lifelessly to the mat.

Chapter 27

Boston

The slot in Silberman's door opened.

"Don't look so dejected, Doctor. Your new friend is a more competent fighter than you, but that's not why he is here."

"Who is he?"

"You asked for a PCP—you got one. He's here to fix you, or at least give it his best try."

A clipboard was pushed through the slot for Silberman to claim.

"What's this?"

"It's your intake form. Fill it in. Please answer all of the questions to start your treatments—and none of this doctor's handwriting nonsense. Please write legibly."

"Seriously? You seriously want me to fill this out?"

"Seriously!" Steve struck a sarcastic tone. "Aren't you the one who asked for a PCP? Anyhow, it's not like your self-treatments are working."

Silberman sat silently in the ridicule of Steve's comments.

"I'll be back in fifteen minutes to collect it. The doctor is very busy today. His next available appointment will be in one week."

"Wait, wait. I've got one question."

"Go ahead."

"If I'm supposed to be in a rehab clinic, where's he supposed to be?"

"Doctor Yoshida tendered his resignation yesterday at the hospital and private practice where he worked, something to do with his Medicare fraud case. He's never been married, has no kids, and really needed a vacation. Nobody is going to miss him."

"Vacation," Silberman muttered with disgust.

"Interestingly, I'm not sure Dorothy really misses you anymore either. Maybe this was a good vacation for the two of you." Steve chuckled as he walked away.

Fifteen minutes later, Steve returned to pick up the form. He perused it to ensure everything was complete.

"So basically, you are listing everything here bothering you before you attempted to medicate yourself."

"Your point is?"

"Just checking. So, the drugs aren't helping at all?"

"They help, but in a vaguely superficial way. It's obvious they are only masking the problems temporarily. The symptoms will return the minute I go off them."

"Wait. Don't you have patients on these drugs to manage their conditions for life?"

"Yes." Silberman thought for a minute. "But they are all older and have no other choice. My body wouldn't be in this sort of disrepair naturally."

"They weren't all older. In fact, you tried to convince me to take Viagra because you had 'many patients my age' on it. How many quick fixes did you prescribe to get the patient out the door?"

"That's because they were all desperate like you!" Silberman turned angry that his judgment was being called into question again. "It's not a pretty sight when someone breaks down in your office, not to mention their body breaking down, and they are sitting before you like you are God. What would you do?"

"Look who's finally admitting he thought he was God."

"As if you're any different. Look at what you are doing to us here."

Chapter 28

Boston

For the next week, Yoshida took over where Silberman had left off weeks earlier. He was placed on the same gastronomic schedule, and required to report to the platform before each toxic meal. Since he was younger than Silberman, Yoshida's constitution held up better against the nutritional assault. Nevertheless, when acupuncture and three square beatings a day were combined with the diet and fear, sufficient symptoms manifested to let Yoshida begin to feel what Steve had experienced.

The slot in Doctor Yoshida's door opened and a clipboard slid through.

"Your patient's intake form. Study it. He'll be here in a minute."

"Alan Silberman—the urologist who went into rehab? He was all over the TV."

"Do you still think he went to rehab? Well, I guess you could call it a new kind of rehab."

"Impotence? Isn't that his specialty?"

"Yes." Steve's smile could be heard in his voice.

"How am I supposed to solve this if he's not able to?"

"Two minds are better than one."

"I guess. But I'm not so sure in this case," Yoshida replied.

"That's true. His mind will likely suck all of the oxygen out of the room. How's this for incentive? Your lives are depending upon it. Is that sufficient motivation?"

Silence fell over Yoshida as the slot closed.

Yoshida had a few minutes to study the forms before he heard the deadbolts retract. The door opened, and a feeble old man hobbled in. Silberman looked twenty years older than his actual age. In four months, his hair had turned white. His face had become drawn, pale, and wrinkled with red splotches. The black bags under his eyes had deepened, and he had gained twenty pounds from the heavy diet and constant stress.

Horror filled Yoshida's eyes. The old man before him looked nothing like the vibrant middle-aged urologist he had seen on television. Instead, he looked like someone a few heartbeats away from death.

The door closed behind Silberman.

"Are you okay?" Yoshida asked.

"What the hell do you think?" Silberman snapped. "I can hardly walk. I can't use the bathroom without pissing my pants after. My eyes are always in pain. I'm constantly freezing. And, I can't have sex anymore. You read it all. It's all there in your hands. Who the hell are you anyhow?"

Silberman didn't like the idea of working with another doctor, especially one who was much younger and likely less experienced than him. His natural disposition toward other physicians was that his word meant something, and everyone else needed to listen and learn.

"I am James Yoshida. I was Steve's PCP."

"A PCP, great. What are you going to do, take my friggin' pulse?"

"I'm an endocrinologist. And yes, I'm going to start by taking your pulse because you look like you've got one foot in the grave. Now give me your wrist. Did this all start here? Or did you have any of these problems before you came here?"

"Everything started within the first two weeks of arriving. At this point, I can't remember which symptom started first. Every morning I wake feeling a little worse and can't even tell what's causing it. I thought it might be an infection from the needles, so I prescribed myself antibiotics."

"Prescribed yourself?"

"I write a script, and this psycho fills it at a local pharmacy. I heard you fighting him. It sounds like you were doing better than me."

"Yeah. I started learning karate at a young age from my father and uncle, but I've not practiced in years—and nothing like this. His knowledge is well beyond anything I've ever seen. It's as if he knows what I'm going to do before I even know it. I was hoping that with two of us we could have taken him. However, seeing your condition and his skill, I don't think it's possible."

Silberman waved off his comment. "I've thought about this for the past week, since you arrived here. I honestly have no idea what's going on in my body. I've used a number of drugs to try to solve this, and they haven't made a dent in curing the symptoms. If the two of us can't solve this, I think I'm going to need him. From what I can hear through the door, it sounds like he's put you on the same path. You'll likely need him, too."

"Need him? Are you delusional? What makes you think we're getting out of here alive if we don't solve this?" Yoshida asked. "Even if we do solve it, I doubt he's letting us out of here at all. This is about getting even. All we can do for now is play his game to stay alive. So, let's get back to your symptoms."

"Fine. My symptoms pointed to a prostate infection. So I prescribed a shotgun approach—antibiotics, smooth muscle relaxants, blood pressure meds, and alpha blockers to shrink the prostate. Initially, it was helping. However, it never got me fully back to normal. When the first round of antibiotics ended, I noticed that the symptoms returned, which made me think that the anti-inflammatory effect from the antibiotics was what was helping. So I prescribed myself some anti-inflammatories, Cox-2s. Ironically, my gastro tract started bothering me—acid, indigestion, and so on."

"That's strange. Cox-2s shouldn't upset your stomach."

"I know that!" Silberman's ego got the better of him. "I think it was a symptom left over from the antibiotics."

"I'm not sure I buy that. Looking at your medications, the antibiotics might account for the pain you feel in your knees as they are known to weaken the tendons. However, I'm sure you *already knew that*. I don't think they would still bother your stomach this long after going off them."

"No, I'm still on them. I replaced Floxin with Macrobid. It's not so harsh on the stomach, but I'm starting to develop rashes."

Dr. Yoshida grabbed the *Physician's Desk Reference* from the desk to look up some of the drugs on the intake form.

"It says that impotence, painful and difficult urination, fever, chills, inability to sleep, and intestinal disturbances are all side effects of these drugs. Basically, your drugs can also cause the symptoms they are supposed to treat."

"Come on, Doctor." Silberman rolled his eyes. "You know that they're required to list every side effect during a clinical trial. If I say my left nut hurts when coughing while on the drug, they have to put it in there. These drugs treat an older population suffering from these symptoms to begin with. If the patient lists a symptom, even if it has nothing to do with the disease, it will be listed as a side effect."

"I guess I can agree with that. However, you are taking an awful lot of drugs here. Why the acid reducers?"

"I was having such discomfort, I needed something. I also figured it must be contributing to my poor sleep."

"Right, acid in the esophagus triggers asthmatic reactions at night."

"Correct."

"So now you are on Macrobid, Propecia, Hytrin, Flomax, Nexium, and Vesicare? That's an awful lot, don't you think? Some of these seem redundant, too."

"I guess so, but they help me manage most of the symptoms," Silberman defended his choices.

"It says here that you have a feeling of fullness in your rectum, and that you're chronically constipated. That could be putting pressure on the prostate and creating more symptoms."

"As if I'm not aware of that. Look, I'm the one living this nightmare. Might I remind you that if we don't figure it out, you'll be living it, too—probably sooner than you know! Now, stop wasting my time questioning my diagnosis and treatment plan and start thinking outside of the box. We've got to come up with some real friggin' suggestions. If he could figure it out, we certainly can too."

"Here's a real friggin' suggestion. I recommend you go off of all the drugs as these may be causing additional symptoms, such as your constipation. The more drugs you take, the more side effects you will have, creating additional layers of symptoms to sort through. This makes it difficult to understand what's happening here. I suggest we get down to the basic symptom profile. Go off the drugs for a week and we'll see how you feel after that. Does this sound good?"

"Fine," Silberman said with a tone of annoyance. He wasn't looking forward to having his symptoms return to full strength.

"Let's see what's going on in your prostate area now." Yoshida snapped a latex rubber glove over his hand and lubricated it. "Please bend over the table."

As Silberman dropped his pants and assumed the position, the door opened, and Steve entered.

"I'm sorry—your time has ended."

"What?" Silberman spat out as he struggled to quickly pull up his pants.

"What did you think? You'd have all day to work on this? As I recall, neither of you gave me an entire day of your time. What's your conclusion? Do you want to prescribe your patient anything, Doctor?"

"No, we are going to take him off of everything to start." The look on Yoshida's face implied he was searching for some indication as to whether he was moving in the right direction.

"Sorry, Doctor, I can't give you any help. You will have to figure this out on your own. Your next meeting will be in one week."

"One week!" Silberman screamed.

"One week. The doctor's schedule is completely booked."

Yoshida interjected, "That's fine. It will take about a week for the drugs to completely work their way out of his system."

Steve escorted an irritated Doctor Silberman back to his room.

Chapter 29

Boston

Without the drugs holding him together, Silberman's condition deteriorated at a faster clip, and his sleep deficit accelerated. As his sleep worsened, the pain he felt in every muscle and joint became exacerbated. He spent most days of the ensuing week shivering under his blanket, only getting up for meals and to use the toilet. The large binding meals he had grown accustomed to continued making his abdominal symptoms worse.

By the next meeting, it was clear that removing the drugs was not helping Silberman. Furthermore, Dr. Yoshida began to better understand his patient's plight through his own experiences. The effects of his new diet, visits to the platform, and acupuncture sessions were quickly wearing him down. His sleep was becoming turbulent, and he noticed the effects on his digestion.

Seeing Silberman a second time after beginning to feel the effects of his new lifestyle frightened Yoshida with what was to come.

"Today you will have thirty minutes in the event you want to run some tests. Call through the slot if you need me. Plan your time accordingly." Steve closed the door and bolted it.

"Okay, let's get started. How do you feel now that you are off the drugs?"

"Horrible. All of the symptoms are still there, but worse. My sleep has gotten worse. I wake in the morning feeling like I just ran a marathon. I'm not getting any real rest. I doubt I've seen REM sleep in months now. I wish he'd just kill me already because this feels worse than death."

From outside the door, the doctors heard, "You are such a complainer. You've only been here for four months. Wait until you've been here for a year. Then, you'll really wish you were dead."

"Don't listen to him. We don't have much time. Let's take care of that prostate exam."

Silberman dropped his pants and grabbed the table. He shot up onto his toes when Yoshida's lubricated, gloved index finger penetrated his rectum and massaged his prostate.

"It all feels normal here. It's not enlarged or excessively warm." Yoshida withdrew his finger. "Okay, you can pull up your pants." Yoshida threw out his rubber glove and handed Silberman a few tissues to clean up. "I don't think you have a prostate problem. I'm not sure what it is, but your prostate doesn't feel abnormal."

"How the hell would you know?"

"Give me a little credit, Doc. Flaunting your ego isn't going to help either of us. Apparently you've not noticed that I'm not exactly feeling so hot myself. I've started getting up in the middle of the night to urinate as well. I've begun experiencing hot flashes in the morning, too, among other issues. I'd say I'm pretty invested in finding a cure to this, wouldn't you?" Yoshida's eyes sent Silberman his message loud and clear.

"Sorry, sorry. I'm just at my wits end here. I've never been sick like this."

"You aren't sick—it's all psychosomatic!" Steve taunted them from the platform. A big smile came across his face.

"Go to hell!" Silberman yelled back. "I'm gonna kill you when I get the chance!"

"You are welcome to spend your remaining twenty minutes here with me on the platform."

Silence. It appeared Steve was enjoying their plight in a way only a sociopath might. This scared both doctors more than the prospect of living with their symptoms for the rest of their lives.

"That's what I thought." Steve laughed.

"Forget him. Let's get back to work." Yoshida tried to focus Silberman on the task at hand. "I suggest we do a blood panel, stool analysis, and urinalysis. We need some data to work with."

"Fine, you call the bastard to tell him."

Yoshida yelled through the slot in the door, "We want to run some tests. How do we go about doing that?"

The door unlocked and swung open.

"This way," Steve led them to the lab. "You'll find all of the equipment you need over there." He pointed to the door in the far wall that said "Lab." "You have five minutes to draw blood and store it in the mini-fridge over there."

Steve supervised the procedure. When they finished, Yoshida asked, "What about the other tests, urinalysis and stool analysis?"

"Each of your rooms is equipped with specimen collection kits. He can do that outside of your appointment."

Steve returned them to Yoshida's room where they finished up their appointment. When Steve came to take Silberman back to his room, Yoshida informed Steve of his latest recommendation—a change to Silberman's diet.

"Since you control the food, we need your cooperation."

"Sure, I'll agree to that."

"Will this be for my food as well?"

"Once you demonstrate you can cure Dr. Silberman, then you'll have earned your cure, too. Until then, your routine will continue as planned. Keep the pen and paper. Provide me with a menu and list of recipes later today. Only include items found in a standard grocery store."

Once Silberman provided his samples, Steve took Yoshida to the lab to work up the results.

"You want me to do this? I've not used these machines in years. My lab techs do this work for me, or we ship samples to an offsite lab."

"You'll find the manuals and assays over there to test for every kind of condition. I suggest you get busy reading and educating yourself on the equipment. It's not like you have much else to do here."

"Fine," Yoshida retorted.

Chapter 30

Boston

After three days of experimenting, Yoshida finally figured out how to use the equipment by testing his own samples. This way he would not waste Silberman's samples sitting in the refrigerator.

A follow-up appointment had been scheduled to review the test results.

"So what are the results, Doc?" Silberman asked as he limped into the room. Yoshida picked his head up from the clipboard in his hand. His eyes were dark and puffy. His weary-looking face told Silberman that his condition was now moving into a full-blown state. "God, you look awful!"

"Look who's talking," Yoshida responded.

"So what do I have?"

"High cholesterol and high blood sugar."

"What? That's it? I could have told you that," Silberman replied.

"That's it. There is nothing in your blood work to indicate anything wrong. In fact, your cholesterol and blood sugar aren't even that high. Both your urine and stool samples were free of pathogens. I don't know what to tell you."

Steve's voice intruded as he locked the door behind Silberman. "It's psychosomatic!" He began laughing loudly.

"If I didn't know what you've been exposed to here, I'd probably say that, too. But clearly something is going on," Yoshida said.

"Obviously something is going on! Don't you think I know that? Let me see those papers!" Silberman snatched the results out of Yoshida's hand.

"Those are both of our results," Yoshida said. "I used my own samples to calibrate the machines."

When Silberman was sufficiently satisfied with the accuracy of the results, he handed them back to Yoshida with a disappointed look on his face.

"How's the new diet working out for you?" Yoshida asked.

"Some of the gastro issues have subsided. However, my constipation comes and goes, along with other issues. The diet has not had much impact on my sleep, nocturia, hot flashes, etc. Are you now suffering from all of these, too?"

"Unfortunately, yes," Yoshida said. "Okay, let's do a quick rundown of your vitals." He took Silberman's pulse, measured his blood pressure, listened to his lung capacity, tested his reflexes, measured his gait, and observed the alignment of his hips and spine. The efforts were fruitless.

Frustrated with Yoshida's lack of creativity, Silberman took control of the meeting. "Let's start with what we know. First, our symptoms. We both can't sleep. We wake in the middle of the night to urinate, among other urogenital issues. You said you are starting to get hot flashes, too. Our eyes hurt. My hair has turned gray already—gray! In four months! We have issues digesting food. And it feels like more symptoms come each week—itchy skin, nose bleeds, abdominal distension, cold feet, vertigo, and numb fingers, to mention a few. Would you agree that covers the major symptoms as they stand now?"

"Agreed." Yoshida nodded as he jotted down the symptoms.

"Now let's identify all the things that have changed in our lives. Stress is the obvious one. I'll give him that. There is a part of this that's probably psychosomatic. However, if you are feeling what I feel, I think you'd agree this doesn't feel psychosomatic."

"How can you say that? The fact that you feel it due to stress is the definition of psychosomatic," Yoshida said sarcastically. "We're basically walking definitions of the word."

"I know what it means!" Silberman's temper was rising. "This goes way beyond the tense muscles and indigestion most people get when they are overly stressed. Constantly living in fear is in a whole other category. Let's just finish the list and debate the semantics later. We have stress, both physical and emotional, a terrible diet, and a terrible bed."

"Acupuncture. What the hell is he doing to us with the needles?" Yoshida asked.

"I don't know," Silberman muttered.

"That's only five things—five seemingly innocuous things. While I actually do agree with you that the symptoms feel very real, stress is known to cause all of these problems—and he stopped giving you acupuncture weeks ago. In fact, he hardly even attends to you now. You're eating a healthy diet and shouldn't fear being beaten."

"You always fear being beaten here!" Silberman countered. "It's like I've developed PTSD. Don't you feel that way?"

"I guess. All I'm saying is that of the five things we've listed, the only things you're dealing with are a terrible bed and the stress of being held against your will. What if we prescribe you something for anxiety? Lorazepam. It won't solve the causes of PTSD, if that is in fact what's going on here, but it will help with your main symptom—anxiety. If that doesn't work, we can try Ambien or Lunesta for your sleep. Improving your sleep may help solve some of these problems."

Yoshida handed Steve a prescription when he returned to take Silberman.

Lorazepam (1 mg x 2 per day)

Chapter 31

Boston

For the next six weeks, Silberman remained on Lorazepam. While he was sleeping better and experiencing fewer hot flashes, the drug-induced calm did nothing to improve his urinary, sexual, or digestive functions. During this period, several other drugs were added and removed with all of them failing. Without fixing his most important symptom, impotence, the doctors would never be freed.

Dr. Yoshida was now experiencing full-blown symptoms. His pain became more evident each time he staggered to the platform. Like Silberman, Yoshida was now waking every two hours to urinate and experiencing alternating chills and hot flashes throughout the day. He was also showing dark circles under his eyes and a growing midsection as his body stored fat in response to the elevated stress levels.

Despite the multitude of symptoms, it was evident that the inability to have sex was the most bothersome symptom for both men. Every time Steve opened either doctor's door slot, he found him lying in his cot with his pants around his ankles trying frantically to obtain or maintain an erection.

"How's it going down there, Dr. Silberman? Still not working?"

"Go to hell!"

"I'd say 'you first,' but it looks like you're already there."

"Get me some Viagra so I can test it." Silberman's eyes were full of despair.

"Do you really want Viagra? What if you develop priapism?" Steve asked.

"I don't care!"

"Seeing as we don't have the meds to cure it, I'm pretty sure you'll care once it happens. Anyhow, you know the rules. If you can't solve your sexual issues naturally, how can you claim you're the leading expert in male sexual dysfunction? It will taste that much sweeter when your claims are merit based. Wouldn't you agree?"

"I'm not so naïve to believe you're actually going to let us go. After all of this, you'd be arrested and incarcerated. While I think you're crazy, I don't think you're stupid."

"Thanks for the compliment—I think," Steve said. "But if the day comes when you've finally solved your issues, it means you'll have learned something useful with which to help others. I can't stand in the way of progress. If I did, it would make my efforts a waste."

"Learned something? What the hell am I supposed to be learning here—how to torture someone?"

Chapter 32

Boston

Seeing the doctors suffer through the same symptoms gave Steve a feeling of vindication from the psychosomatic label that had burdened him for years. However, pain and humiliation alone would fall short of his intended goals. Until the doctors experienced his complete journey—pain, fear, humiliation, reeducation, and recovery—they would never see the world differently. They would never fully understand their patients' plights, or develop the compassion required to heal them. True vindication would only come if the doctors could discover and experience the healing process for themselves.

It was clear that they weren't making any progress. In fact, they weren't even close. Silberman was right. The only thing they had learned was pain. On occasion, Steve had to remind himself that pain was only the first step—a necessary step—to bringing about any sort of reeducation. It was a motivator. He knew simply making an appointment to tell the doctors about his healing process would have been dismissed as psychosomatic symptoms that spontaneously resolved themselves. He also knew that they would return to business as usual—poisoning patients from the same pharmaceutical punch bowl that made them rich year after year.

While he could rationalize the necessity of torture, a feeling that he was losing sight of his goals, and himself, grew stronger the deeper he got into his plan. This feeling was reinforced on multiple occasions when the objective part of his mind witnessed a darker side emerge. There was a perverted sense of joy he felt, a pleasure he was taking in the doctors' suffering, something he had hoped to guard against. Despite feelings of guilt that sporadically surfaced, he found it difficult to stop. He had no intention of turning back, but he was no longer sure where he was going from here.

Once Doctor Silberman reached a pathological state, he realized that he was stuck somewhere between the introduction he had carefully orchestrated and one of two fates awaiting the doctors. He wanted to give them enough time to find their way from point A to point B. However, more time meant more pain. He was wrestling with questions about how much was enough, whether it still served as a proper motivator, and how long he should give them to solve their problems.

He thought suffering through his symptomatology would have provided enough motivation to find a cure or at least think outside of the box. However, with time marching on, and their faculties waning, he realized he might have to make a decision that he had hoped to avoid.

Chapter 33

Boston

A cold look came over Steve's face. "If you aren't learning anything, you might be right."

"Right about what?"

"That I should just kill you both and get on with life."

"No! That's not what I said! Those are your words, not mine!" Silberman's voice quivered.

"Sure. But, at this point, I think it's time to admit defeat. My little experiment here doesn't seem to be going as planned. In reality, it was flawed from the beginning."

"Flawed?" Silberman shouted as his eyelid began twitching nervously.

"Yes, flawed. My initial assumption was that you, and all the other doctors I saw, simply dismissed my symptoms as psychosomatic without ever putting any real effort into researching the underlying causes. I figured that if you had proper motivation, such as actually experiencing the symptoms, you might take it seriously enough to find a cure. I was wrong. You were never capable in the first place. I gave you too much credit. My bad."

"My bad?" Silberman hollered. "What the hell does that mean—my bad? My bad, so now I'm going to kill you?"

"Look, it's not been a total loss. Watching someone who repeatedly told others he had all the answers—someone who believed he was God—fail to find his own answers made this all worth the effort. In the end, I was asking too much of you."

"If you could solve it, I can solve it too! You had fifteen years to do it, I've only had a few months!"

"That's just it. I don't have another fifteen years to waste—especially on someone like you. To be clear, I didn't solve it—someone else did. Furthermore, I was never trained in medicine. You've had more than twenty years in practice, not to mention medical school before that. That's it. I've made up my mind. We're done here."

Steve opened the door.

"Get up. Let's go. You're going to the platform with me."

"Wait! Two more weeks! Give me two more weeks—I can do it—" Silberman cowered in the corner.

"No. You've had your time."

Steve grabbed Silberman's foot and dragged him off the cot. The doctor crashed to the floor, slamming his tailbone on the concrete as he let out a loud yell. Steve stepped behind the doctor and dazed him with a strike to the back of the head. He then pulled Silberman's arm behind his back and drove it up until the pain snapped the doctor out of his dazed state. Silberman began panting like a dog to alleviate the pain. Steve forced the doctor to his feet and proceeded to walk him to the far corner of the platform, guiding him with the trapped arm.

Silberman tried to struggle, but every effort only served to tighten the lock, making him comply even quicker. He tried to stay ahead of the pain, but Steve was pulling backward on his shoulder, preventing him from escaping the lock.

Once they reached the corner, Steve forced Silberman onto his knees and unleashed two strikes to his head and neck, landing on earth and wood points. The doctor lay sprawled out on the platform. As Steve descended the stairs, he thought, *it's time to bring this all to an end.*

Next, the slot to Yoshida's door opened. "You, too?" Steve asked sarcastically. Yoshida was also on his cot with his hand in his pants and having no success. "Button up your pants and meet us on the platform." The door unlocked and opened a crack.

"What? What are we going to the platform for?"

"Just get to the platform," Steve ordered.

When Yoshida reached the top of the stairs, he saw Silberman lying unconscious in the corner and quickly assumed a fighting stance. The mechanical way in which he stepped backward, drew his arms up, and clenched his fists caught Steve's attention. Years of blind repetition had become visible, sending his thoughts down a path.

His mind began skipping along tangential thoughts between Yoshida's attacks, focusing on the doctor's arsenal of blocks, punches, and kicks. They were linear and hard, similar to his Western approach to fighting disease. *He has all the right techniques, but no understanding of what they mean.*

Steve's mind emerged from its internal dialogue to put an end to the fight. Parrying a punch to his face, he moved in and unloaded a series of strikes that moved up the doctor's arm and finished with an elbow to the torso. Yoshida collapsed a few feet from Silberman.

Steve stood over the unconscious doctors for a minute thinking through his next steps. *Practice doesn't make perfect. Perfect practice makes perfect. How can you make perfect practice if you don't even know what perfect means?*

Ten minutes later, the doctors came to, aided by Steve. Yoshida was the first to wake. He looked on as Steve repeatedly drew his hand up Silberman's spine. Each time he reached the neck, he gave it a moderate slap and clutched it vigorously to massage it. Silberman's eyes were slowly turning lucid as life returned to his face.

A blank whiteboard and easel sat before them. On the easel hung an anatomical poster detailing the different energy channels, including their associated acupuncture points and Chinese names translated into English.

"What's this?" Yoshida asked, pointing to the boards.

"A test."

"A test? I thought you were going to kill me!" Silberman yelled.

"I was—and still might," Steve replied with a matter-of-fact tone.

"What kind of test?" Yoshida continued probing.

"It's pass-fail," Steve said. "Pass and you live. Fail and you—well, you don't want to fail."

"Oh, that kind of test," Silberman said sarcastically.

"When I started this, I wanted you to suffer as I had—"

"Well, it worked!" Silberman blurted out.

Steve ignored Silberman's antics and turned his attention to Yoshida. "I anticipated that your training would have hindered your progress, but eventually you would find a solution. However, we've reached a point where your training has now become the debilitating factor. Neither of you have produced a single new idea in weeks. You started out strong with the change in diet, but then you fell right back into treating it with drugs. If you want a good analogy to your progress, think about your martial arts training. Why does a martial artist practice the same movements over and over?"

"To make them second nature," Yoshida answered. "You don't have time to think in a fight, only react."

"Exactly," Steve said. "In a fight, your adrenaline takes over, and all fine motor skills go out the window. You're only left with gross motor skills. Most students who get into fights will tell you that, regardless of their level, they relied upon the things they learned as white and yellow belts to win. These are the simplest movements that they've been practicing the longest—and they require the least amount of dexterity. This is what's happening to your minds. The stress has dampened your creative abilities to think outside the box. You are falling back on the same things you've done in your practices for the past twenty years—throwing drugs at the problem."

"So now what?" Silberman asked in a skeptical tone.

Steve continued to ignore Silberman. "The biggest irony here is that you're actually sitting on all of the answers and don't even know it."

"I am?" Yoshida looked perplexed.

"It struck me as you assumed your fighting stance. You practiced *katas* as a child, didn't you?"

Growing more irritated by the minute, Silberman ripped his way back into the conversation, "What the hell's a *kata*?"

Yoshida turned to address him. "*Kata* is Japanese for 'form.' It's a choreographed routine of movements—blocks, punches, kicks, and other types of strikes that are often accompanied by colorful stories. When I was young, I was made to practice them in our backyard. Neighborhood kids used to watch through a hole in our fence and make fun of me at school—"

"There are 108 common *katas*," Steve said, interrupting Yoshida, "that a teacher would pass on to students. Most practice these routines over and over without ever understanding their meanings. If you were an obnoxious student, like yourself," his eyes zoomed in on Silberman. "The teacher probably wouldn't trust you with such knowledge. When you understand the meaning of the *katas*, you will finally have the tools to start healing yourself." Steve turned to Dr. Yoshida. "Do you remember any *katas* from your childhood?"

"Sure, my first *kata*. It was quite simple, but my grandfather still made me practice it twenty-four times a day, saying the same story over and over. God, I hated him for it at the time."

"Ironically, it just may be the thing that saves you here," Steve said. "Show us the *kata* and describe the motions you make. Tell us the story."

Doctor Yoshida stood and walked to the center of the platform. Standing firmly with his feet together, he snapped his elbows backward, bringing his fists next to his waist, and stepped laterally into a horse stance. His knees were bent with his feet slightly more than shoulder width apart. This was the starting position of the *kata*.

He stepped backward with his right foot creating a left foot forward fighting stance. "To reach enlightenment, travel the inner passage of the mountains." His left arm scooped across his body and swung up over his head to imitate a block with his forearm. His right fist remained next to his waist.

"Look for the point where rivers run dry." Yoshida feigned a grab of the imaginary attacker's arm with his left hand, which was still positioned over his head.

"There you will find the muddy waters of the valley." He stepped forward with his right foot and brought the attacker's arm down to chest height. He then chopped downward with his right hand.

"Break down the flood gates to water the fields." After completing the downward chop, Yoshida made a horizontal chopping motion, as if to strike his opponent in the chest.

"When food grows in the fields, store it in the great tower gate." The doctor executed two punches, one with each hand before stepping backward into a defensive posture.

"Very good, doctor. Now, what does it all mean?"

"I don't know. I was only seven years old."

"Okay. I want you to start again, and stop after the initial movement," Steve instructed.

Yoshida nodded and got into position. He stepped backward with his right foot and blocked overhead with his left arm. "To reach enlightenment, travel the inner passage of the mountains."

Steve walked over to the doctor. "In this move, you are the mountain. Look at your firm stance." Yoshida's wide triangular stance made his body look like a sturdy mountain. "Your arm carves a path through the mountain, through the inner passage. What is the purpose of this movement?"

"To block a punch," Yoshida said emphatically.

"'To reach enlightenment, travel the inner passage of the mountains.' Your arm carves a path through the mountain, through the 'inner passage.'" Steve emphasized the last phrase as he pretended to throw a punch that would have been blocked by the ridge of the doctor's forearm, which was still hanging in midair. His eyes looked toward the easel where the anatomical diagram littered with acupuncture points hung. Intent on directing Yoshida's eyes to follow, he continued tapping the doctor's forearm as he repeated the phrase "inner passage" and turning his head toward the board.

Yoshida eventually understood. Within a minute of scanning the diagram, his eyes landed on a point a few inches above the wrist, precisely where Steve was tapping. He quietly read aloud, "Inner Pass." His voice indicated an air of disbelief.

Steve tapped his forearm against Yoshida's again and asked, "Do you still think it's a block?"

Astonished, Yoshida answered, "So everything I was doing was incorrect."

"Not exactly. You had the right movements, but no understanding. The only way your karate would be effective is with a lot of luck." Steve pointed to Silberman. "Get up. You're going to be his *uke.*"

"His what? What the hell just happened?" Silberman demanded.

"He just bridged the gap in my family's legacy that was broken thirty years ago," Yoshida answered. "The block was not a block."

"Wow. The block was not a block," Silberman said sarcastically. "Then what the hell was it?"

"It was a strike—to a pressure point." Yoshida turned back to Steve. "Does every line in this poem have the same type of hidden meaning?"

"I would bet every line in all of the *katas* you learned have these embedded meanings. This is where your test will begin. For the next thirty minutes, you will use Doctor Silberman as your *uke*—'training partner'—to find all of the points." Steve turned to Silberman. "You're going to give him your arm to work with as he pieces together the *kata*."

Silberman was slow to stand up. He stood in front of Yoshida and held up his fist as if he had just thrown a punch.

Yoshida pretended to make the initial block, tapping the Inner Pass point. He then grabbed Silberman's arm where he blocked it and said, "Look for the point where rivers run dry." They both turned their heads to look at the diagram. Yoshida repeated the sentence a few more times as they scanned the points.

"It could be any of these," Silberman said out of frustration as he pointed to the myriad of dots running along the inside of the wrist.

"Use the sentence to figure it out," Yoshida replied.

"What do you think I'm doing?" Silberman retorted. He began reading the points aloud, "Broken Sequence, Channel Ditch, Great Abyss, Spirit Gate, Yin Cleft—as if I know what the hell a Yin Cleft is."

"It's obvious from the sentence that we are looking for something related to water. I'm going with Channel Ditch—a channel is a waterway." He looked to Steve for some indication of approval.

"It's your test, not mine. Write your answers on the whiteboard and call me when you're finished." Steve threw Yoshida a marker and walked into the kitchenette to prepare lunch.

A half hour later, he heard a hesitant voice call out, "We're done ... I think."

When he returned to the platform, Steve saw the list of points on the board and instructed Yoshida to perform the *kata* on Silberman, describing how they arrived at each point.

Doctor Yoshida assumed a horse stance as Silberman punched cautiously into the air. Yoshida stepped backward to execute the first movement. "To reach enlightenment, travel the inner passage of the mountains. Inner Pass. You gave us that one."

Steve nodded.

Yoshida's voice faltered as he began moving into unfamiliar territory. He grabbed Silberman's wrist and said, "Look for the point where rivers run dry. Channel Ditch?"

"Is that a question?" Steve asked.

"Yes."

"When you grab someone's wrist, aren't you grabbing two points—one with your thumb and the other with your index or middle finger?" Steve asked.

"I told you there were two points," Silberman remarked.

"Look for the point where rivers run dry," Steve added. "Go ahead—actually look. Turn the wrist over. Where is your middle finger pressing?"

Yoshida scoured the diagram. "It looks like the fifth point on the heart line. The Connecting Li point."

Steve fought to restrain his smile. *Channel Ditch, one of a few Jing River points in the body, combined with Connecting Li, a point for incontinence and excessive bleeding. Very clever—a river that suffers from incontinence will run dry,* he thought. "What happens to his body after you turn the wrist?"

Yoshida torqued Silberman's arm a little further. "He's forced to twist, opening his body up for the next strike."

"Correct. What does it say next?"

"'There you will find the muddy waters of the valley.' His arm creates a *V.* Is this supposed to be the valley?" Yoshida asked.

"Yes. Good. Now, what's the next point?"

Yoshida lightly chopped the crease of Silberman's elbow. "Cubit Marsh. This was the only name in the vicinity that resembled muddy waters."

"Okay. What's next?"

"Break down the flood gates to water the fields." Yoshida chopped horizontally with the hand that just struck downward.

"What are you striking?" Steve asked.

"The Cycle Gate."

"This is the last point along the liver meridian," Steve added. "Please continue."

"When food grows in the fields, store—"

"This is two verses," Steve interrupted. "You have two strikes. Separate them."

"Right." Yoshida nodded as if he was bowing to his sensei. "When food grows in the fields—" He punched with his left hand.

"The point?" Steve motioned to the diagram.

"When food grows—Food Hole." Yoshida's face revealed an increased level of confidence.

"What the hell's a food hole?" Silberman continued showing his frustration.

"What the hell do you think it is?" Steve shot back sarcastically.

"I don't know. Why else would I ask—?"

"Really? In your body, you can't think of an organ that you could call a food hole?" Steve replied. "He's punching a point along the spleen meridian. In Chinese medicine, the spleen, stomach, and pancreas are related organs. As such, this system involves food."

Still confused, Silberman continued probing, "What's the purpose of all of this? And what the hell is a meridian?"

"Meridian is another word for channel. The points you just spent the last half hour staring at form channels—or meridians. Didn't you notice the lines running through them? Each channel corresponds to an organ. Don't confuse these channels with nerves or veins. It's a different concept, and it's what I've been using to knock you out and make you sick. If you can learn the theory behind this, you can use it to reverse the process and make yourself better. So I suggest you start paying closer attention." Steve looked at Yoshida. "Okay, continue."

"Store it in the great tower gate." The doctor executed the final punch and then stepped backward.

"And, which point?"

"Great Tower Gate." The doctor pointed to the center line of the body, a meridian known as the Conception Vessel. "They saved the easiest one for last."

"Good, this point causes heart-related issues," Steve added.

Silberman interrupted again, "This is all just fine and dandy! Now, what the hell does it all mean? How does this help me get better?"

"It doesn't. This is called *dim mak*, or death touch. It's a combination of pressure points that will subdue your opponent by either knocking him out or killing him. When your friend here learned *katas* as a child, he was actually learning *dim mak*. If he knew what it all meant, he could be lethal."

"So he could kick your ass once he learns the meaning?"

"I wouldn't go that far." Steve laughed as he reflected on the years of private instruction he was afforded in the back alley schools of Chinatown. "What you should be focusing on here is that martial art practices, like those Dr. Yoshida learned, found their roots in Chinese medicine. The same medicine I've been using to make you sick can be used to cure you. You know, it's the same medicine that you laughed at years ago."

"Medicine? More like poison," Silberman retorted. "I don't care what you say. This is not medicine. It's torture!"

"There's a saying in Chinese medicine—'that which heals also kills.' If you take Chinese medicine in excess, you could exacerbate the very problem you are trying to cure. It's similar to how pressure points can be used for both healing and death. So far, I've only used them to bring you one step away from 'death.'"

"You never actually said if any of these points are correct." Yoshida interrupted.

"That's right, I didn't. I told you this was a test."

"If you don't tell us the answers, how do we know if we passed?" Silberman snapped.

"You're about to find out."

"What do you mean?" Yoshida asked.

"The test isn't over yet." Steve looked at Silberman. "Give me your shirt."

"Why?" Silberman challenged him.

"You can either give it to me or I'll take it. Option two will hurt a lot more. It's your choice," Steve calmly replied.

"Fine." Silberman glared at Steve as he peeled off his shirt and tossed it on the ground.

Steve directed Yoshida's attention toward the marker. "Take the pen and draw the points on his body. Tell me the names as you do it."

Yoshida grabbed the pen and began marking up Silberman's pale skin. He repeated the *kata* under his breath as he located the points on the chart and called them out. When he finished, he turned back to Steve.

"Good. Now, knock him out," Steve said.

"Excuse me!" Silberman roared.

"This is the test. It's the only way you'll know if you found the right points."

"Why don't you just tell us if we're right?" Silberman shouted.

"Where's the fun in that? If he knocks you out, you'll see another day. If not, I'll finish what I started earlier." Steve glared back at Silberman. "You have forty-five minutes. You better get going."

Sweat began pouring from Silberman's brow. His body tensed up as Yoshida approached him.

"Don't worry." Yoshida tried to calm Silberman's nerves. "How many times have you been knocked out here? It's nothing you haven't already experienced."

"How about if I knock him out?" Silberman pleaded with Steve.

"When you have a *kata*, he can be your *uke*." Steve was enjoying this.

"Just put your arm up and let's get this over with," Yoshida said as he got into position.

"That's easy for you to say," Silberman replied as he put his right fist level with Yoshida's head.

Yoshida cautiously blocked Silberman's forearm, grabbed his wrist, turned it over and chopped at his elbow. He then twisted his torso to tap Silberman's chest before executing the two punches. His guarded movements showed a focus on accuracy over power.

"Who are you planning on knocking out with those pansy taps? I want you to hit him!" Steve yelled.

"I need to become comfortable with the points," Yoshida replied.

"That's why I had you draw the points on him. Hit him. Now!" As Steve became more animated, Silberman's body grew visibly tenser—exactly what Steve wanted. Tension disrupts the flow of energy, which would make it easier for Yoshida to knock out his *uke*.

Silberman appeared apprehensive as Yoshida signaled him to start. Yoshida snapped his arm up to block Silberman's punch.

"Ouch!" Silberman retracted his arm and began waving it around to relieve the sting.

"That's not helping. Let's go. Again!" Steve commanded.

As Silberman punched again, the bones in Yoshida's wrist met the black ink on his forearm. He let out a shriek as the strike intensified the pain of the prior hit. Yoshida clutched Silberman's wrist before he could pull it away again. When Yoshida turned the wrist over, his fingers were naturally digging into the two pressure points.

"Hit him harder!" Steve yelled, raising the tension in the room.

Yoshida stepped in with his right foot and smashed his fist into the inside of Silberman's elbow, using enough force to pull the aging doctor off of his feet.

"Keep going! Faster!" Steve continued pushing them.

Yoshida rotated at his waist to snap the ridge of his hand into the flabby meat of Silberman's peck.

"Wrong point!" Steve yelled. "Start over!"

Silberman's face was turning red as the pain sent his heart into overdrive. He wearily threw another punch and the edge of Yoshida's left wrist whacked the point. The sting echoed across Silberman's face. Yoshida gripped the wrist and turned it over as he stepped in. He drove the ridge of his right hand into the Cubit Marsh point, and Silberman let out a loud cry. Yoshida rotated at the waist and landed a chop into Silberman's ribcage, catching the correct point—slightly below the right peck.

Silberman's natural reaction was to recoil in response to the pain, however, he was held in place by Yoshida who was still hanging onto his wrist. Yoshida dropped the arm and stepped in to punch with his left fist, landing a blow on the outside of Silberman's peck. He took another step to finish off Silberman with the final strike, landing it an inch below the sternum.

Silberman crashed to the mat. He was hurt and gasping for air, but not knocked out.

"Again!" Steve demanded. "Twenty-two minutes remain on the clock if you want to live."

The two doctors repeated the *kata* a dozen more times. Silberman screamed, recoiled, and objected with each new round of punishment. Pressured by Steve, Yoshida continued hitting harder with each new series of strikes.

Round after round repeated the same moves—overhead block, rotation of the wrist, downward chop, chop to the chest, and a series of punches. Yoshida was moving through it at a blinding pace. With little time left on the clock, he began sacrificing accuracy for speed and power in an effort to complete as many attempts as possible. He moved in for the final blow but Silberman wasn't there—he had collapsed. With three minutes remaining on the clock, Yoshida had knocked Silberman out.

Whether it was from the sheer amount of pain or accurate striking didn't matter, Yoshida had done it. He turned to Steve with a big smile, only to meet Steve's hands landing knock out blows to his head and neck.

"It's only fair," Steve said as Yoshida collapsed next to Silberman.

Chapter 34

Boston

Early the next morning, Steve summoned the doctors to the platform. He watched as Silberman hobbled up the stairs—his balance was wobbly. The prior day had taken its toll on him.

"Welcome to the second day of your test." He directed the men to take their seats at a folding table he had positioned in front of the whiteboard. Notepads and pens sat on the table next to concierge bells, one for each man.

"What's all this?" Silberman asked.

"Since you didn't like being the default *uke* yesterday, I decided to make it a merit-based decision today. You'll be asked a series of questions, eleven in total, valued at one point each. The loser will be today's *uke*. The paper in front of you is for notes and answers, and the bells are your make-shift game show buzzers. Yesterday, you got a taste of the theory. Today, you will begin deciphering the nuts and bolts of it." Steve turned to Yoshida. "Dr. Yoshida, did your grandfather talk about the five elements?"

"No, but my mother did."

"Good. What are they?"

"Let me think." Yoshida paused for a minute. "Fire is one of them."

"What's the opposite of fire?" Steve asked.

"Water?"

"Correct."

Yoshida took another minute. "I think earth, metal, and wood are the others—right?"

"Yes, that's right." Steve wrote them on the left side of the board. "How did you hear about them? In what context did she mention them?"

"She used to talk about them when cooking."

"Do you remember any examples?"

"The only one that comes to my mind right now isn't even food related."

"That's fine. Let's hear it," Steve insisted.

"I remember her saying that a house shouldn't have a bathroom that faces into the kitchen because having water too close to fire is bad luck. I wasn't sure what she meant by this. Most of these saying were like a foreign language to me—a bunch of superstitions I never understood."

"This is an example of how the elements might be used in feng shui. For thousands of years, the Five Elements Theory permeated all aspects of Chinese culture from martial arts to sexual practices." Steve paused to let his words sink in. "Can you think of anything specific from her cooking?"

"Yes, now I remember something she used to say, 'every meal needs something from each element to keep you balanced.'

I always thought she meant something from the four food groups, but it looks like that too was just another saying I never understood."

"According to the Five Elements Theory, everything in nature belongs to one of these elements. Each element has its own set of qualities that help define it. For example, each element has its own distinct flavor, emotion, smell, and color. Since each of your organs are also labeled as earth, water, fire, wood, or metal, they are associated with the flavors, emotions, smells, and colors of their corresponding elements. Your mother was probably talking about flavors."

"My organs have flavors?" Silberman asked, conveying a hint of ridicule.

"Yes, in the sense that each organ has a flavor that influences it. Personally, I think it's easy to see how flavors can influence your organs. Consider a spicy dish. What happens when you eat something spicy?"

"My sinuses clear up," Silberman answered. "But other people might sweat or get overheated. Everyone presents different symptoms."

"Let's stick with your sinuses. Which internal organ are your nose and sinuses most closely related to? Kidneys? Spleen? Heart? Lungs? Liver?"

"Lungs," Yoshida answered.

"Good."

"The flavor of the lungs is spicy?" Silberman laughed. "This is supposed to be medicine!"

"What if I had said sugar? What would your answer have been?"

"The pancreas," responded Silberman, "because there's scientific evidence that the pancreas produces insulin in response to sugar. What evidence is there that spicy foods affect the lungs?"

"And, what if I had said salt?" Steve continued.

"Kidneys, obviously. They regulate blood pressure by balancing sodium levels in the body."

"And coffee?"

"Coffee isn't a flavor," Silberman retorted.

"Neither is sugar, but you didn't have a problem giving me an answer. What flavor does coffee have?"

"Are you trying to tell me that because coffee is bitter it has an effect on the heart?"

"No. I'm saying that all bitter foods have an effect on the heart. So far, you've told me four body parts that are affected by four foods, each with distinctly different flavors," Steve said, as Silberman smirked. "From the expression on your face, I can already see you're getting ready to challenge me on the lungs example, so I'll say this—in Chinese medicine, the skin is related to the lungs. Since the other spice-related symptoms you described were skin related, they are in turn related to the lungs, which means the lungs are influenced by spicy foods."

"Convenient," Silberman muttered.

"I guess you'd also say it's convenient that most people with respiratory conditions suffer from skin related symptoms—i.e. asthmatics. Or, maybe you'd say it's convenient that the two most common forms of cancer are skin and lung cancer—and people who have had skin cancer are at higher risk of developing lung cancer. In Chinese medicine, we treat the whole person because everything in the body is connected. When you specialize, you limit your ability to see the entire patient and diagnose their condition. Now, moving on. Which element do you think the lungs and pungent flavors are associated with? Any idea? Earth? Water? Fire—?"

"No clue," Yoshida said as he turned to Silberman, who just sat looking aggravated.

"I guess that part isn't as obvious, but it does lead us to our first question." Steve drew a pentagon next to the list of elements on the board. "One of the keys to finding your health lies in the Cycle of Creation."

"What the hell is that?" Silberman interjected.

"The Cycle of Creation describes one way the five elements interact with each other. For the first question, you need to figure out the pattern—the order in which each element helps the next. To show you what I mean, I'll get you started with an example. We'll start with wood." Steve wrote "Wood" next to one of the points on the pentagon. "Look at the list of elements and tell me which element is made stronger by wood. Is it water? Does wood make water stronger? Or, is it metal? Maybe fire—?"

"Fire," Yoshida answered.

"Good. I think this question is simple enough," Steve said as he wrote "Fire" adjacent to the point following wood. "Now, you need to find the element that fire helps make stronger. You need to do this for each element until you complete the pentagon. The first person to answer correctly wins this round. Ring your bell when you've finished."

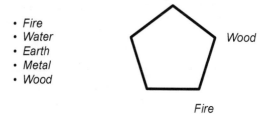

- *Fire*
- *Water*
- *Earth*
- *Metal*
- *Wood*

Wood

Fire

"Piece of cake," Silberman uttered under his breath.

A minute later, Yoshida slammed his bell.

"Hell, he had an unfair advantage," Silberman complained. "He grew up with these things. You should have given me a head start."

"Why don't you wait to see if he even got the answers right?" Steve replied. "Go ahead, tell us what you have."

"Wood, fire, earth, metal, and water."

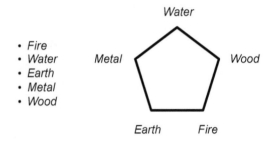

"Correct. Can you explain how you got there?"

"It was simply a process of elimination. Fire wasn't going to help metal or water, so I chose earth, and so on. It had nothing to do with my heritage. I'm just smarter than you." Yoshida laughed.

"We'll see about that," Silberman replied.

"Okay, enough," Steve interjected. "Here's your next question. Match the elements on the pentagon to the organs you believe provide the best match. We'll start with another example. Which of these elements can grow organically?"

"Wood," Yoshida answered.

"So can fire," Silberman countered. "A wild fire consumes everything in its path, growing organically."

"That's true," Steve said. "Let me ask it a different way. Which of the elements has the ability to regenerate itself? If a fire goes out, can it regenerate itself?"

"No," replied Silberman, "not without external help."

"What about a tree? If you cut a tree's branch, does a new branch grow near the site of the old branch? When you think about it this way, which of these elements would you say has the ability to regenerate itself?"

"Wood," both doctors said in unison.

"Good. Which organ in the body also has this ability?"

"The liver," Yoshida answered. Silberman nodded in agreement.

"Do you understand the assignment?" Steve asked. "Match each element to an organ. You may begin."

A few minutes passed and Silberman pounded on his bell.

"If you break it," cautioned Steve, "you won't be able to answer future questions. Explain your answers."

"After wood and liver, I matched water with kidneys. The kidneys filter waste and produce urine—water. Next, I matched earth with pancreas because of the *kata*. 'Food grows in the fields.' Fields are earth, which you said was the spleen, pancreas and stomach. So, I chose pancreas. Then, I was left with fire and metal. The heart seemed like the most logical match for fire. And, by process of elimination, I matched metal with lungs. Am I right?"

"Yes, you are correct. The score is one to one." Steve drew a matrix on the whiteboard and began filling in the answers. "These organs you've listed are called *zang* organs. They are solid organs that perform most of the body's more complex processes. They are paired with *fu* organs, the hollow organs that transport much of what is taken in and excreted out. As you've probably guessed by now, your next question is to match the *zang* organs with the *fu* organs. As before, I'll provide you with an example to get you started. Doctor Silberman, you mentioned that the kidneys produce urine. How is urine transported out of the body?"

	Wood	Fire	Earth	Metal	Water
Zang	Liver	Heart	Spleen / Pancreas	Lung	Kidney

"Technically, it's transported out through the urethra," Silberman answered with a smile.

"There's no need to be so difficult all the time," Yoshida said. "He's obviously looking for bladder."

"Thank you," Steve said. "Same rules as before—ring the bell when you finish. Please begin."

A few minutes later, Silberman rang his bell. "Done!"

"Let's have it."

"After kidneys and bladder, the next logical combination is the liver and gallbladder. The liver secretes bile, which is transported through the gallbladder. I then paired the lungs with the large intestines. Every time you breathe in, your lungs impact the large intestine, increasing peristalsis. The pancreas is paired with the small intestine because pancreatic enzymes pass directly into the small intestine to digest food. And, finally, the heart is paired with the stomach because they were the only two left—maybe it's because stomach acid causes heartburn." Silberman laughed with confidence as he sat looking proud of his answers. It was the first genuine laugh Steve had seen him make during his captivity.

"Sorry, but you're wrong."

"What?" Silberman shot back.

"Some of your answers are right, but some are wrong. Care to take a stab at it Doctor Yoshida?"

"I had the same pairings," Yoshida replied.

"That's fine, you have nothing to lose by taking a guess," Steve encouraged him.

"Okay, I'll switch the last two. Heart goes with small intestine and pancreas with stomach."

	Wood	Fire	Earth	Metal	Water
Zang	Liver	Heart	Spleen / Pancreas	Lung	Kidney
Fu	Gall Bladder	Sm Intestine	Stomach	Lg Intestine	Bladder

"Correct. The score is two to one in Doctor Yoshida's favor."

"This is bullshit!" Silberman exclaimed.

"You're just a sore loser," Yoshida taunted his opponent.

An hour later, the matrix was complete and the two men were tied at five points apiece. After a short break, they had returned to their seats to hear the tiebreaker question. The pressure at the table was palpable. Whoever answered incorrectly would be the *uke* and receive an unknown number of blows until they were knocked out.

	Wood	Fire	Earth	Metal	Water
Zang	Liver	Heart	Spleen / Pancreas	Lung	Kidney
Fu	Gall Bladder	Sm Intestine	Stomach	Lg Intestine	Bladder
Color	Green	Red	Yellow	White	Black
Flavor	Sour	Bitter	Sweet	Spicy	Salt
Smell	Rancid	Scorched	Fragrant	Rotten	Putrid
Emotion	Anger	Joy	Worry	Sadness	Fear
Tissue	Tendons	Vessels	Muscle	Skin	Bones
Facial	Eyes	Tongue	Mouth	Nose	Ears
Seasons	Spring	Summer	Summer	Autumn	Winter

"Here's your final problem for the day. If there's a Cycle of Creation, doesn't it make sense that there's a Cycle of Destruction?" Steve asked.

Both doctors nodded, hanging on every word.

"Which cycle do you think the *kata* uses? The Cycle of—?"

"Destruction!" Silberman shouted as he smashed his bell. "Did I win?"

Steve disapprovingly shook his head. "No you didn't win. I haven't even gotten to the problem yet. Yes, it's the Cycle of Destruction. But, what is it? That's the problem. You must construct the Cycle of Destruction—tell me the order of the elements. I've written the *kata* on the board to serve as your example. Use it to help determine the relationships between the elements. Considering everything you've learned over the past two days, I think you have enough information to solve this. You may begin."

There was a stark contrast in the way each doctor approached the problem. Yoshida appeared to be focused on understanding the principles rather than being first to finish. He was working with one pentagon, carefully pondering each relationship before labeling them on his paper. Silberman, on the other hand, had scribbled out five pentagons with arrows pointing every which way. His logic appeared scattered across the page without any direction.

When Yoshida finished, he took a few seconds to look over his work and nodded—most likely a subconscious reaction to agreeing with his conclusions. The unconscious action signaled Silberman, who appeared far from reaching any solution. Without hesitation, Silberman's hand darted to the side, whacking his bell off the table.

Steve burst into laughter. "Do you actually have the answer or are you just trying to beat Dr. Yoshida to the bell?"

"I do," Silberman said. "It's backward. The cycle moves backward. Instead of water, wood, fire, earth, and metal, the cycle moves from metal to earth, then fire, wood, and finally—water."

"It's a good guess, but you're wrong," Steve replied. "Dr. Yoshida, do you have an answer?"

"Yes. I matched the order of the points in the *kata* with their corresponding elements." Yoshida looked at Silberman. "You even said it yourself. The *kata* uses the Cycle of Destruction, which is the order of the strikes."

"What can I say? I choked," Silberman responded.

"Come show us the order here on the whiteboard and explain how you got there."

Yoshida took the marker from Steve as he approached the board. He drew the first arrow—fire to metal. "The initial block, Inner Pass, was a fire point. Next, there was the grab which includes both fire and metal points. And, finally, the chop to the inside of the elbow is metal. The energy moves from fire to metal."

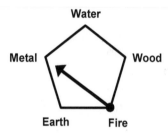

"Correct. Fire melts metal," Steve said. "Continue."

"After the chop to the elbow, there's the chop to the chest—a wood point." Yoshida drew an arrow from metal to wood.

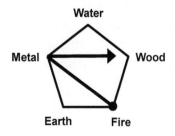

"Metal cuts wood," Steve added.

"After wood, there are two punches—one strike to an earth point and the other strike to a meridian we've not discussed." Yoshida drew an arrow from wood to earth.

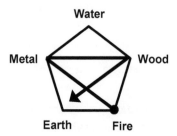

"The last punch is to the Conception Vessel, a meridian that runs down the center of your body. It's one of eight meridians called extraordinary meridians. It's not important for this discussion."

"Is that it? Shouldn't there be more arrows?" Silberman asked. "He hasn't won yet."

"Yes," Steve sighed. "Can you finish the diagram Dr. Yoshida?"

"Sure. Using this logic, I drew an arrow from earth to water and another from water to fire."

"The Cycle of Destruction is also called the Cycle of Control. I've already mentioned that fire melts metal and metal chops wood. Can you think of an example in which wood controls earth?" Steve asked. "Think of a tree."

"A sidewalk!" Silberman shouted. "The tree roots in front of my house have destroyed the sidewalk. Do I get—?"

"You already lost," Yoshida cut him off. "Just accept it."

"He's right. You're the *uke* again," Steve stated. "With that said, it's time to clear the table and chairs so you can get to work. This time you'll have thirty minutes."

Yoshida turned and bowed to Steve. He had a strange look in his eye—a hint of gratitude, as if he were thanking the man who spent the past eight weeks torturing him. Steve couldn't help but wonder if Stockholm syndrome started setting in. He suspected that these simple lessons, these little bits of knowledge, probably made the doctor feel the closest he had ever felt to his own heritage.

Once the platform was cleared and the men got into position, Silberman removed his shirt to reveal the ink covered bruise marks from the prior day. He held up his fist and the *kata* began. Yoshida stepped backward as their forearms clashed together. He grabbed Silberman's wrist and pulled him down to his height before stepping in to strike the crease of the elbow. The strike jerked Silberman forward to meet the chop to his chest that followed. Yoshida released Silberman's fist and stepped forward to execute the two final strikes. Silberman lay on the ground holding his abdomen and trying to catch his breath.

"There's no need to brutalize your *uke*. Good strikes leave no marks, yet hurt more than strikes that do," Steve advised. "Find your natural rhythm—stay relaxed."

"Why didn't you tell him that yesterday?" Silberman shouted.

Yoshida bowed to Steve. He then paused for a minute to reflect on the words before signaling Silberman to continue. Silberman threw a punch and Yoshida stepped his way through the routine, fluidly striking each point firmly.

"Better," Steve commented. "However, you're still thinking too much. Quiet your mind—don't think, just do it."

The two men began again. With each new series, Yoshida appeared increasingly comfortable, transitioning through the movements less mechanically. On his fifth attempt, Silberman hit the mat, rendered unconscious by a strike to the chest. The smile on Yoshida's face told Steve there was no doubt in his mind that he had executed the *kata* correctly.

"How did that feel?"

"Effortless," Yoshida answered. "It was as if I hardly touched him."

"From the look on your face, I think I've made a believer out of you. What about your friend here? Do you think he's coming around?"

"I doubt it."

"Let's wake him up and find out," Steve said.

Chapter 35

Boston

The next morning, the men assembled on the platform for the third consecutive day.

"When we started two days ago, I told you that the *kata* holds one of the keys to finding your health. Since then, you've deciphered and tested it, as well as discovering some of the traditional Chinese medical theory behind it." Steve paced back and forth in front of the whiteboard as he addressed the doctors. "Today, we enter the final phase of your test. For this part, you'll work together using this knowledge to develop the best plan for restoring your health."

"How do you propose we'll do that?" Silberman asked. "We still don't even know what's wrong."

"You know more than you think and that's what you're going to uncover today." Steve replied. "I know these theories appear vague, however, I assure you that they're anything but superficial. For now, your assignment is to simply create a plan that points you in the right direction using what we've discussed so far. What do you think you're going to use to create this plan?"

"The Five Elements Theory," Yoshida answered.

"Which cycle?"

"The Cycle of Creation," both doctors answered.

"See. That wasn't so hard. Once you decide upon a direction, I'll help you execute it with herbs and acupuncture, among other things. If you're right, you'll start feeling better immediately. If not, you'll probably feel worse and our time here will come to an end."

"What the hell does that mean?" Silberman asked.

"I think you know what it means. Let's get started. You can begin by copying the matrix to your paper." When the doctors finished, Steve continued, "You're going to start by analyzing each row and circling the items that best match your symptoms. For example, if your eyes hurt, circle it. For items such as flavors, you can circle the flavors you think you've been consuming regularly or any change in taste that might have developed during your stay here."

"'Our stay here.' You make it sound like we're at a fucking resort." Silberman muttered as his eyes sent a scathing message.

Five minutes later, the doctors indicated they were finished.

"Let's begin," Steve said. "Tell me which *zang* organs you circled and why."

"We have liver, pancreas, and heart," Yoshida volunteered, "because everything you fed us was high in fat, sugar, and caffeine—so much so that it seemed toxic. I feel like all three of my organs are shot now."

A sheepish look came across Steve's face. "As you might have guessed by now, your food contained additional ingredients—herbs meant to bring about specific effects according to the Five Element Theory."

"I knew it!" Silberman shouted. "I knew those muffins and coffee were laced with something. Is that why I always felt on overdrive?"

"Correct," Steve replied. "Let's move on. Which *fu* organs did you choose?"

"We circled two—bladder and large intestines," Yoshida said. "Bladder because we both have lots of problems with nocturia, and large intestines because of the digestive problems we're experiencing."

They continued through each line until they had identified all of the applicable signs and symptoms on the matrix.

	Wood	Fire	Earth	Metal	Water
Zang	Liver	Heart	Spleen / Pancreas	Lung	Kidney
Fu	Gall Bladder	Sm Intestine	Stomach	Lg Intestine	Bladder
Color	Green	Red	Yellow	White	Black
Flavor	Sour	Bitter	Sweet	Spicy	Salt
Smell	Rancid	Scorched	Fragrant	Rotten	Putrid
Emotion	Anger	Joy	Worry	Sadness	Fear
Tissue	Tendons	Vessels	Muscle	Skin	Bones
Facial	Eyes	Tongue	Mouth	Nose	Ears
Seasons	Spring	Summer	Summer	Autumn	Winter

"Which elements have the most circles?" Steve asked.

"Water, wood, and metal," Yoshida said.

Steve drew a pentagon on the board and labeled each point with its corresponding element. "Look at the columns for each element and think about the significance of the items you circled. For each element, do the symptoms you've circled point to a weak or strong element? For example, are your water related symptoms stemming from weak or strong water?"

"Aren't they all weak?" Silberman countered. "If I feel this weak and awful all of the time, how could any of them be strong?"

"Good question. Think of your body as a house with each organ representing a different appliance—washing machine, dryer, dishwasher, etc. They are all connected to each other through the electrical system. When one appliance uses too much electricity, it takes energy away from another—literally stealing it. Appliances that use too much or don't receive their fair share won't function properly. As a result, the other appliances around it also suffer. To answer your question—yes, they could all be weak. Or, it could be one of a dozen other combinations. My basic point is that since all of the appliances are connected to each other—when one is off, the rest will be off."

"So, it's more important for the elements to stay in balance?" Yoshida asked.

"'Every meal needs something from each element to keep you balanced.' Does that sound familiar?"

Yoshida smiled.

"Now, take time to reflect on these symptoms and what they mean for each element," Steve continued. "When you are done, place an up arrow next to the elements you think are too strong, and a down arrow next to those you think are weak."

The doctors debated the semantics of their symptoms for an hour before Yoshida called out to Steve, "I can't work with this guy any longer. He's impossible. He won't agree on anything."

"That's because you're a moron," Silberman quipped.

"In case you forgot, you're the patient."

"He's right," Steve said, addressing Silberman. "The only reason he's even here is to treat you. He's got the final word."

With minimal help from Silberman, Yoshida selected a final set of arrows and beckoned Steve, "We've finished."

Steve held up the marker and said, "Draw your answers on the board and explain your rationale."

Yoshida took the pen and began. "We started with the three elements that had the most circles—water, metal, and wood. In the water column, bladder was the first circled item, causing us the most confusion and fighting. Since our bladders are constantly going, does this mean they are weak or strong? Dr. Silberman concluded it means they're strong—"

"It's still my conclusion," Silberman pounced. "I'm going to the bathroom every two hours—it's going nonstop—"

"I already overruled you!" Yoshida shouted at Silberman before turning to Steve. "There's an undeniable weakness about everything related to our bladders, from the quality of the stream to the inability to control it. Regarding our running to the bathroom every two hours—they don't call it a weak bladder for nothing." He smirked at Silberman. "Additionally, since it's connected to our genitalia and we've had so much trouble down there, it makes sense that it's weak. When I factored in the other issues we've been having—aching joints, ringing ears, horrible body odor, and fear—all symptoms in the water column—there's no doubt in my mind this stems from weakness."

"I see," Steve commented.

"Next we looked at wood. We circled liver because of the high amounts of fat you've been feeding us, making the liver work harder. Then, we discussed its associated emotion—anger. One of the few points we actually agreed upon was how quickly we switch between feeling fearful and angry. Fear makes you retreat, while anger makes you want to take action. This is a strange combination because they are completely opposite reactions. The bouts of anger we're experiencing feel extreme, coming on very fast. When we considered the order of the elements—water feeds wood—it fit with your comments about one organ stealing energy from another. In the context of the Five Elements, it seems possible that wood might be stealing energy from water and turning fear into rage. Therefore, it would be logical to label wood as a strong element."

"Good. Maybe Dr. Silberman can discuss the next element," Steve said.

"Fine," Silberman said, striking an indifferent tone. "Fire. There wasn't much to this one. We had lots of caffeine and we both have bitter tastes in our mouths. We went with strong. Anything else?"

"Yes," Steve pushed back. "How does it fit within the context of the Five Elements Theory? What in the theory would indicate that it should be strong?"

"He basically said it—wood is strong—wood feeds fire," Silberman answered, sounding annoyed.

"Is that all you see? Where's the value in what isn't there ... the value in what's weak?"

"Huh? I'm not following you," Silberman replied.

"Water!" Yoshida shouted. "Without water controlling fire, fire can become stronger."

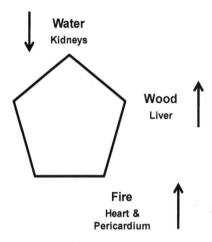

"Exactly," Steve said. "Not only does strong wood add to fire, but weak water allows fire to grow unchecked. What's next?"

"Metal," Yoshida drew a down arrow next to the metal point. "It's weak. Using your example of the house, it seems like there's a lack of energy in the large intestines causing our digestive issues—primarily constipation and bloating—not enough energy to move things along. In addition, the constant sweating and sensitivity to touch are skin related symptoms, which you said are related to metal."

"Sounds a lot like hot flashes, don't you think?" Steve queried.

"Hell, if it weren't for the fact that we're both male, I'd already have prescribed hormone replacement therapy—" Yoshida joked.

"Not to mention an increase in the risk of breast cancer and heart disease," Steve countered. "Let's move on to earth."

"Using the same logic as wood, I also labeled this as strong." Yoshida drew an up arrow next to the earth point. "Considering the amounts of sugar you've been feeding us, not to mention the amount of worry stewing in our heads, this element has got to be overworked."

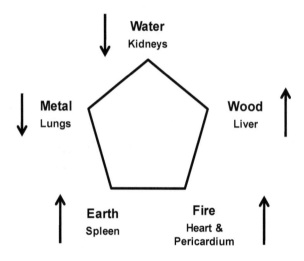

"Now that you've labeled all five elements, you've basically done the work required to create your plan. You've told me where you think the problem areas are, as well as their qualities—strong versus weak. Using this framework, what do you think the solution will look like?"

"The arrows will be reversed," Yoshida answered. "Strengthen metal and water while simultaneously weakening wood, fire, and earth."

"Is that correct?" Silberman asked.

"You're going to have to wait to see."

"How long before we know if it's working? And, how long is it going to take to heal from this?" Silberman continued probing.

"Typically, it takes one month for every year you've been sick. For me, I was sick for fifteen years. That meant a year and three months of healing. For you, it comes to three weeks.

However, since I accelerated your conditions using herbs and acupuncture, you'll probably need at least a month. In addition to herbs, acupuncture, and diet, we'll supplement your healing with yoga and qigong."

"Qigong?" Silberman asked.

"Qigong is a branch of martial arts that focuses on developing internal energy. *Qi* means energy and *gong* means practice. So, you'll literally practice influencing your internal energy by using meditative and breathing techniques, as well as prescribed movements. Some people practice qigong for spiritual and health reasons ... others for fighting. We will be practicing for both health and spiritual enlightenment."

"Internal energy?" Silberman sounded confused.

"Hold out your arm." Steve took the doctor's arm and pressed his finger firmly into the inside of Silberman's wrist. "Focus on the point where my finger is pressing." After a minute, he let go. "Can you still feel where my finger was pressing?"

The doctor nodded as the blood began pooling under his skin again.

"Can you take that feeling and move it?"

"Move it? Where?"

"Here," Steve repositioned his index finger further up the doctor's forearm, hovering it above the skin located an inch below the crease in his elbow. "Using your mind, I want you to feel a line of energy connecting both points. Can you feel it?"

"Not really. I can imagine the point where your finger was, but I can't move it."

Steve pressed his finger into the second point on the doctor's forearm. "How about now?"

Silberman nodded. "The minute you touched my skin, my mind made the connection. I could feel a line connect the dots."

"Good. That's the basic concept. Now, see if you can do it on the other arm. Try to use your mind to generate that feeling without having to touch yourself. Dr. Yoshida, you give it a try, too."

After experimenting with a few different body parts, Steve walked over to the easel with the anatomical diagrams and asked, "Where do you think we'll move that feeling?" His finger was tracing its way along the different meridians.

"Through the acupuncture points," Yoshida answered.

"Good. Is there a particular order we will use?" Steve prodded them to think.

"The Cycle of Creation?"

"Good. The qigong practices I'll give you will match your plan—strengthening metal and water, while reducing the energy of wood, fire, and earth. If the plan you've chosen is correct, you'll start feeling better in the next few days."

Chapter 36

Two weeks later

With a lot of patience and hard work, the doctors' bodies had regained most of the suppleness they had lost over the past few months. Able to sleep more consistently and replenished with nutrients, their muscles no longer ached and their tendons no longer felt dry and brittle. Their stamina grew day by day, made evident by the ease with which they could hold each sun salutation posture on the platform.

Each day began the same way. They woke at 4:30 a.m. to harness the earth's energy. The first hour was spent engaged in meditation to raise their qi levels. Standing motionless, they focused their minds on moving their internal energy. As they inhaled, the energy traveled up their spines and over their heads. On their exhale, the energy moved down the front side of their bodies to their perinea. Each breath completed a cycle. As the energy traveled this path, it grew longer and stronger. Once they accumulated enough qi, they would distribute it through the different energy channels according to the qigong exercises prescribed by Steve. At the end of this routine, they would spend five minutes grounding their energy.

Once they finished waking up and expanding their internal qi, they would engage in a few hours of yoga before eating breakfast.

All meals and snacks were simple, containing high-quality plant-based protein, whole grains, and vegetables. There were no packaged foods, condiments, or any other ingredients that might influence the body outside of the herbs Steve prescribed each day. He explained that they were on an elimination diet meant to reset their metabolism, detoxify their livers, and reduce inflammation affecting the three elements they wanted to decrease.

Every day after breakfast, Steve administered acupuncture to both men before allowing them to return to bed for a late morning siesta.

After lunch, afternoons were spent delving deeper into Chinese medical theory. Steve used Dr. Yoshida's *katas* to demonstrate new concepts, instructing the doctors to practice on each other to facilitate their understanding.

Walking through the motions, calling out the points, and uncovering the meanings behind the poetry of each movement offered additional benefits. It made them feel alive again. While meditation, qigong, and yoga had reintroduced their bodies to the healing process, the *katas* gave them something extra. The *katas* helped the doctors develop a deeper appreciation for the theories they initially scoffed at. As their understanding grew, so too grew their confidence in the process, ultimately making them feel hopeful. This was an important component in their healing process.

"Tell me about your progress so far," Steve directed his comment to Yoshida.

"Considering the symptom profiles we started with, I think we're improving quicker than I thought possible."

"I disagree," Silberman interjected. "I have plenty of symptoms that haven't improved at all. For example, my eyes still hurt. I think we've hit a roadblock."

"I know," Steve said.

"What do you mean you know?" Silberman replied.

"I know because I've not started treating the symptoms you're still struggling with."

"Why not?" Silberman snapped.

"How many times have you heard me say that you need both Eastern and Western medicine to solve your problems?" Steve asked. "While you've learned a lot over the past few weeks, you've been compartmentalizing most of it based upon East and West. I've not seen any efforts to marry the two. Once you do that, you'll finally be able to answer the question of why your eyes hurt and I'll add it to your treatments."

"That's not true," Silberman countered. "I've postulated on multiple occasions that our eye pain is related to liver damage from the herbs you were giving us—a Western diagnosis. Since both liver and eyes are wood related organs, this proves that I've attempted to match Eastern with Western medicine."

"If your liver were diseased, why aren't you walking around in the mental fog that plagued you for the past six months? Where are the dark circles under your eyes, and the foul body odor, not to mention the itchy skin—all signs of liver disease? Your liver isn't the problem and you know it," Steve said. "Eastern and Western medicine are like two foreign languages.

You can't simply translate them word for word—a lot gets lost in translation. For the past two weeks, I've had you both practicing the *katas*. Why?"

"To decipher the points—" Yoshida answered.

"Ah, the points," Steve said. "If the points are the 'words' of Eastern medicine, does it make sense to apply the 'syntax' of Western medicine to them?"

"I guess not," Silberman replied.

"That's basically what you did, which is why you got lost."

"How did I do that?" Silberman asked. "I'm not following you."

"Two weeks ago, you used the five elements to determine that water and metal are weak, and wood, fire, and earth are strong. However, instead of plotting your path using acupuncture points and a Chinese framework, you continued charting your course using Western medicine."

"Plot a path with points? But, you're the one who's giving us acupuncture and herbs," Silberman said.

"It's only a metaphor to say that you continue thinking in Western medical terms and don't understand the connection. For example, two days ago, I saw you palpitating Dr. Yoshida's liver. Why?"

"To check for hepatic inflammation."

"Think back to the house example in which I likened each organ to an appliance. Just because the dishwasher is receiving too much energy doesn't mean it has broken yet. Similarly, the Chinese medical diagnosis of excess liver heat doesn't mean that your liver is diseased yet. The five elements are a compass meant to guide you to the liver and gallbladder channels. From there, you follow the points. Had you looked at them, you might have found another cause." Steve walked over to the easel. "Before you two geniuses spent the past two weeks knocking each other out, who was doing it?"

"You were," Silberman said with a biting tone.

"And, where was I striking you?"

"Everywhere," Silberman retorted. "The arms, abdomen, back, head, neck—"

"The neck!" Yoshida interrupted, pointing to the easel. "These points at the base of the skull are on the gallbladder meridian—they're wood points."

"What's located in this area, anatomically?" Steve pointed to the easel.

"The occipital nerve!" It dawned on Silberman. "Occipital neuralgia could cause this pain behind the eyes, which is why it hurts to keep our eyes open."

"Finally! We'll make a diagnostician out of you yet," Steve remarked. Interestingly enough, this also happens to be the same point used by acupuncturists to treat certain types of eye pain—specifically, the kind you are suffering from. With that, you've now married the two systems, and I'll start treating your eye pain. Most of your symptoms can be diagnosed this way. I suggest you try it with another symptom."

"What about digestion?" Silberman asked.

"Sure. It will work for all of your symptoms. However, digestion is a bit more complicated. I believe you are experiencing more digestive issues than Dr. Yoshida. Is that correct?" Steve asked.

"Yes, I am," Silberman replied.

"My problems are rather mild compared to his," Yoshida added.

"Since you're the PCP, maybe you can tell us why your symptoms differ," Steve said.

"I don't know why."

"Then start by telling me what the primary complaint about doctors' prescribing practices are today," Steve continued.

"We overprescribe," Yoshida answered.

"Which kind of drugs in particular?"

"Antibiotics," Yoshida said. "Ah—that's how we differ. That was Dr. Silberman's first choice for treating his prostate-related symptoms. I never took any drugs."

"And, what's the big deal about taking antibiotics?" Steve asked.

"They kill off your flora. That's why they suggest eating yogurt when taking antibiotics," Yoshida answered.

"This is one of the reasons it took me so long to figure out what was wrong when I went through this. Studies by researchers at the University of Michigan have shown that certain broad spectrum antibiotics, specifically the kind Dr. Silberman prefers when treating prostatitis, can *permanently* wipe out the good bacteria, or flora, in your intestines."

"What do you mean?" Silberman demanded.

"There are over four hundred different types of bacteria in your gut," Steve continued. "They perform many tasks, from helping you digest foods to synthesizing vitamins. Researchers believe they play a vital role in your immune system. However, the entirety of their role in our health remains unknown."

"You can just buy them. I've seen them in specialty health stores," Silberman rebutted.

"Sure, if you know which bacteria you're now deficient in," Steve replied. "Unfortunately, there aren't very accurate tests at this point, and the products on the shelves have only a fraction of those found in your gut. At most, eighty different types are sold, far short of the four hundred-plus strains you were playing host to six months ago. Now that you've lost them, research has shown that it may not be possible to permanently replenish them. In studies, they only colonized for up to six months in mice before passing out of their intestinal tracts. This is what I suspect is making your digestive problems so much worse."

"Great, so what does this mean for me?" Silberman asked.

"It means you get to live in discomfort like the hundreds of patients for whom you indiscriminately prescribed antibiotics," Steve said. "Or you could live like me and limit your diet to the foods you know you can tolerate. It's not exciting, but I don't suffer from the issues you currently have. The five flavors dull the taste, Doctor."

"What the hell does that mean?" Silberman spat back.

"It means, everything in moderation, including your prescribing practices," Steve responded as he turned toward the easel. "It's time to play another round of connect the dots. Let's see what else you can find."

Forty minutes later, the doctors called to Steve in an excited tone.

"What do you have for me?" Steve asked.

"We believe we've identified the cause of our sexual and urinary issues," Yoshida said.

"Really? Tell me," Steve replied.

"We decided to look at water since it's related to our inability to have sex. We figured if we followed the points along the water meridians they might lead us to something. We also decided to included the earth meridians because earth controls water—" Yoshida started.

"Three of the four meridians run right over the pudendal nerve in our abdomens," Silberman interrupted, hitting his hand to his head. "That's when it hit me. It's pudendal neuralgia!"

"These were points you struck on a daily basis." Yoshida added.

"So, that's it then," Silberman said. "We figured out how to solve our sexual issues. You've got to let us go now."

"No. The deal was that you will go free once you've cured yourselves," Steve said. "Right now it's just theory. Once you prove it—"

"I knew it!" Silberman shouted. "I knew you weren't going to let us out of this place. You know this is the answer. You repeatedly struck our pudendal nerves—the nerve that innervates the bladder, sphincter, rectum, and penis—causing pudendal neuralgia. This accounts for all of our urogenital symptoms. It's not that complicated."

"Says the urologist who needed six months and a lot of help to find his way to this proposed solution," Steve said. "What if it's not correct? You wouldn't have proven you are the leading expert in your field. I'd let you go and you'd ignorantly think you understood this. Two months from now, you'll probably be running from one acupuncturist to the next searching for a cure to the same symptoms."

"I'll take my chances. If that happens, I'll just get one of the doctors in my group practice who offers acupuncture to treat it," Silberman said.

Steve started laughing. "Those aren't acupuncturists. MDs only need three hundred hours of continuing education to practice acupuncture. By now, you've already had more than that. Do either of you feel qualified to treat someone with needles?"

"Hardly," Yoshida answered.

"Most accredited acupuncture programs require over two thousand hours of study, with some requiring more than three thousand hours," Steve said.

"Could any trained acupuncturist solve this?" Yoshida inquired.

"As far as a real acupuncturist curing this, I will cautiously say yes. While I think the average acupuncturist is better trained and capable of handling this type of diagnosis, it took eight to find someone who understood what I was going through. As you know, there were a lot of symptoms to sort through. However, when you compare eight acupuncturists against the more than one hundred allopathic doctors I saw, not to mention the countless chiropractors and other types of practitioners, I think it's safe to say that your chances are much better with an acupuncturist. And, your best chances are right here." Steve smiled.

"Great," Silberman said sarcastically.

"I'll give you the next three weeks to prove your theory."

Chapter 37

Three weeks later

I t's been a few weeks. I know you've made some progress during this time. However, for every two steps forward, you've been taking one step backward," Steve said. "Who can tell me why certain symptoms keep returning—some within a few hours of your treatments and others every few days?"

"I think you are sabotaging our treatments to keep us here longer," Silberman said. "I don't trust your acupuncture."

"From that comment, can I assume that your urogenital symptoms have returned?"

"Yup," Silberman muttered.

"Which symptoms are you both continuing to experience?"

"Hot flashes," Yoshida answered. "They've become less frequent but never fully went away. My urogenital issues were completely resolved a week ago but returned over the past few days—primarily dribbling and ED."

"I find it convenient that these symptoms returned right as the three weeks came to a close," Silberman added.

Steve ignored Silberman. "Have either of you noticed any unusual patterns when the hot flashes occur?"

"They always happen right before I have to defecate," Yoshida answered.

"And, now we're back to the pudendal nerve," Silberman interjected.

"Why do you say that?" Steve asked.

"The pudendal nerve affects both the somatic and autonomic nervous systems—accounting for physiological responses that we control and those below our conscious radar. Pressure on this nerve could induce a number of involuntary reflexes, including sweating and changes in heart rate—potentially imitating hot flashes."

"Okay, but why would there be pressure on the nerve?" Steve asked.

"Ah, let's see," Silberman's voice struck a sarcastic tone. "Maybe your punching us in the stomachs for the past few months has something to do with it. Latent trigger points could have built up around the nerve causing signal disruption and referred symptoms."

"The physical therapy and acupuncture you've had over the past three weeks would have resolved these points," Steve remarked. "Could something else be putting pressure on the nerve?"

"Constipation," Silberman answered.

"Are you constipated now?"

Both doctors nodded.

"But, you've been eating a very healthy diet. Why would you still be constipated?"

"While a loss of flora could explain his constipation, I didn't take antibiotics. So it doesn't explain why we're both experiencing this," Yoshida said.

"It's all related to the pudendal," Silberman said. "The neuralgia can cause the external sphincter muscle to spasm, leading to constipation. The constipation then pressures the nerve, causing the autonomic responses."

"You still haven't said what causes pudendal neuralgia in the first place."

"Anything that puts prolonged pressure or stress in that region can cause it—sitting, cycling, childbirth, even chronic constipation," Silberman answered.

"So, constipation can cause pudendal neuralgia, and the neuralgia can cause constipation. Sounds like a vicious cycle," Steve said. "However, if the neuralgia was cured for the past few weeks, why would your constipation return and aggravate your pudendal again?" Steve asked. "It sounds like Western medicine is about to take you in circles, which tells me it's time to start over," Steve said. "Go back to the five elements and travel the acupuncture points until you find your answer."

Thirty minutes later, the doctors called out to Steve, "We've got it!"

Steve returned to the platform to find the whiteboard coated in a layer of dry marker. Symptoms and body parts were scrawled around a pentagon in the middle of the board. Arrows were drawn from metal to the other four elements.

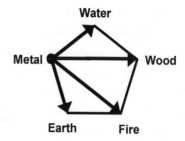

"What's this?" Steve said, pointing to the board.

"We matched our symptoms against the matrix," Yoshida said. "Constipation and sweating are syndromes of the large intestines and skin, respectively—both of which are metal. We then followed the points along the large intestine meridians, starting with the tip of the index finger and moving up the arm to the head. At each point, we asked ourselves if it was a place you had struck or if it served some important anatomical function from a Western perspective. When we reached the eighteenth point, a point you repeatedly hit on our necks, we realized that it's the location of—"

"The vagus nerve!" Silberman interrupted. "This nerve innervates practically everything. That's the reason for the arrows pointing to every element. If the vagus nerve has a problem, it could lead to constipation that would put pressure on and possibly reinjure the pudendal nerve."

Steve thought back to his initial meeting with Doctor Tam in which he learned that his vagus nerve had been playing the primary role in his problems. The vagus nerve passes through the carotid sheath in the neck and innervates a number of organs in the body, including the heart, lungs, liver, gallbladder, pancreas, stomach, bladder, esophagus, and large intestine. The majority of its function is to communicate with the central nervous system, sending sensory signals that, in turn, lead to autonomic and somatic reflex responses. As such, it is a pretty important nerve, impacting many of the body's processes, including heart rate, digestion, and sweating. Simply massaging the nerve can slow your heart rate down, and excessive stimulation can stop your heart completely.

The word *vagus* means "wanderer," a fitting name as its reach extends to so many organs. For years, crossed signals had sent Steve's body into overdrive, producing uncontrollable sweats and hot flashes, disrupted digestion, breathing issues, and sleep disturbances.

Silberman continued, "Since the vagus and pudendal nerves both transmit sensory data back to the central nervous system, each has the ability to cause a multitude of symptoms, making it virtually impossible to determine the underlying pathology. Just when you think you had one symptom solved, it pops up again from a different source."

"I agree. I think it would be unlikely that any one doctor could figure this out," Yoshida added.

Chapter 38

Three weeks later

D ay by day, the atmosphere on the platform gradually changed, reaching a cordial tone. Skepticism had been replaced by understanding as the doctors' rapid and unequivocal recovery helped them develop a deeper level of respect for their counterparts in the East. Simplistic theories had given way to more complex concepts revealing a powerful marriage between Eastern and Western medicine.

"When you look at the interaction between the two nerves—the pudendal and vagus—it's rather poetic if I say so myself. Strikes to your abdomens and necks set the stage by creating constipation, hot flashes, impotence, and other urogenital symptoms. Add to that a culinary assault according to the Five Elements Theory meant to exacerbate all of your problems, especially constipation. That forced you to put more pressure in your lower abdomen—specifically on the pudendal nerve—creating a never ending cycle," Steve said.

"Even if a doctor realized it was a nerve related issue, the other nerve would reintroduce the problem—frustrating both the patient and doctor. In the end, he'd probably just classify your symptoms as psychosomatic," Silberman said.

"As I mentioned before, even many Chinese doctors I saw were fooled by it," Steve said. "They successfully balanced the elements, just like I was doing for you in the beginning of your treatments. The points they chose along the meridians never included the latent trigger points near these nerves. Therefore, after a short period, the impeded nerve signals would throw everything off again."

"If I understand you correctly, the Five Elements Theory wouldn't have been enough?" Silberman asked.

"Correct. Without understanding the role of latent trigger points and their effect on these nerves you could have spent a lifetime constantly rebalancing the elements," Steve replied. "While some acupuncturists do specialize in trigger point therapy, you'd have to know that this option was available and that it best matched your condition."

"Did you do all of this just to show us you could make us better again?" Yoshida asked.

"No, I did it so you could learn how to make yourselves better. Would have believed such physiological changes were possible if I simply told you? You'd never have thought such vague clusters of symptoms had legitimate causes. You'd keep frustrating patients by telling them everything is psychosomatic, pumping them full of toxic drugs, and never shaking that uneasy feeling that you were really just ignoring a large segment of your patients. On average, before you arrived here, what percentage of your patients' symptoms did you routinely dismiss as psychosomatic?"

"Twenty percent," Yoshida answered.

"I did it so should you see your patients again, you'll look at that twenty percent differently, compassionately, and with a new understanding of how to help them."

Chapter 39

One month later in Boston

I t was a cold day in mid-April. Paul had settled back into his normal weekday routine of going to work, cranking out a couple of hours at the gym, and then returning home to an empty apartment. This was the isolated single life to which he and his city dweller friends had grown accustomed.

After seven months, his malaise had not completely lifted. His mind returned often to Prague, imagining how wonderful the city could have been under different circumstances, and to Klára and her childlike innocence.

Work had been exceptionally stressful that day. He was blindsided by an impromptu meeting in which his boss had pulled him into a conference room and laid into him about his downtrodden attitude. No matter how hard he tried to fake it since returning from Europe, he just couldn't get his head back into debits and credits. To make matters worse, his micromanager of a boss had a knack for making him want to do less rather than more.

In recent months, his workouts had grown more intense, a necessary antidote to his persistently elevated stress levels. Each night, he lifted until failure, leaving his muscles throbbing with a feeling that his body was three jacket sizes bigger than his actual physique.

After picking up his mail in the mailroom of his Back Bay apartment building, he boarded the elevator with one of his neighbors. His thoughts focused on the banana protein shake waiting for him upstairs. They stared forward, never making actual eye contact or acknowledging each others' presence. She turned toward the opposite corner of the elevator and typed away on her phone, sending out rapid-fire text messages and updating her social media sites. When their floor arrived, they exchanged a few bland pleasantries and went their separate ways.

"Have a nice night," Paul called out as he turned right.

She mirrored the sentiment and turned left.

He flipped through his mail on the way to his door.

"What's this?" he muttered.

It was an envelope from the life insurance department of National Assurance Corp.

He tore it open and unfolded the letter. The sound of his neighbor's door closing behind her at the other end of the hall pulled him out of his thoughts, and he fiddled for his keys. After opening the door, he wrestled with the letter.

> Pay to the order of: Paul Benson
> Amount: $20,000

Life insurance? But Steve wasn't working for corporate America. Paul couldn't believe the school in Prague would have provided such benefits. *$20,000. Such a small amount?*

He picked up his cell phone to call the number at the top of the letter.

"National Assurance Corporation. This is Jennifer. How may I help you?"

"Hello, I just received a check from your company related to a policy for my brother."

The woman on the other end of the line sensed the youthfulness of his voice. "Oh. I'm very sorry to hear that. Can you provide me with the account number at the top of the letter?"

"34-34895."

"Thank you. What is your question?"

"I was hoping you could tell me about this policy. My brother was working overseas for a language school. I doubt they would have offered employees this type of benefit. Can you tell me if there was a group associated with it?"

"I see it was a group policy. However, the group name is not visible on this system. One second while I access my other screen."

"Also, can you tell me how much the policy was for?" Paul probed.

"I'm sorry. I am not at liberty to discuss those details."

"I'm just curious because the check was for $20,000. I don't mean to sound greedy, but it just sounds like an odd amount for a life insurance policy," Paul said.

"Again, sir, I'm sorry, but I am not able to provide those details. I can tell you that you were not the only beneficiary."

"Other beneficiaries?" Paul repeated her comments. "Who?"

"Again, sir, I'm sorry, but privacy laws prohibit me from disclosing those details. You may wish to check with your other relatives or have your lawyer contact our company."

"I understand," Paul replied. "Have you found the group name?"

"Ah, that's why."

Paul could hear her fingernails tapping away on the keyboard on the other end of the phone line.

"It looks like this policy was issued by one of our foreign-based subsidiaries," she said. "I only handle domestic policies. Our systems here do not have access to all of the information for these policies. I can provide you with the number of the foreign branch where the policy was issued."

"Sure. Where is the branch located?" Paul asked.

"The Czech Republic." She provided Paul with the number and concluded the call. "We are very sorry for your loss."

Paul hung up abruptly to call his parents and learned that they had not received a check. When they heard there was another beneficiary, they were equally perplexed. His father offered to contact the family's attorney to obtain more information from the insurance company. Paul's thoughts flashed back to the mafia. *If they took out a policy and killed him, why include me?* He decided it was best to omit this from their discussion and ended by saying he would contact the school to find out if it was customary to provide teachers with life insurance policies.

Chapter 40

Boston

The next morning, Paul woke early to call the school. He turned on his computer and opened the voice-over-IP software he had used to speak with Steve every week. Dialing in his credit card number allowed him to cheaply place calls to phones abroad.

Paul searched his desk for Klára's phone number, eventually finding it mixed in with the pile of Steve's notebooks. Upon dialing the number, he received an automated recording in Czech. At the end, a pleasant British woman's voice provided an English translation.

"The phone number you have called is no longer in service."

A sinking feeling came over Paul. *Why would her phone be out of service?* After a few minutes of searching the Internet, he found the school's Web site.

"Dobry den. King Charles Language School." The woman's distinctive Czech accent transported Paul back to Prague.

"Uh, may I speak with Klára?"

"Klára? Is she a teacher here?" The woman sounded puzzled.

"No, she is Czech."

"Sir, many of our teachers here are Czech. Does she work in the administrative offices?"

"Sorry, yes, she works in marketing."

"I'm sorry, sir," the operator replied. "We don't have anyone by that name working in any of our administrative offices. Would you like me to connect you with marketing?"

"Okay?" Paul was confused.

The phone went silent. Paul wasn't sure if he had been hung up on as often happens with call transfers.

"Marketing. This is Dita."

"Hello, my name is Paul Benson. My brother was Steve Benson. He was a teacher at the school last year."

"Steve Benson? I don't know who that is."

"He was the teacher who was killed."

"Killed?" she screamed.

"Yes, seven months ago. I'm sure you heard about it."

"Sir, I'm very sorry. Are you sure you have the right school? I've never heard of this."

The sinking feeling in Paul's stomach grew heavier.

"Listen, I was working with a woman from your school named Klára. She said she worked in marketing, and that the school had sent her to help me navigate the situation."

"We've never had a Klára in marketing. In fact, I don't know of a Klára who has worked here. Would you like me to transfer you to scheduling? They deal with the teachers' schedules. They would have a record of your brother if he worked here."

"Okay, fine." Paul was becoming concerned by the lack of answers.

"Scheduling, this is Monika."

"Hello, my name is Paul Benson. My brother was Steve Benson."

"Benson?" Her voice indicated she did not recall the name among the hundreds of teachers passing through their doors each year.

"Yes, he was a teacher at your school. He had started almost two years ago."

"Ah, yes! Now I remember your brother. I remember him because he was the one with the work experience in investments. Not common for teachers here."

"Exactly!" Paul felt a sense of relief.

"Yes, we were sorry to see him go. He was a very popular teacher with the senior executive students."

"To see him go?" The way she described his death offended Paul.

"Yes, we have many teachers who are runners, but we were surprised when he left."

"Runners?"

"Yes, we have a few teachers each year who quit without telling anyone. We call them runners because they are typically young, recent college graduates, and working is a big shock for them. So they run."

"My brother didn't leave. He was killed."

"What?" Monika said. "The police never contacted us. We never heard this. It was not in the news."

"I spent a week in Prague working with a woman claiming to be from your school."

"Who?"

"Klára. She said she was in the marketing department and the school sent her to help me with the police as they investigated Steve's death."

"I'm so sorry. We just figured he was a runner. We rarely follow up with these teachers. I don't know this Klára. She is not from our school."

"Are you sure?"

"Yes. Have you tried the police? Do you need their phone number?"

"Yes, please."

Paul's head was buzzing with thoughts. He peppered Monika with additional questions trying to figure out who Klára was, but it was useless. *Who did I spend that week with?*

After writing down the number, Paul placed a frenzied call to the police department asking for Lieutenant Marek. The operator, who spoke very little English, put Paul on hold until someone who spoke English could take his call. Five minutes later, they tracked down Marek.

Marek spent a few minutes conversing in broken English. He didn't understand who was on the other end of the phone and quickly grew frustrated. Eventually, he just hung up. Paul called back to speak with the English speaking operator again who agreed to help translate, but did so grudgingly. When Marek finally understood that it was Paul calling, he still didn't understand the purpose of the call.

"He says Klára works for forensic team. Why do you ask?"

"She told me she worked for the school," Paul realized that such details sounded trivial, but for some reason, she wanted him to believe she was from the school.

"Lieutenant Marek says you are mistaken. He is very busy and does not have time for such questions. He is very sorry for your loss, but he cannot help you." She took a dismissive tone that seemed influenced by Marek's presence behind her.

Desperate not to be hung up upon again, Paul spouted off, "She gave me a phone number that is now out of service. The number no longer works. It's like she didn't want me to know who she was. Why didn't she just say she worked for the police?"

"Yes, this happens all the time. People get new phones and numbers."

"No! That's not it! Forget it! I want to speak with her. Can you just connect me with her?"

"I'm sorry, but she has gone on vacation. She left yesterday for two weeks."

"Two weeks! Can you give me her mobile number?"

"I'm sorry, sir, but I cannot do that."

"Why not? She gave it to me before."

"So you say. I do not know that. Sir, do you have any other business here? Lieutenant Marek thinks you have made a mistake and did not understand her. We know you must still be very upset about your brother, but we cannot help you anymore."

"Does Lieutenant Marek know that the school did not know anything about my brother's death?"

In a dismissive tone, Marek told the operator the details are not important and hung up.

Chapter 41

Boston

Two days later, Paul returned home from the gym to go through his usual routine. He picked up his mail and waited for the elevator. Over the past few days, he noticed that the same neighbor was waiting there every night. He wondered if it was just a coincidence or if she was stalking him. He was becoming suspicious of everyone. He began flipping through his mail as he often does to avoid eye contact. However, he realized there was silence. She wasn't madly typing away. *Her phone must be broken.*

"What's this?" he muttered aloud.

He found a postcard among his junk mail. The glossy front of the postcard showed three rotund stone windmills, each painted white with thatched roofs. They sat against the deep blue Mediterranean. In the top right corner, "Mykonos" was spelled in gold script. Paul flipped the card over. It was blank. The postmark was stamped a week earlier.

"Someone on vacation?" his neighbor asked.

"I don't know. It's blank." He held up the back of the card and then turned it over to show her the scene.

"I wouldn't mind being on vacation there."

"It would beat this never-ending winter. Forty degrees in May," Paul said in disgust.

"Only in Boston."

Something about the card looked familiar. It reminded him of a family vacation they took while he was in college.

Their floor arrived, and they exchanged the same small talk as they did every night and parted ways.

He entered his apartment and began searching the Internet for terms related to Mykonos. He searched images on the different search engines and even used a program to zoom in on the windmills using satellite photos. *What does this mean? Do I know anyone on vacation in Mykonos? Is it even warm there right now? Lord knows it's not warm here.*

He had been feeling uncomfortable after the phone calls with the school and police in Prague. He believed he would never receive the full story. After an hour of Web-based distraction while drinking his protein shake, he decided to shower.

While disrobing, he saw the boxes from his brother's apartment in the corner of his closet. *That's why the postcard looked familiar,* he thought. *It wasn't the family vacation.* He had seen it on his brother's corkboard in Prague. Standing naked in his apartment, he grabbed the box and sifted through its contents until he found the collection of postcards. He flipped through them until he found the card. *It was the same.* He turned it over.

"Run! Don't walk on lava."

The handwriting looked like Steve's. A date was written below the cryptic phrase—*three days from today! This can't be a coincidence.*

Paul spent the next thirty minutes in the shower contemplating what it meant. *Should I go? Is it really him? Is it his handwriting? I think so!*

After toweling off and getting dressed, he tormented himself for another hour before finally relenting to the thought of boarding a plane in the morning to get the answers to his questions. He let out a loud sigh to dissipate his spinning thoughts. He figured that he received the $20,000 for a reason and should use it to pay for this trip. He already knew that his mind would never let go of this until he knew the truth. He researched flights and hotels online. *Where exactly am I going? Mykonos? Lava?*

Chapter 42

Two days later on Mykonos, Greece

Lieutenant Marek stepped off the narrow-bodied commercial Airbus A320-100 and descended down to the tarmac at Mykonos Island National Airport. The sun was strong, penetrating the clear blue sky and radiating off the black asphalt. Marek's pale northern European skin was quick to burn. However, seeing the sun made him feel alive. The intense heat was a nice contrast to the cool Prague spring.

Three of Marek's associates followed him off the plane to meet a small battalion of Greek police officers who stood in formation waiting for their Czech guests to arrive. The captain approached Marek with his hand extended.

"Welcome to Greece. I am Captain Gianakos. We are happy to assist you in this matter. I have summoned officers from the neighboring Cyclades islands to participate in this effort. You can see them here behind me."

A junior officer stepped forward to translate for Marek.

"We appreciate your assistance." Marek managed to complete the sentence on his own.

The junior officer explained to the captain that the forensic team in Prague had found the postcard while combing through Steve's apartment. The postcard contained a date when it appeared Steve Benson might be on Mykonos.

Shortly after Marek had dismissed Paul's call four days earlier, a pop-up notification on his computer's calendar reminded him of the postcard's message and date. He had added it to his calendar during the case to see if any unusual activity would occur around that time.

When he saw the message, he dropped everything and began digging deeper. He thought more about Paul's phone call and the tasks he had assigned to Klára—contacting the school and Steve's family, and performing media relations. *What media relations?* He never got one phone call from reporters. He just assumed she had made sure it stayed out of the media. Now, he realized she might have had other motives and needed to speak with her.

He tried to call her, but got her voice mail. Just as the operator had told Paul, she was already on vacation. When he tried her new mobile number, it too was disconnected. A vacation coinciding around the time on his calendar, Paul's phone call inquiring about her employment status, and two out-of-order phone numbers made him realize it might be more than just a mere coincidence.

After having dispatched a detective to investigate Klára, Marek called the school and was connected with Monika in scheduling who recounted her conversation with Paul.

"I am looking at Steve Benson's records. He started working in January and left by mid-March."

Marek drew a timeline on his desk blotter and realized that there were six months unaccounted for. "Where was Steve Benson during the time he left school and committed suicide in September? Did he commit suicide? Why would he fake his own death?"

"Money," a junior detective answered, as Marek talked to himself.

"What do you mean?"

"I finished looking into Klára Hruska, the forensics analyst you asked me to research. In the past week, twenty million dollars passed through her account."

"Twenty million dollars?" Marek gasped. "Passed through?"

"Yes, it printed on her account for one day."

"And?" Marek demanded.

"The next day it was gone."

"I want to know where that money went!" Marek was burning red. The embarrassment of a junior forensic analyst pulling the wool over his eyes was something he did not want to be remembered for. "Find out who sent it!"

"Yes, I'm waiting on the bank for that."

"What the hell is a junior forensic analyst doing with twenty million dollars in her account? I want to know Steve Benson's whereabouts between March and September. What was this guy doing before he supposedly jumped from the Nusle? And have forensics retest the DNA. If it's not a match, then we need to retrieve the body from America and inform the right family. This is a goddamn mess!" Shame washed over Marek as he remembered how proud he had felt at the ease with which he thought he had solved the case.

An hour later, the junior detective handed Marek a printout of several flights between Prague and Boston. "He was gone for weeks at a time."

Unbeknownst to Marek and his men, Steve had used this time to set up the warehouse for the arrival of the doctors.

What was written on the postcard?" Captain Gianakos asked. "'Run! Don't walk on the lava,'" the detective replied. "Do you know what this means?"

"We are in the Cyclades islands. I'm sure you've heard of our two most famous islands—Mykonos, the island on which we stand, and Santorini. Santorini is one of two volcanic islands in this chain. The other is Milos. If I were to guess, I would say he is referring to the black sand beaches on Santorini. They are black because they come from the volcano's lava. You cannot walk on black sand. It's too hot. Maybe this is what it means."

The junior detective translated for Marek. "Lieutenant Marek suggests we divide our resources among the three islands."

"Good idea. If they come to these islands, there is a good chance they will pass through Mykonos," the captain replied. "One group will go to Santorini, one group to Milos, and one group to remain here. We will have men stationed at each port and airport to search every ferry and plane."

After disbursing the two teams to Santorini and Milos with photos and orders, Marek and his men joined the captain for an evening at a local taverna. Sounds from a bouzouki filled the quaint restaurant, charming patrons like the sirens in the sea. The wait staff returned every fifteen minutes to deliver a new dish or bottle of wine. Marek was the most jovial his men had ever seen him, laughing and toasting with the captain to the impending capture of his prey.

After midnight, the wait staff cleared the tables on one side of the restaurant and began plucking patrons from their seats one by one to join in the line dancing. Marek was too drunk to refuse a taste of the traditional Greek folk dances. Hopping, skipping, and sidestepping—forward and backward—was a little too confusing for him and his men, who were too drunk to care. The good-natured locals were simply happy that their guests were experiencing the exotic culture they had to offer.

Chapter 43

Athens, Greece

The next morning in Athens, Paul boarded the Highspeed 5, a catamaran headed for Santorini. He was still jetlagged from the transatlantic flight the night before. He spent the flight from Boston thinking about the summer vacation they spent touring Greece. The majority of the trip was spent exploring the Peloponnese and developing *teenage ruinitis*, the utter boredom experienced by teenagers forced to visit too many ancient *ruins* by good-intentioned parents.

Once they got to the islands, Paul and his brother were free to run around the narrow streets of the local towns and play with the other children, most of whom were tourists just like them. The part of the island they were looking forward to the most, the beaches and ocean, were not as much fun as they had hoped. Instead of throwing the Frisbee or walking along the beach, they were towel bound. The black sand absorbed the intense Greek sun and scalded their soles, making it impossible to leisurely walk barefoot. Occasionally, Steve would throw a little black sand onto Paul's back, singing his flesh. Paul would snap out of his sun-induced dream state to throw some back.

On the flight, Paul had thought back to the chair boy, the young Greek boy whose job it was to rent chairs under the thatched umbrellas along the beach. He told the brothers that the black sand was lava from the volcano. In his broken English, he would say, "Run! Don't walk on lava!" Every time they would go for a swim, they would yell this to each other with a Greek accent as they ran to the water.

He could hear his brother mimicking the boy's accent. Who else would know such a saying?

Passengers were packed into the high-speed ferry that shuttled travelers between the islands in half the time as its larger cousins, the car ferries. Trapped between his neighbors who had just finished their last cigarette butts and reeked of smoke, Paul could barely catch his breath. *Europeans!* He was reminded of how much people in southern Europe smoke as compared to the people he met in Prague.

Paul spent the five-hour ride catching up on sleep. When he woke, he could feel the back of his sinuses were inflamed from the constant smoke-related irritation. He kept swallowing, but the swelling wouldn't go away.

Upon disembarking with the other passengers, they were accosted by the numerous hoteliers who waited at the port to sell new arrivals on their accommodations. Tourists walked through a flurry of brochures and photo albums that showed off the different amenities of each hotel and pension. Prices were quoted, and most importantly, free rides to the center of town were offered.

Paul got cornered by one woman whose bed and breakfast had a small room that would be perfect for a single traveler. She offered to give him a special price of thirty Euros for the room, which included a shared bath and breakfast. However, it was not near the beaches. He was set on being near the black sand beaches, which he learned through his Web search were in a town called Kamari. She assured him it was close and that he could take the scooter there whenever he needed.

In a community this small, owners did not interrupt each other when presenting their offering. When Paul decided to move on, other owners saw this and pounced. She yelled something in Greek, and they all disbursed. Paul thought she put the hex on him until a man emerged from the back of the group.

"You want to go to Kamari?"

"Yes, that's where the black sand is, I hear," Paul replied.

"Okay, you come with me. If you don't like my accommodations, you can pay me ten Euros for the ride and select another hotel there. That's cheaper than a taxi. And I know you will stay with us once you see our hotel," he said proudly.

Paul agreed.

"My name is Spiro." The hotel owner extended his hand.

"Paul."

After showing Paul to the hotel van, Spiro spent a few more minutes gathering passengers bound for his hotel and off they drove.

Chapter 44

Santorini, Greece

An officer from Captain Gianakos's battalion spotted Paul from a platform overlooking the crowd of hoteliers swarming on the street. He radioed Gianakos on Mykonos, who ordered him to follow Paul until they could arrive.

Driving an unmarked police car, the officer kept his distance as he followed the van. Already knowing the hotel van's destination, there was no need to maintain a close tail—a difficult feat considering the nature of the roads. Barely wide enough to fit two compact cars, motorists passed each other in opposite directions hugging the crumbling edges of the dilapidated road. Occasional clearings where the vegetation had been mowed down provided safe detours for cars forced off the road by passing buses.

The officer followed the van until it turned into the resort parking lot. He continued on a hundred meters before circling back to park in a clearing down the road. Palm trees sheltered the impressive white and blue resort that was set back from the road. The sign next to the gate read "Kamari Beach Resort."

The officer could hear guests splashing about in the pool on the other side of the hotel, facing the ocean. He radioed in his location and was ordered to wait until they arrived from the other island, which could be another five hours. He reclined his seat and imagined he was lying poolside in a lounge chair, sipping a drink, and enjoying the warmth of the Greek sun.

The hotel owner brought Paul into the compound through an arching white stone hallway that tunneled its way through the building. The cool shade of the tunnel contrasted sharply with the intensity of the sun. They passed the hotel's office on the right before stepping into the pool area. Large beige and white tiles checkered the patio around the pool. Blue lounge chairs sat under thatched umbrellas shading bikini-clad guests from the powerful rays. From the far side of the pool, spacious private balconies with ocean views were visible.

"Each room has a balcony with a view of the ocean," Spiro commented in response to Paul ogling the blue-railing balconies.

"Great!"

"Breakfast is included with your room. As you can see, the boardwalk is just below the trees there." The patio area sat five feet above a boardwalk that ran along the beachfront. "You can exit there to the beach." Spiro pointed to a door in the corner of the courtyard.

"Can I see the room you have free?"

"Sure, I'll take you now."

The other guests from the van were in the office waiting for Spiro's wife to finish registering them. He said something in Greek, and she tossed him a key. For the past twenty years, guests could be heard making jokes about how it was all Greek to them. It was a cliché that described the privacy locals enjoyed knowing their guests couldn't understand a word they said.

The room was modern with sleek black furniture. Sheer linen blinds caught in a gentle breeze flapped across open French doors leading to the balcony. Light reflecting off of the white cloth diffused in all directions, and the breeze turned the ceiling fan ever so slowly.

Paul crossed onto the balcony and leaned against the railing, gazing out over the beach. His eyes traveled down the beach in one direction and back up the boardwalk in the other until they finished their journey back in the patio area of the hotel. His eyes stopped abruptly. It was a delayed reaction by his mind's facial recognition software. He ran his eyes backward along the journey and then forward again until they honed in on a pair of sunglasses staring back at him from the patio just beyond the pool. He clutched the railing. His legs locked at the knees and heart pounded. The man in the sunglasses tipped his drink toward Paul as a big smile canvassed his face. It was his brother, in living flesh.

"What the—" Paul turned to run out of the room. "I'll take the room."

"The room has actually been reserved for you already by the man you see on the patio. He said you are brothers."

"We are!" Paul yelled as he careened out of the room.

He sprinted down the hall, jumped the flight of stairs, and rushed out to the patio. He reached the table and practically fell over.

"You!" Paul exclaimed with anger, pointing at the woman sitting next to Steve. "Who the hell are you?"

"Meet my wife. I believe you've already met in Prague." Steve laughed as he held Klára's hand up to show off her diamond ring.

"Your wife?"

Steve stood up and gave his brother a hug to assure him everything he was experiencing was, in fact, real, but Paul pushed him away with a look of disbelief.

"Where the hell have you been?"

"We'll get to that."

"What did you get out of faking your own death?" Before he finished asking, he uttered the answer to his own question. "You—you're the other beneficiary."

"Actually, it was Klára. And 'why?' I spent my entire life's savings to find a cure—a cure that was as simple as getting deep tissue massage on the nerves in my neck, physical therapy for my pelvic floor, and avoiding certain foods. Modern medicine with all of its technology and high-priced doctors was a complete waste. I was angry that so many doctors failed me and did their best to make me, the patient—their customer—feel two feet tall due to their own ineptitude and insecurities. I was angry at the numerous mishaps with insurance and how their structure only serves to promote disjointed care. In reality, the insurance company is the real customer, which is why nobody is looking out for the patient. Finally, I'm tired. It's been fifteen years, and I just want a vacation—a long vacation. Is that too much to ask?"

"I guess not," Paul replied.

A smile came across Steve's face, "Run! Don't walk on lava!" He imitated the Greek boy from decades earlier, as he had when they were young. All three broke into laughter.

Spiro brought over a round of cocktails as Steve and Klára filled Paul in with as many details as they safely could. Paul told Steve that he had finished reading his journals. Having experienced some of it with Dr. Huang in Prague, he now understood more about the journey his brother had been on for those fifteen years.

After a few drinks, the three ventured down the boardwalk to find a place on the water to dine. As they were seated, Steve threw out a few Greek words to the waitress, "*Ena boukali levko parakalo.*"

Paul was thoroughly impressed with his brother's new language skills after inhabiting the island for less than a month. "What does that mean?"

"A bottle of white, please."

After four hours of appetizers, main courses, wine, and dessert, the three couldn't cram another ounce of food into their stomachs. The island cooled off quickly at night, and it was time to head back to the resort.

Chapter 45

Santorini, Greece

The three climbed the stairs to the patio and dialed the code to unlock the iron gate. Upon entering the resort, Klára clenched Steve's hand.

It was Marek, sitting under one of the umbrellas with Captain Gianakos. Two officers standing at the gate readily closed it and blocked their retreat. Ten other officers stood around the premises.

Paul grew anxious despite reassuring himself that he had not done anything wrong. However, he felt protective of Steve, the way only a big brother would. He stepped forward to stand next to Steve.

Reaching slowly into his pocket, Steve withdrew his mobile phone. Officers nearby stood ready with their revolvers drawn in anticipation of a weapon.

Marek began screaming at Klára in Czech, drawing the other hotel guests onto their balconies to witness the events unfolding below them.

Marek's eyes turned red as they popped out of his skull. "We found the insurance money that passed through your account."

"There's no money in there. You can't prove anything," Klára replied.

Marek appeared to grow increasingly agitated. "We know you switched the DNA evidence."

"I never tested those samples. Check the records." The edges of her mouth turned up. While bagging evidence at the crime scene, Klára had replaced the hair samples with Steve's before passing them off to another analyst for analysis. This way, she never had to doctor the records or results after the fact. There was nothing tracing the test result inconsistencies Marek's men were about to unearth in Boston back to her.

"We know you pretended to be from the school to prevent Paul from learning that his brother was a runner. That way he would never dig deeper, and we would never learn about Steve's flights between Prague and Boston during the six months unaccounted for."

Speaking in broken English with a wide grin and sarcastic tone, she said, "My English not very good. He mistaken."

"Speaking of Boston—who the hell is buried in the U.S.?" Marek yelled.

"One of Steve's private—"

"A student?" Marek screamed.

"Juri Vichta."

"Mafia sex trade, Juri Vichta? Those appointments in his calendar were legitimate meetings?"

"Yes—English lessons. Vichta lived in the penthouse unit of Steve's building."

"So, he just threw Vichta off the Nusle?"

"Nothing in life is ever that simple, now is it?" Klára's voice contained a hint of ridicule. "As you saw in Steve's calendar, Vichta wasn't his only student with an unsavory reputation. When Steve learned how Vichta ruined people's lives for a living, and that he was being targeted for assassination, Steve realized the stars were aligning—he had his jumper. Everything happens for a reason. Wouldn't you agree? He just didn't know when, and he saw no reason to intervene."

Seconds after Steve closed his phone, the captain's phone rang. Gianakos's voice turned angry, yelling into his handset. The conversation lasted for two minutes with Gianakos pacing back and forth on the tiles. As the dialogue wore on, he was forced to assume a conciliatory tone. Once he hung up, he turned to his men and barked out an order in the fit of rage he was forced to conceal on the phone. The twelve officers marched off the patio in a hurry to avoid his wrath.

Marek looked on in astonishment. "What the hell is going on?"

The junior detective translated into English.

Gianakos answered in anger, "No matter how many austerity measures you put in place, there is always room for corruption in this country!"

"Especially when your bank account packs twenty million dollars," Steve added. "Tell the lieutenant that most battles are won well before you ever step foot on the battle field, or in this case, the lava."

"Twenty million dollars!" Paul exclaimed. "What do you plan to do with all of that money?"

"I struck a deal with the Greek government," Steve smiled.

"What do you mean? What kind of deal?"

"I will use the money to set up a free clinic here to treat people suffering from terminal, debilitating, and undiagnosed ailments. Having experienced firsthand how quickly disjointed care can bankrupt you physically, emotionally, and financially, I don't think you could find a better place to recuperate. In return, the Greek government has placed me into their version of witness protection."

"How on earth did you arrange all of this?"

"I had glowing recommendations from *two prominent physicians* in Boston."

• • •

Thank you for reading!

To view story line images,
find a local practitioner,
and add your review,
please visit:

http://godcomplexbook.com

Bibliography

Chen, Ellen M. *The Tao Te Ching: A New Translation with Commentary*. St Paul: Paragon House, 1989.

Chia, Mantak, Maneewan Chia, Douglas Abrams, and Rachel Carlton Abrams, MD. *The Multi-Orgasmic Couple: Sexual Secrets Every Couple Should Know*. New York: HarperCollins Publishers Inc., 2000.

Dilman, George, and Chris Thomas. *Advanced Pressure Point Fighting of Ryukyu Kempo*. Reading: George Dillman Karate International, 1994.

Omura, Yoshiaki. *Acupuncture Medicine: Its Historical and Clinical Background*. Tokyo: Japan Publications, 1982.

Pitchford, Paul. *Healing with Whole Foods: Asian Traditions and Modern Nutrition*. Berkley: North Atlantic Books, 1993.

Price, Troy. *Kyusho-Jitsu/Dim-Mak: Pressure Point Striking Using the Five Elements/Phases Theory*. Chapel Hill: Columbia School of Karatedo, 1998.

Tam, Tom. *Tom Tam Healing System*. Boston: Oriental Culture Institute, 2001.

Yang, Dr. Jwing-Ming. *Eight Simple Qigong Exercises for Health: The Eight Pieces of Brocade*. Jamaica Plain: YMMA Publication Center, 1988.

Yang, Dr. Jwing-Ming. *The Root of Chinese Chi Kung: The Secrets of Chi Kung Training*. Jamaica Plain: YMMA Publication Center, 1989.

Yudelove, Eric Steven. *Taoist Yoga and Sexual Energy*. St Paul: Llewellyn Publications, 2000.

11966420R00182

Made in the USA
Lexington, KY
18 November 2011